Christmas
Cow Bells

Books by Mollie Cox Bryan

The Buttermilk Creek Mystery series

CHRISTMAS COW BELLS

The Cora Crafts Mystery series

DEATH AMONG THE DOILIES

NO CHARM INTENDED

MACRAMÉ MURDER

ASSAULT AND BEADERY

The Cumberland Creek Mystery series

SCRAPBOOK OF SECRETS

SCRAPPED

SCRAPPY SUMMER eNovella

DEATH OF AN IRISH DIVA

A CRAFTY CHRISTMAS

SCRAPPILY EVER AFTER eNovella

SCRAPBOOK OF THE DEAD

as
Cow Bells

Mollie Cox Bryan

KENSINGTON BOOKS
KENSINGTON PUBLISHING CORP.
www.kensingtonbooks.com

KENSINGTON BOOKS are published by

Kensington Publishing Corp.
119 West 40th Street
New York, NY 10018

Copyright © 2019 by Mollie Cox Bryan

All Kensington titles, imprints, and distributed lines are available at special quantity discounts for bulk purchases for sales promotion, premiums, fund-raising, educational, or institutional use.

Special book excerpts or customized printings can also be created to fit specific needs. For details, write or phone the office of the Kensington Sales Manager: Attn.: Sales Department. Kensington Publishing Corp., 119 West 40th Street, New York, NY 10018. Phone: 1-800-221-2647.

Kensington and the K logo Reg. U.S. Pat. & TM Off.

First Printing: October 2019
ISBN-13: 978-1-4967-2132-7
ISBN-10: 1-4967-2132-2

ISBN-13: 978-1-4967-2133-4 (eBook)
ISBN-10: 1-4967-2133-0 (eBook)

10 9 8 7 6 5 4 3 2 1

Printed in the United States of America

Cast of Characters

Brynn MacAlister—Cheesemaker, dairy farmer, sleuth

Nancy Scors—Brynn's neighbor

Nathaniel & Hannah Scors—Nancy's son and daughter-in-law

Wes and Max Scors—Nathaniel and Hannah's sons and Nancy's grandsons

Tom Andrews—Farmer and teacher

Elsie Andrews—Tom's wife and a pie baker

Josh O'Connor—Honey farmer and president of the Shenandoah Springs CSA

Kevin Ryder—Owner of Bluebell Farm, producer of Christmas trees and pumpkins

The O'Reilly Family (Miriam and David, and their children, Frank & Tillie)—Owners of the local apple orchard

Willow Rush—Organic vegetable farmer

Reverend Ed Higard—Local Presbyterian church leader

Mike Rafferty—Fire marshal

Schuyler Rafferty—Vet-acupuncturist

Paul & Sheila Hoffman—Owners of Hoff's Bakery

Zach Flannery—Owner of Flannery Contracting

Jacob Flannery—Zach Flannery's nephew

Cast of Cows

Buttercup—One of Brynn's three Red Devon
  milking cows, docile and sweet

Marigold—The shyest of the three cows

Petunia—Vocal and stubborn, in mourning for
  her lost calf

ACKNOWLEDGMENTS

Thank you, dear readers, for spending your time reading my books.

The research for this book was so much fun—and delicious. I spent a day at Creambrook Farm in Middlebrook, Virginia, learning how to make cheese from Louella Hill. Special thanks to Ben and Kristen Beichler, the owners of the farm, and Louella, who also has a gorgeous book out about making cheese: *Kitchen Creamery*.

Special thanks to my beta readers, Jennifer Feller and Mary Sproles Martin, so generous with their time and energy. A shout-out to my "Down on the Farm" Mystery Writers Facebook Group sisters: Lynn Cahoon, Edith Maxwell, and Peg Cochran. We're having so much fun on that page, swapping recipes and craft ideas, and enjoying fellowship. What a fabulous and supportive group of writer friends.

A heartfelt thank you to my editor, Martin Biro, and my agent, Jill Marsal. I couldn't ask for a better editor or agent. Not only are they sharp professionals, but they are both good people. I'm so blessed to have you both in my life. In fact, the whole team at Kensington is amazing! Thank you to my new publicist,

Larissa Ackerman, for her excitement and fabulous attitude about this series, and James Abbate, editorial assistant, for keeping me informed.

Thank you to my daughters for all the love and support and for putting up with a mom who writes, which might mean things like road trips where my plots are the main conversation, and Saturdays spent helping me haul books to an event. You both are the best. Thanks, Emma and Tess.

XO,
Mollie

Chapter One

Sometimes a place reaches deep inside of you, flows through you with light and warmth, and fills you with a sense of belonging, a sense of home. Brynn MacAlister's first view of the Shenandoah Valley from the Blue Ridge Mountains—a blanket of green, yellow, and brown rolling fields and farms spread for miles into the mists—had grabbed her with certainty. The village of Shenandoah Springs, a blip in her view, was small and tattered but oozed charm, tucked in the valley between the mountains and the town of Staunton, Virginia. She and Dan had figured this was the area for them to grow their dreams: a micro dairy farm to support their cheesemaking. Some dreams fade, such as her marriage plans with Dan, but Brynn was determined to make a go of the cheesemaking and dairy farm.

"Yoo-hoo!"

Brynn would know that voice anywhere.

She opened the door for her closest neighbor, who was dropping by for tea, and then quickly shut it against the cold December wind.

Nancy held a plate of scones, wrapped in plastic. "My grandmother's recipe, straight from Scotland."

Brynn took the plate. "Thanks so much. The kettle is on." She led Nancy back to her favorite spot in the house, a kitchen nook where the table sat beneath a window with a view of her rolling backyard pasture and three Red Devon cows. Three cows were just enough for her to handle on her own. Maybe too much.

Nancy settled into her seat, and Brynn poured the tea. Earl Grey was the tea they had first bonded over in the grocery store, and then realized they were neighbors, both new to town, both into local, artisanal food, and both into farming, as were most of the residents of Shenandoah Springs.

"How's it going with the renovations of the church?" Brynn asked.

"Things are going well. It was difficult to find contractors. They acted interested until I told them I was turning the old church into a farm shop. I don't get it." She stirred sugar into her steaming tea and set the spoon on the saucer. "I had to hire contractors all the way from Lexington."

"Strange. Your plans support the local community. It's too bad." Brynn sipped from her tea.

"The locals are all lovely," Nancy said. "But they do have some strange ways."

Brynn hadn't been in Shenandoah Springs long, but she agreed with Nancy. Most locals had roots that stretched back generations, and they didn't feel the need to make new friends. Still, Brynn thought it would just take time to get acquainted.

"I thought I'd be doing something for the local economy by offering farmers a place to sell their goods every day, rather than just one weekly farmers' market. I plan to sell produce, beer, wine, and even crafts. I just met a weaver who makes the most astonishing rugs and things." She paused while taking sip of her tea. "But I don't know. I sometimes get the feeling they either don't get what I'm doing, or don't support it."

"Why wouldn't they?" Brynn said. "You're doing a wonderful thing for the area. Once it's up and running, it will be a mad success. I know I can't wait to see my cheese on display at the Old Glebe Market."

Nancy cracked a smile. The crinkles around her eyes seemed to smile, too. Her big, droopy brown eyes reminded Brynn of a puppy. She wasn't sure they were good enough friends for her to mention that.

"How's it going with you?" Nancy asked. "I take it Petunia is still giving you trouble."

Brynn's stomach fluttered. Was it that bad? "Yes, unfortunately. I know she's loud. The vet said cows have a strong maternal instinct, but she should get over the loss of her calf any day now."

Petunia had given birth to a stillborn calf a week ago. Each morning, the moment she left the barn, the cow ambled right to the hillside where her calf lay, buried beneath an old oak tree, and bellowed through the day. To make matters worse, she wasn't eating right, and she wasn't getting along with the other two cows, Buttercup and Marigold, both docile and sweet. Marigold was the shyest cow Brynn had ever known. Yesterday, when Petunia came into the barn, she kicked over a bucket with a stubborn deliberation Brynn had never seen from her cows—and it scared Marigold.

"I'm worried about her." Brynn picked up her cup of tea and drank in the strong brew.

"Perhaps you should call that hunk of a vet to come over again," Nancy said, with one white eyebrow cocked. "I may be old, but I ain't dead, honey. That man is something else."

"He's okay," Brynn said. "But he's a good vet, and that's all I care about." It had been almost a year since she caught Dan cheating, and she had no interest in men at this point in her life. She couldn't imagine trusting one long enough to have a relationship. Not even the vet. Besides, he was married, which didn't seem to concern Nancy.

"Boy, that Dan did a number on you. You're young, and there's plenty of time to find a new love," Nancy said. "But then again, my husband's been dead for years, and I've yet to find one man anywhere near as good as him."

Brynn's face heated. "Let's eat the scones." She unwrapped the plate and cinnamon wafted. She lifted a scone to her lips and bit into it. "Mmm." She couldn't speak because her mouth was full. "So good!" she said after she swallowed.

"Grandma Sadie wasn't kidding around when she baked. She used real butter, real eggs and sugar, and the freshest cinnamon she could find." Nancy bit into her scone. "I followed her recipe to a *T*."

"It makes a difference," Brynn said and took another luscious bite.

"I'm glad you like them. Now let's talk about that cow of yours. You need to do something. I can hear her all day long. And I'm not the only one."

Brynn dropped her scone. What did Nancy think she could do about it? Poor Petunia was in mourning. Dr. Johnson said she was depressed, and it would run its course.

"I'm sorry, Nancy. I'll call the vet again."

"Can't you muzzle her? I mean it sounds cruel, but at least it'd be peaceful."

Brynn's heart broke at the thought of muzzling her sweet Petunia—and because her new friend didn't realize that she adored her cows. She'd no more muzzle them than she'd muzzle a person.

"No, Nancy. I can't do that." She took another sip of tea, even as her stomach soured.

Chapter Two

One of the many reasons Brynn and Dan had decided on Shenandoah Springs for their own farmette and cheesemaking hub was its active Community Supported Agriculture program. Residents bought shares and received locally grown or sourced goods once a week.

Brynn and Dan had responded to an ad in *Mother Earth News*: "Be a part of our farm community revitalization in the heart of the breathtaking Shenandoah Valley of Virginia. Land is cheap, and the community practices organic, healthy, artisanal farming. We have a very active CSA and farmers' market."

They were both living in Richmond, with her family, until they could figure out their next step. When they found that Buttermilk Creek Farm was for sale at a reasonable price, it seemed like kismet. Buttermilk Creek was the small creek that ran through the property, though nobody seemed to know why or when it was named. But the name added to Brynn and Dan's sense that it was the perfect place for them to grow their dreams. Brynn decided to keep it, rather than come up with a new name.

Brynn first fell in love with cheesemaking as a

chemistry student in college. She'd taken the class on a lark because she needed the credit. But there was something so magical about the way milk turned to cheese, even though she understood the chemistry behind it. She couldn't get ideas for cheese out of her mind. Throughout the rest of school, she experimented with making cheese. After she graduated from college, she searched for cheese school, much to her parents' dismay. They'd paid for a degree in chemistry. Where was this cheesemaking thing coming from?

Brynn briefly considered Murray's, a high-end cheesemaking school in New York City, but just as quickly dismissed it. She wanted a place with cows. A place that she could see and control the cheesemaking process from the start. She found St. Andrews Creamery, which is where she met Dan. He had the same mindset for wanting to control the cheesemaking process from start to finish, which meant knowing exactly what your cows ate and how the food affected the cow's health and the flavor of the cheese. "All organic" and "grass fed" were not just buzzwords. They were a way of life. It took time and care to create good cheese—why wouldn't you want to know your cows and see that what they ate was the best for them?

Not only was there an artistic and healthy element to Brynn's way of handling cheese and cows, but there was also a spiritual one that seemed to be in development at all times. She realized happy cows give better milk—just like Granny Rose had always said. She was always experimenting with what made them happy— music, a scratch behind the ears, a rubbing of the nose, and speaking to them as if they understood her. Sometimes she swore they understood her more than most people do.

And, when she tended her girls, a sensation she described as spiritual often came over her. She felt at one with the universe, like she was taking part in something bigger than herself.

Dan used to tease her when she expressed this sentiment to him. Yet, he understood that happy cows make better milk and cheese.

But Brynn didn't want to think about Dan. Or the dreams they shared. Not today. Not ever. She needed to stay present as she drove to the fire hall.

Brynn had volunteered to help box the products for the CSA, and she'd brought along tiny linen-wrapped wedges of her Buttermilk Creek Farmstead Cheese to introduce to the locals.

As she arrived at the fire hall, a meeting place which doubled as the center where they held bingo on Thursday nights and square dancing on Saturday nights, she heard raised voices inside. She stopped awkwardly at the door, apprehensive, not knowing what to do with herself. She pressed on and opened it.

A large man with a Jack Daniels ball cap shadowing his face cleared his throat. "It's an old church, and it should be preserved, that's all I'm saying."

"But it's just sitting there," a woman said. "It'll be restored to its former beauty, and it will be a great place to sell our products."

"But that's what the fire hall is for! I'm just saying, people come from out of town and think they know what's best for this community. I don't like her or her ideas."

Brynn tried to pretend not to hear him talk about Nancy, but as she set her box of cheese down, it landed with more of a thud than she wanted. All eyes were on her.

The woman who had been speaking in Nancy's defense stood. "Hi, Brynn. How's it going?" Willow Rush was an organic vegetable grower. "What do you have there?"

"Cheese, what else?" She tried to lighten things up with her tone. She felt as if she'd walked into a hornet's nest, instead of a working meeting of the CSA. She moved along and inspected the boxes, brimming with organic, local, and artisanal products. Baggies full of winter greens, like arugula, rocket, kale, bok choy, collards, mustard, and turnips, along with brussels sprouts and small cabbage. "The brussels sprouts are almost too pretty to eat."

"Thanks," Willow said, beaming. Long and lean, mocha-skinned Willow had the freshest face Brynn had ever seen. And she had been the biggest help since Brynn had moved here.

A large, young man came into the room carrying jars of applesauce with ribbons on them. He placed them in the boxes, and, as he moved by Brynn, she smelled the strong scent of apples, nutmeg, cloves, and cinnamon—scents that always comforted her. She recognized him as a part of the O'Reilly family, who own the orchard near her place. He turned his gaze toward her. He had the iciest blue eyes she'd ever seen.

The man wearing the Jack Daniels cap also looked at Brynn. The shadow lifted from his face as he looked up. "Hello. I don't believe we've met." He extended his hand as he stood. "I'm Tom Andrews."

"Good to meet you," Brynn said, although she

wasn't too sure about that. He was clearly a man with a temper, and his face was still red from his machinations. "I'm Brynn MacAlister. I'm living at the old rectory with my cows. Buttermilk Creek Farm. I'm a cheesemaker."

"Nancy is your neighbor then. I don't know what that woman's doing," Tom said. "I wish she'd go back to where she came from!"

Brynn's mouth dropped as she tried to search for the right thing to say. She wanted to defend Nancy, but she didn't want to make enemies.

"Now, Tom," someone said from behind Brynn. "Now is not the time. We need to get work done here today and decide about raising our membership fee in the new year."

Brynn turned to face the person who'd spoken. It was Josh O'Connor, the president of the CSA and a honey farmer. He held a box full of small jars of fresh honey—some still had bits and pieces of honeycomb in them. Brynn's mouth watered. She made a mental note to seek out that honey, for both herself and for her sister, Becky, who loved honey.

Josh placed his brimming honey jars in the boxes. Brynn followed suit with her cheese.

"Besides, you'll scare away our newest member." He looked at Brynn, and his green eyes twinkled as if in acknowledgment of Tom's mischief.

Brynn looked away. "No worries. I'm not so easily scared away."

"Don't pay any attention to me, sweetie, I'm just an old guy with old ways," Tom muttered.

It had been a few years since a man had called her sweetie, other than Dan. It raised her hackles, but she stopped herself from telling him it was unacceptable. Just this once. If he said it again, she'd inform him. She was nobody's sweetie—and certainly not his.

A few more people entered the room. They made introductions, and Brynn was certain it would take her months to remember all their names. But she would remember their products. Lavender. Radishes and rutabaga. Persimmons. Apple butter. And to top it all off, the local Christmas tree and pumpkin farmer brought miniature Christmas trees, which gave the boxes a festive flair.

She reached into a box and held up one of the tiny trees. "Adorable."

"Thanks," the man standing next to her said. "It's a great way to use up scraps on the farm, and people seem to like them. I'm Kevin." He extended his calloused but warm hand.

"Okay everybody. Listen up. We have a decision to make," Josh said, after clearing his throat. "Some of us think we need to raise prices. We're barely earning out."

"But earning out is just one of our goals," Willow said. "We wanted to support the community by offering healthy products and exposing them to what we're producing. More people have ordered from my website since I joined the CSA."

Which reminded Brynn that she needed to find someone to do a website for her. She planned to sell her cheese online and ship it. But first she had to find someone to create the site—she was not technologically astute.

"I say we give it another year before we raise prices," Kevin said. "You know the local economy isn't that

great. If we raise prices now, I'm afraid we'll lose sub-
scribers."

Mutters of agreement sounded from around the
table, where they had gathered in a deluge of earthy-
colored flannel shirts and wool sweaters.

"Tom?"

"Well, I suppose you're right. It's just that I sometimes feel like we're giving our products away for
nothing. I'm still teaching, so we're doing okay, but if
we were just trying to survive by our greens and such,
we'd never make it. I wonder how some of you are
doing it."

Willow spoke up. "We all have other gigs, Tom. You
know that."

The group decided to table the issue until next
year. After the meeting, they loaded the boxes into
Willow's truck, as it was her turn to make deliveries. If
a member had a truck, they took turns. Brynn had
thought about getting a truck, but she hadn't followed through yet. A pang of regret plucked at her.
There were a lot of things she needed to follow through
with, but she had no time. Maybe Dan was right. Taking
care of three cows on her own was too much for her,
even if she was just milking one of them. But she
could manage the cows—it was the rest of her life that
fell away.

"How's that cow of yours?" Willow said. "Is she still
giving you problems?"

"Unfortunately, yes," Brynn said.

"I have a friend who specializes in acupuncture and
herbs for animals. She's a vet of sorts."

Acupuncture? Herbs? Petunia was too valuable to

mess around with New Age pseudomedicine. "I don't know if I'd trust any of that."

"I know what you mean," Willow said. "But she's got a great track record. It might be worth a shot."

"Complete and total mumbo jumbo," Tom said. "What your cow needs is a muzzle."

Chapter Three

Brynn didn't expect people to understand how she felt about her cows. She was a cheesemaker, not a farmer. She didn't see her Petunia, Marigold, and Buttercup as "agricultural," but more as a part of the team it took to make the artisanal cheese. The reason she owned cows was because she'd become a freak with wanting to control every part of the cheese-making process—right down to what the cows who gave her the milk were eating.

She tossed and turned that night worrying about sweet Petunia. The cow had been blessed with such a sweet personality, a church at the edge of town had asked for her to be part of the local living nativity scene. Brynn thought it was an excellent way for the community to get to know her and her cows. But Petunia was mourning her calf. And her grief was taking longer than the vet said it would, so it worried her—and it broke Brynn's heart. And it was starting to annoy the other two cows, who were avoiding Petunia.

Somehow, she fell asleep, jolted awake by sirens screaming a few hours later. She glanced at her clock: 3:03 AM.

She stuffed a pillow over her head, but the sirens

were getting closer. The girls would be frightened and on edge. So she untangled herself from her quilt and slipped on her jeans and sweater. She padded down the stairs, realizing the sirens were close indeed. As she peered out the window, several fire trucks were flying down the road—toward the Old Glebe Church. She looked off toward it and saw flames.

"Oh my God!" She rushed outside, and then went back inside as the cold smacked her with an icy grip. She reached for her coat and slipped on her boots.

While struggling to get her coat on, she raced toward the church, over the hilly field connecting her property to the church property.

She almost tripped over several clumps of field grass as she made her way, heart racing as she came up over the small hill where the church came into view. Flames engulfed the old building.

She continued to run across the field toward the church, now surrounded by fire trucks and ambulances, along with several cop cars with red lights flashing.

Where is Nancy?

As she moved closer, the fire's blistering heat enveloped her and the flashing lights shot through her eyes. She squinted, examining each person she saw. The firefighters were hosing off the place, and the police had gathered in a corner. The ambulance was lying in wait.

Where is Nancy?

She ran toward the group of police officers. "Where's Nancy?"

One of them turned toward her, yelling over the roar of the fire. "Excuse me?"

"Where's Nancy? The woman who lives here?"

"And you are?" He pulled her over to the side.

"I'm Brynn, her neighbor. I live right over there," she said. *As if that makes a difference.*

The officer took in a breath and released it. "We don't know if she's inside."

That can't be right. "Do you mean she didn't call?" Brynn's heart was pounding in her ears.

"It was called in by another neighbor, up the road," he replied, still yelling over the noise.

A firefighter unraveled another fire hose about ten feet from Brynn. Tufts of wiry red hair sprang from the bottom of his fire helmet. His partner was the same large young man from the CSA meeting. The one who smelled of apples. The one with icy blue eyes.

"Well, she's inside." Brynn tried not to scream. "Where else would she be?"

"Our guys are inside. If she's in there, they'll find her."

Brynn took in the blaze. It was destroying the old church, the place Nancy wanted to renovate to make into a market, the place she lived in, the place she'd always dreamed of.

A great gust of wind blew smoke in Brynn's eyes and burned her throat.

The cop reached for her and led her farther away from the smoke and fire.

Her head was spinning, her heart was pounding, and a stream of hot salty tears ran down her face.

"Calm down, okay?" the officer said, in a gentler voice. They were now farther away from the noise of men yelling, engines roaring, and fire consuming the church. "We don't know anything yet."

"There's no way she could survive that fire!"

"You never know. I've seen people survive fires all

the time. Sometimes they're hospitalized with smoke inhalation, sometimes with burns. But it happens."

Brynn's stomach was churning now. She gasped for air. How could this happen? Nancy was always so careful.

A wave of sick came over her, and she turned to wretch, dizzied, as her knees wobbled.

The officer held her up as her knees resisted. The flames blurred as she fell forward onto the officer.

"Can I get oxygen over here?" she heard him say.

Another firefighter ran up to her, with a sooty, sweaty face and kind blue eyes, and he scooped her up in his arms right before she passed out. Her last thought was: *So many blue eyes around here.*

When she came to, Brynn was in a warm ambulance with a cheerful paramedic. "Hi Brynn," she said, smiling. "You'll be okay. You passed out."

Brynn took the oxygen mask off. "What about Nancy? The woman who lives here?"

Her smile vanished. "She was just taken away. Zach Flannery, the guy who carried you over here, said they're taking her to Augusta Medical, weirdly enough. She's burned, but not badly, and suffered a lot of smoke inhalation."

"Will she be okay?"

"Let's hope so." The paramedic looked at her watch as she held Brynn's wrist. "You're good to go. But take it slowly, okay?"

Brynn tried to sit up, and it turned out, the paramedic was right. She dizzied and lay back down.

The paramedic smiled. "Let's try again, shall we?"

Brynn sat up and inhaled.

"That's better. Now, can we give you a lift home?"

Brynn nodded. "Thank you. I live at the old rectory, next door."

"I've always loved that place," she said. "The way it sits tucked in that long driveway against that green field and the hills."

"Yes, it's lovely, but I'm sure I've got three upset cows to deal with."

"You're the cheesemaker, right? I'm Casey, Doc Johnson's daughter."

It was a cliché, but certainly true about small towns: everybody was either related or knew each other. In a community like this, it was difficult to be a newcomer, and it would be even more difficult to keep secrets, Brynn imagined. Everybody would be all up in everybody's business.

"Nice to meet you, I'm Brynn MacAlister." She coughed. She tamped down the fear creeping into her guts about her girls. They must be nervous, with all the commotion from the fire. Petunia would need milking, and they all would need to graze.

The vehicle's engine started, and they crept along the road.

When Brynn stepped out onto her driveway, the rank scent of the charred building invaded her senses. She tried not to think about the fire as she made her way to the barn. Cows were sensitive creatures. Her Granny Rose always said to approach them only with happy thoughts in your head. To some it might be a silly superstition, but Brynn had learned to take her granny's advice about everything. She wished she had done so when saying yes to Dan's marriage proposal. She remembered Granny Rose's words vividly: "It's not that I don't like him. I just don't think he's good enough for you. And he's not husband material."

Brynn had inwardly scoffed. Husband material. Who talked like that these days? Funny expression—but exactly right. Finding her fiancé with a woman named Jolene had just added salt to her gaping wound. Dolly Parton was Brynn's personal country music guru, and she'd not been able to listen to any of her music since. Her stacks of albums and CDs sat unplayed.

After milking and letting the girls out, she'd head over to the hospital to check on Nancy. At the very least, Nancy would be heartbroken. Brynn was certain the Old Glebe Church, which had been sitting there since 1835, was in ruins.

But, ultimately, it was just a building, old or not. Nancy, on the other hand, was still alive, and Brynn was eager to see and comfort her—and find out what the heck happened.

Chapter Four

After she tended the cows, Brynn headed to the Augusta Medical Center, which was thirty minutes away.

The strange, zigzag parking lot brimmed with cars, and it took longer than she expected just to find a space to park. Who knew it would be so crowded?

But the minute she entered the building, she felt calmer. Full of light, and featuring a huge Christmas tree in the lobby, the place felt welcoming.

She approached the receptionist. "Hi, I'm here to check on Nancy Scors."

The receptionist looked up at and smiled. "Just a moment. Let me check to see where she is." Her long fingers plucked at the keyboard, her festive red nail polish glimmering.

Brynn realized she hadn't even showered after being in the barn that morning.

"She's on the schedule to be transported to Charlottesville. Hang on. Let me see if we can sneak you in there to see her." The receptionist picked up the phone and spoke into it.

It hadn't occurred to Brynn that they might not allow visitors. She was only a neighbor, not family. And it also hadn't occurred to her they'd move her to a bigger city hospital. It must be more serious than Casey, the paramedic, had let on. Or maybe she didn't know.

"Miss, she's waiting for transport and is in the hall-way, waiting for the mechanics to give the go-ahead for the 'copter," the receptionist said, and then gave Brynn directions.

They had just placed Nancy on the gurney to take her down the hall to the helicopter landing pad when Brynn arrived. Nancy looked so small and pale, en-gulfed by attachments and tubes. She spotted Brynn and reached out her hand. A whimper came from her bandaged face.

"Shhh," Brynn said. "It'll be okay."

"Ready to go," the flight nurse said as he walked into the hall.

"Looks like they're flying you over the mountain," Brynn said, trying to sound cheerier than she felt.

Nancy motioned for Brynn to come closer. As she did, Nancy tried to say something, but it came out a garble.

Brynn shook her head. "You can tell me later."

"No! Paul the contractor," she said. Or was it "*Call* the contractor?"

With that, they whisked her off.

Brynn watched as they took her to the pad.

What was she saying? Paul the contractor? Or call the contractor? In either case, Brynn had no idea who Paul the contractor would be or even which contrac-tor to call.

A nurse standing near Brynn cleared her throat. "She's out of her mind on pain meds. I wouldn't take anything she said too seriously."

"Okay, thanks." Brynn found her way back to the lobby to find a group of schoolchildren gathered to sing near the sparkling tree. Their teacher was at the baby grand piano, and all eyes were on her as they sang "O Holy Night."

Brynn's emotions tangled inside her. Poor Nancy. She'd be hospitalized for Christmas. Brynn had always heard that was the worst time because the doctors with the most experience were all off on vacation. Another tangle pulling at her was Christmas, which she'd be spending alone. No Dan. No family. Her sister and niece couldn't afford to make the trip this year. And her brother was off God knows where on a cruise ship, of which he was the captain. They'd gotten used to not seeing him for any of the holidays.

Brynn's parents weren't in any shape to make the trip this year either. And Granny Rose had passed last year, leaving her a little money, which helped to pay for the farm.

She closed her eyes and let the sweet voices of the children lift her spirits. Even if for just a few minutes. The sound circled her, as if the hospital lobby was built for song.

Christmas is just another day. Next year it would be different—hopefully her house would be full of family and friends. Maybe including Nancy.

Yes, that's the hope her heart clung to. She just needed to get through this Christmas. It would be a challenge.

"She never should've been brought here in the first place." A voice lifted out of the crowd. "A fire victim like that goes directly to Charlottesville."

Brynn blinked. She must be talking about Nancy.

"That's protocol."

She scanned the crowd to find the person speaking.

"The woman will be lucky if she makes it through the night."

Brynn's chest tightened and burned. *Lucky if she makes it through the night?* They must not be talking about Nancy. Nancy was going to be fine.

She glanced at her phone.

Did she have time to go to Charlottesville and make it back to her cows before dark?

Charlottesville was another forty-five minutes away. And she'd never been there before. She had no idea where the hospital was located. Not a good idea. But she was the only person Nancy knew locally, and she felt the tug of guilt. She should try to see her again.

The beep of her cell phone caught her attention, and she scooted into a corner before answering. "Yes?"

"Ms. MacAlister?"

"Yes, this is she."

"This is Reverend Higard. I stopped by to see how things were going with our Petunia."

Our Petunia. She already had a reputation as one of the gentlest cows any of the locals had met.

"I'm sorry, but there's been a fire, and my neighbor Nancy has just been life-flighted to University of Virginia Medical."

"Oh dear. I've met Nancy. How awful. I saw the burned church. I didn't know she was inside."

"Yes, I think the Old Glebe is lost."

He paused and cleared his throat. "I wanted you to know Petunia seems very unsettled. She's mooing loud. I heard her while sitting in my car—with the windows closed. It really is disturbing."

Brynn's heart sank. She needed to get back to her cows. She'd see Nancy tomorrow. It would be better to go home and tend to Petunia before figuring out directions to the Charlottesville hospital.

"I know. I'm so sorry. The vet said she's in mourning, depressed because of the stillborn calf."

"I never knew an animal could be depressed," he said, with the emphasis on the word "animal." "I find it hard to believe. In the meantime, she's causing quite a disturbance in the community. Isn't there anything you can do?"

Brynn bristled at the way he said the word "animal" and didn't like his tone. He wanted Petunia for his living nativity, and that's the only thing he cared about. Clearly.

"I'll be home soon to settle her," she said, trying to sound more cheerful that she felt.

What could she do about her sweet, depressed Petunia?

Chapter Five

Owning animals of any kind was a responsibility—one that Brynn knew many people took too lightly. But she didn't, which is why she had steered clear of adopting a cat or a dog until this point. But now that she was tied down with her cows, she might consider another animal. If she could afford one. And if she could find the time to go to the local animal shelter.

When Brynn drove up to her house, she noticed a young woman, who she'd seen before, standing at the fence. When she exited the car, the girl turned as if to leave.

"Hi there," Brynn said. "Can I help you?"

The girl turned back toward her, and, beneath a swath of long, straight, strawberry-blond hair, two huge amber eyes took her in.

"Nah. I'm just checking out the cows. The big one over there seems sad."

"She is. Her baby died, and she's depressed."

The girl's eyebrows shot up. "Man, that bites. Poor girl."

Brynn wasn't certain, but she thought the girl blinked away the start of a tear.

"Would you like to meet her? She's not quite herself, but she's still as sweet as pudding."

The girl graced Brynn with a quick smile. "Okay, but I can't stay long. My parents will worry."

"Are you the O'Reilly girl?" Brynn said as she motioned for her to follow.

"Yes. I'm Tilda, but my friends call me Tillie."

"Nice to meet you."

Tillie smiled.

Brynn remembered meeting Tillie's parents and brother, nice folks and the owners of a local apple orchard.

Tillie shuffled along a pace or two behind Brynn, who opened the gate. All of her girls looked up, and Buttercup headed her way.

"Wow, I didn't realize how big they are."

"Big, but gentle." Brynn held up her hand, and Buttercup nuzzled her. Buttercup loved attention.

"She likes you," Tillie said. "I figured cows have some kind of feelings, but she's like a dog."

"They have feelings and get attached to each other and to people."

Petunia bellowed and rocked back and forth. Side to side. A mother grieving.

Brynn walked over to her and stroked her face, careful of her huge horns, as always. Petunia dropped her head and nuzzled Brynn's shoulder. "I know, girl. I know you miss your baby."

Brynn turned and headed to the barn, and the cows took their place in line. Tillie followed close behind.

"She needs an evening milking. Do you want to try?"

Tillie's eyes widened. "Seriously? Heck yeah. What about the other two?"

"Neither one of them are lactating. A lot of dairy farmers keep them artificially lactating. I'll do that, but only to one cow at a time. It's all I can handle on my own."

After Tillie washed her hands, Brynn showed her how to place her hands on the udders. "Tug and squeeze at the same time."

Brynn had milking tubes and a machine, but hand milking was better for her ailing Petunia. More gentle.

"You're a natural."

"I guess I am." Tillie seemed startled by that fact.

"Do you help your parents with the orchard?" Brynn grabbed the broom and swept the floor.

"Sometimes. But I help in the shop more. Sometimes I play music there."

Brynn looked up from her sweeping. "What do you play?"

"Guitar, and I sing. It's what I love."

"Do you write your own songs?"

"Yeah, sometimes." She laid her head against Petunia, and Brynn noted how her hair almost matched the color of the Red Devon breed. "She's so warm."

Brynn continued to sweep. "That she is. You see those speakers up there? I play music for them all night long and sometimes during the day. Maybe you could play sometime for them?"

"They like music? That's so cool."

"I think most living creatures like music." Just then, Brynn's cell phone buzzed. She didn't recognize the number, so she let it buzz and continued pushing the broom. The young woman had captured her attention. And she was calming Petunia—just a bit.

"What kind of music do you play for them?" Tillie asked.

"Sometimes classical, sometimes jazz, sometimes acoustic guitar. But it has to be kind of mellow. You know?"

"So no hip-hop, right?" She laughed at her own joke.

"Right. They seem to like country music, especially Dolly Parton." Brynn's phone buzzed again.

"Everybody loves Dolly. She's a queen. You better get that, don't you think?"

Brynn leaned the broom against the barn wall and held the phone to her ear. "Hello."

"Brynn MacAlister?"

"Yes, this is she."

"This is Officer Owen Edwards, from the fire? We met then, is what I mean to say."

"Yes, Officer Edwards, what can I help you with?"

"I'm sorry to have to tell you about your neighbor, Nancy."

Brynn's heart fluttered in her chest. "Is she okay?"

Tillie's chin lifted in her direction. Brynn tried not to sound alarmed, but she must have failed by the look on the girl's face.

"No, ma'am. She passed away about an hour ago."

"What?" Brynn clutched her chest as she felt the air press on her. Tillie dropped what she was doing and stood. "But I just saw her at the hospital. What happened?"

"I apologize. I wanted to come and bring the news in person, but we're short-staffed tonight, and I couldn't manage. She passed away during her medevac flight."

Brynn dropped the phone as she heard a strangled sob come from deep in her gut. Did that sound come from her?

"Ms. MacAlister?" Tillie ran to Brynn. "Are you okay?"

She tried to tamp down the shock for fear of scaring Tillie, but she couldn't manage.

"I'm sorry. I didn't mean to startle you. I've just gotten some terrible news."

Tillie's face drained of color. "Oh no, what happened?"

"My neighbor Nancy just died," Brynn said.

"The woman who lived in the old church?" Tillie's eyebrows rose.

Brynn nodded.

Tillie's face was hard to read in that moment. Panic? Fear? Worry? Was she scared? Concerned? She offered Brynn a stiff hug. "I'm really sorry."

After a moment, Tillie pulled her hat and gloves on. "I have to go. It's getting late." She spoke with resolve and determination. Brynn had just met the girl, but she perceived Tillie was putting on a brave face.

Tillie waved and shut the barn door, leaving Brynn standing in the barn, with only her cows for comfort.

Chapter Six

Brynn had always heard bad luck or loss comes in threes. She'd lost Dan, or rather, she'd broken up with him after she caught him cheating. She'd lost Petunia's calf, and now she'd lost Nancy. Granted, she and Nancy had just been getting to know one another, but they'd bonded because of their shared property line and interests. Brynn was living in the house previously occupied by the preachers and their families who had tended the congregation at the old church. The other thing she and Nancy had in common was that they were newbies in an area where most people could trace their heritage back for generations.

Brynn had just finished eating her breakfast oatmeal when a knock came at her door. She opened it to a complete stranger. Which wasn't too out of the ordinary since she was so new to the area. He wore a tan uniform, including a hat resembling a cowboy hat.

"Ms. MacAlister?" the man said. "I'm Fire Marshal Mike Rafferty. Do you mind answering a few questions?"

Brynn assumed this was about the church fire, but she couldn't imagine what answers she'd have.

"Certainly," she said, and waved him inside. "Please have a seat. Would you like a cup of coffee? Water?"

"Sure. Coffee would be wonderful. It's getting so cold. I guess we're expecting snow. Might have a white Christmas after all." His green eyes lit as he smiled.

Christmas. Brynn wished people would stop mentioning it.

He sat at her kitchen table as she fixed his cup of coffee. "Cream? Sugar? The cream is fresh from my cows."

"Nah, black is fine."

She set the cup in front of him, and he cradled it in his hands. She sat across the table from him. "How can I help you?"

"I'm here about the church fire." He held the steaming brew to his lips and blew, then took a sip. "Now, that's good coffee."

"Thanks." Brynn just wanted the man to get on with it. Her chores were piling up, and she needed to check on her last batch of cheese and get the next batch started. These things took time.

"So, the police on site last night tell me you were there." He set his coffee down.

"Yes, I woke up because of the sirens. The noise. I got dressed to check on my cows, figuring they'd be nervous from all the commotion, but I never got to them. I saw the flames and took off for the church."

"Did you notice anything or anybody out of place?"

Her face must have shown her confusion.

"I mean, other than the firefighters and police officers. I mean, were there any people around? Onlookers?"

She sifted through her memories of that night. "I was half asleep, worried about Nancy. And it was kind of hard to see, even though it was lit by the firetrucks. No. I guess I wasn't paying too close attention to the crowd."

"Hmm." He took another sip of coffee. "Do you have any idea why Ms. Scors was taken to Augusta Medical? Did you hear any of that decision-making process? Or orders?"

Brynn mulled over what she remembered. Why was the fire marshal investigating the fire? Did they investigate all fires—or was there a reason for this investigation? "No. Nothing. Well, only that one of the paramedics mentioned that it was odd that Nancy was sent to Augusta Medical. I didn't think anything of it at the time. What's going on?"

"Sorry?"

"Why are you investigating the church fire?"

"Any time there's a loss of life in a fire, I investigate."

"Oh, I see."

"I need to rule out arson, which in this case led to the loss of a life, which would be manslaughter or murder, depending. I'm hoping that's not the case here." He looked toward her field.

"Is there something troubling you about this fire?"

"I can't be certain, but I think it's very suspicious."

Brynn's heart sped. "Do you mean someone set the fire? Intentionally? Who would do such a thing?" It didn't make sense.

"Someone either set the fire, or Ms. Scors set it herself."

"I can't imagine either scenario, frankly. She loved the place and was getting ready to turn it into a farm shop. It was her dream." Brynn swallowed the burning sensation in her throat. "Why would she set the fire?"

He shrugged. "I have no idea why some people do what they do."

Brynn had the feeling he was talking about more than fires, but she didn't want to pry. After all, they'd just met, and he was here on official business.

The room quieted, with each of them lost in their own thoughts and Petunia mooing in the background.

"But I guess the other question is, why would someone else want to set it on fire? What purpose would that serve?"

"A lot of people just do it for the thrill. Sometimes it's kids messing around, and it gets out of hand. Other times, it's thrill seekers. People who love to set fires." He took a drink of coffee and set the cup down. "You'd be surprised." He spoke with quiet authority.

When he said "kids," Brynn thought of Tillie, who had acted very strangely when she learned about Nancy's death. But she was a teenager, and maybe she'd never known anybody that died before. Brynn hadn't read too much into it at the time, but perhaps Tillie knew something.

"But who would set that beautiful old church on fire? It seems as if—if someone did set it—they'd need a reason. A personal one. Something like a vendetta."

He cracked a smile. "You've got some imagination there."

Imagination? Brynn's faced heated. He was the one coming in and leveling theories about the fire. She had assumed it was an accident. Never in a million years did she think someone would have set that fire.

"Sometimes when the thrill seeker sets a fire, they hang around to watch their handiwork, which is why I asked you if you noticed anybody else there besides the local authorities."

"I'm sorry. I'm afraid I was just too upset that night."

He nodded. "I understand. If you think of anything, please call." He handed her his card, then he stood, as if to go. "Is your cow okay?"

"She'll be fine," Brynn quipped, but wondered if it was true.

Poor sweet Petunia. And poor Nancy. What a cruel, sad way to die.

Chapter Seven

Brynn's cellar smelled of cheese, which is just how she liked it. The cellar of the old house was a perfect place to age her cheese. The last crock of cheese from before she'd moved here was probably ready, while the new cheese still had a way to go. But she couldn't wait to taste the difference, now that she and her girls were in the Shenandoah Valley of Virginia. And the cows were eating different grasses, with no pesticides. They would also be eating some of the local flowers come spring, adding subtle, but tasty, notes to the cheese.

She wasn't just trying to stay busy to forget about Nancy and the fire marshal's allegations; she needed to taste and cut the cheese to deliver samples to local restaurants. Between the restaurants and the local CSA group, maybe by spring she'd have a few regular customers.

The cellar was perfect, but her make had a long way to go. She currently used a small room in the barn as her make, which wasn't as nice as the cheesemaking room she and Dan had shared. He'd always called it their lab, but she preferred the old terms, such as "make" for the room. So now that it was her place, her own space, she'd call it whatever she wanted—so make it was.

Brynn nudged opened the crock and sliced off a wedge of the milky-white cheese. She brought it to her nose and smelled it. The aroma was spot on, exactly what she wanted. The flavor was mild with a back bite, which is also what she wanted. She'd be able to make her sales calls tomorrow. She would take baskets with her cheese, crackers, and a bottle of wine to five restaurants. And hope she'd get her first local customers. The farmers' market was a long way off—it didn't open until the end of April.

For a moment, she thought about taking Nancy a hunk of her cheese. Her stomach squeezed as she remembered that Nancy was gone. It would be hard to get used to her not being around, coming over for tea, and sharing plans for her shop, or listening as Brynn shared plans about her cheesemaking and cows.

When she came out of the cellar, she heard a strange buzzing and realized it was her phone. She'd forgotten to turn the ringer on. A name popped on the screen, and Brynn almost didn't answer. It was Reverend Ed Higard, probably calling to complain again about Petunia, but she answered anyway.

"Brynn, I'm calling about Nancy's memorial service. We wanted you to know it will be tomorrow at First Presbyterian. Do you know where that is?"

She was surprised there would be a service, assuming Nancy's family back in Massachusetts would handle the arrangements. "Yes, I know where it is."

"Good. We'll see you then. Is everything okay? How are you?"

"Honestly, I'm stunned by all this—the fire, her death. All of it. And it's odd that her family isn't stepping in," Brynn said.

"Oh, they'll be here. I imagine some of them are already here. Her son said she loved this place so much. He knew she'd rather be here than in Massachusetts. She's being cremated, according to her wishes."

All this talk of cremation and death felt like a huge cloud descending on Brynn. It was happening too quickly to process. Everything was being flung at her without a chance for her to catch her breath in between.

"Brynn, are you okay?"

"It all seems to be happening very quickly."

"Sometimes it happens that way, if the morticians and families and lawyers all have open schedules. There's no point in dragging any of it out. After all, Nancy is now with her maker. Her body is nothing more than a shell."

Brynn didn't want to hear any more. She didn't want to think about it. Nancy had just died yesterday, and they were holding a memorial for her tomorrow. And that was that. Here one minute, gone the next.

"You're right, of course," she said. "Thanks for calling. See you tomorrow morning."

"How's Petunia?"

"The same. I'm going to call the vet in a moment."

"Good to know. We'll be needing to rehearse soon."

Rehearse? Petunia's role was to stand there with the other animals and look at people with those big watery brown eyes of hers. She'd charm them all. What was there to rehearse? What had she gotten Petunia into?

She immediately dialed the vet, before she forgot about it. "Doc Johnson, Petunia is still having problems."

"I'm sorry to hear that. There is one measure we could try."

"What?"

"Well, some have success giving their cows antidepressants."

"What? You're kidding me. Right?"

"No. Cows are complicated, deep creatures, and sometimes when they get depressed, they need a little help."

There was no shame in antidepressants, Brynn knew. But for a cow?

"How would it affect her milk?"

"I don't honestly know the answer to your question."

"I think I'd feel uncomfortable medicating her until we know."

"I'll make some inquiries for you."

"Thank you."

What had Brynn's life become? Not only did she lose her neighbor in a fire, but the fire marshal thought there had been foul play. If someone had set that fire, Brynn needed to know. And now, she was considering giving Petunia antidepressants. She'd thought moving to this valley would bring her peace. In fact, it had done just the opposite.

Chapter Eight

After Brynn made up her baskets, she gave in to the temptation she'd been resisting all day—to walk over to where the old church had stood.

The air was bracing, even with her layers of sweaters and her coat. She pulled her scarf closer to her neck. The mottled gray sky in the distance looked like a precursor to the predicted snow.

She walked along the fence of her backyard field where her cows were grazing, Petunia still rocking and mooing. The hillside was an easy walk, with a vista she'd come to appreciate, for just over the knoll was a view of the little white clapboard church—so beautiful in its simplicity, even though it lacked a recent paint job and the landscape was a bit deteriorated, including an untended old graveyard. Still, it was lovely. But as Brynn came up over the top of the hill and gazed in the direction where the church stood, nothing but charred remains were there. The place was still smoking.

She lowered her eyes. She had thought to go over and poke around, to see if there was anything of Nancy's worth saving in her basement abode. But she couldn't do it. She suddenly felt a mix of fear and shame for poking her nose in where it probably didn't belong. Nancy's family would certainly see to her things—whatever was left of them. Brynn looked back up at the landscape and realized yellow tape was surrounding the church. Caution tape.

Unbelievable. The evidence must have pointed in the direction of arson. Wait. It wasn't crime-scene tape. It was caution tape, warning people to stay away. But still, a pang of regret and sadness moved through Brynn, just as she noted a movement coming up through the woods beyond the church. She squinted as the person stood and looked over the smoking remains. It was a girl, she thought, but bundled up so much that she couldn't tell for sure. A jolt of fear hit her.

Hadn't the fire marshal said that thrill seekers like to come back to the scene of the crime?

But the person lifted her head and waved at Brynn, then walked toward her. The closer she came, the more Brynn recognized her. It was Tillie.

What was she doing there?

"Hey, how's Petunia?" she called in Brynn's direction as she ambled toward her.

"About the same, unfortunately," Brynn replied. "What were you doing over there?"

"I was just, I don't know . . . curious." She shifted her weight. "Do you know what caused the fire?"

The hair on the back of Brynn's neck pricked up. Why was Tillie so curious about the fire? Then again, so was Brynn.

"I have no idea." Brynn inwardly chastised herself for her growing suspicions about Tillie. After all, she liked the nice, young woman, who had shown a genuine concern for Petunia, which is more than she could say for the rest of the other community. "Do you want to help with Petunia this afternoon? It's almost time for the last milking."

She grinned so wide her dimples gathered. "I'd love that."

She and Tillie walked in companionable silence toward the field, and then into the barn.

After Tillie was finished with the milking, Brynn took care of the milk, pouring it into huge glass containers and placing them in the freezer, where they could stay until tomorrow or the next day, when she decided which kind of cheese to craft from them. She invited Tillie in for hot chocolate. And as they sat enjoying the sweet brew, Brynn studied the girl who seemed so quietly assured of herself at such a young age.

"Did you know Nancy well?" Brynn asked.

Tillie looked off and then back to Brynn. "She had some really cool books she let me borrow. I really liked the Whitman books. And the Leonard Cohen books. I had to sneak them into the house. My parents are strict about what I read. The only books they allow into the house are my school books and religious books. I'm going to miss her."

Brynn understood when parents didn't want their kids to read certain books, but she thought Tillie's parents were making a huge mistake. Still, they were her parents, so Brynn kept her own counsel. "Me too," Brynn said. "Will you be coming to the service tomorrow?"

"I'm working at the shop, so my parents can go. I don't like those things anyway. Kind of creepy."

Brynn felt a twinge of guilt at suspecting that Tillie knew something about the fire. Obviously, she knew and liked Nancy and was just checking things out, much the same way Brynn herself had done.

"Did you visit her a lot?"

"Yeah, whenever I could. There's a shortcut through the woods. Our orchard is just on the other side of Glebe Woods."

"I didn't know it had a name."

"Everything is Glebe this or Glebe that." She rolled her eyes. "They were so thrilled with that church back in the day, so I guess everything took names from it. But then most of the people who were here moved into town, and this village fell apart."

There wasn't much left of the original village. But there was a bit of a town square, with a few new shops and several old homes.

"It's nice that it's gotten a bit of a new life, though, isn't it?"

"Yeah. I like it here. I like the new stuff, too. New people. New crops. But some people don't like it. Like Mr. Andrews, my history teacher."

"Really?" Brynn took a sip of her hot cocoa. "Why's that?"

"He's a preservationist and thinks nothing should be changed. He really didn't like Nancy. He wanted the church to be left alone."

"I guess he's entitled to his opinion and feelings. But it was my understanding this land had all fallen into disarray, and the new people sort of saved it."

Tillie's cell phone alerted to her to a text message. "It's my mom. I need to go." She stood quickly and reached for her bag. "Thanks so much for the hot chocolate and for letting me milk Petunia."

"Anytime," Brynn said. "You're welcome to come over anytime. I mean it."

Brynn watched Tillie as she walked over the hill and toward the church, until she faded on the horizon.

What was her story? Brynn made a note to stop by and introduce herself to Tillie's parents. Why did her parents feel the way they did about books, prompting the need to go to Nancy for books? She knew Staunton had a great little library—and most likely the school did, too. How odd.

Brynn supposed it was no odder than all of the other occurrences over the past six months of her life. As she thought about it, things just kept getting stranger and stranger.

Chapter Nine

Getting ready for the memorial service was challenging, just after she'd been in the barn. A good scrubbing from head to toe, and what should she do about her nails? She didn't have time to paint them. She'd be lucky if they were presentable. She sighed. Well, as long as they were clean. She lived in a community of farmers and artisans. It wasn't as if she were back home in Richmond, where her mom and grandmother's friends scrutinized her before she went out the door—especially for funerals and weddings. She didn't miss that—at all.

She slipped on a black skirt, tighter than she'd like. She'd have thought tending to the animals was as good as any Pilates class, but so far, that hadn't turned out to be the case. She pulled her sweater over her head and untucked her long brown hair from beneath it. She twisted her hair up into a tight bun, put on tiny pearl earrings, and glanced at herself in the mirror. She recognized her dad's blue eyes and full lips, and it gave her a start. She'd heard about women turning into their mother, but it was her father she saw when she looked at her reflection. Why hadn't she inherited her mother's dainty bone structure and high cheek-bones? She tried not to think about it.

She breathed in deeply. She'd barely had time to process the tragic fire and Nancy's death, and now she was off to a memorial service.

A small crowd had come to say their good-byes at First Presbyterian Church, and after the service, the church had a meal for the mourners.

Brynn piled her plate with green bean casserole, scalloped potatoes, and baked corn. The buffet-style table was full of desserts, too. She made a mental note to return for more. But then she thought about her already tight skirt.

As a newly single woman, finding a place to sit was always tricky. She looked around and spotted the man she'd overheard introduced as Nathaniel, Nancy's son. He had his wife and two sons with him. Nancy had told Brynn about her grandsons' adoption. They'd been born in Pakistan and lost their parents when they were just babies, and then found a home with Nathanial's family. And now they were young men.

"Hello," Brynn said as she came up to their table. "I'm Brynn."

Nathaniel stood. "Oh yes, Brynn. Please sit down. My mom talked about you." His eyes were rimmed in red. "This is my wife, Hannah, and our two sons, Wes and Max." His sons were droopy and sullen.

"Lovely to meet you." Brynn stood with her plate in her hands.

Brynn noted how much Nathanial looked like

Nancy, with the same droopy puppy-dog eyes. Brynn felt a kinship right away.

Brynn sat down next to Wes, who was tucking away a linguini salad.

"We're so confused about what happened to Mom," Nathaniel said. "Do you know anything?"

Brynn had just shoveled a forkful of casserole into her mouth. She held up a finger and swallowed. "I don't know how the fire was started. All I know is the fire marshal came to see me and asked a bunch of questions."

"So they must think the fire was suspicious," Hannah said.

They suspect it was intentional. Your mother tried to tell me something as they wheeled her off to the helicopter. Brynn didn't know how much to say. She didn't want to upset the family further, as they were obviously distraught and in mourning. "Anytime there's a fire where a life is lost, they investigate."

"Oh, I see," Hannah said. She glanced at her husband. It was a look of shock, disbelief, grief.

Nathaniel wasn't eating. He was merely pushing food around on his plate.

"Where are you staying?" Brynn asked.

Nathaniel grimaced. "Well, that's a problem. We stayed at the B&B last night, but they're kicking us out tonight. No room at the inn. They barely fit us in last night. Evidently, with Christmas next week and everything, they're booked. So I guess we'll be leaving tonight."

"Nonsense. Stay with me. I've got plenty of space. I even have a guest cottage, which is just sitting empty." The main house had been partially furnished when she and Dan had bought it, which made it all the more practical for them, since they wanted to spend their money on cheesemaking equipment and their product, not beds, dressers, and tables. The guest cottage was scantily furnished, but there were beds in it. What else did they need?

"We couldn't put you out like that," Hannah said.

"It's no problem," Brynn said with firmness as she eyed up Max and Wes, who remained awkwardly silent. "In fact, I could use some help doing a few things around the house and barn. So if you could help, it would be a huge favor."

Just then, a family walked up to the table.

"We're the O'Reillys. I'm Miriam, and this is my husband, David. We wanted to express our condolences." It was Tillie's parents. Her mom had a baby on her hip, and her dad had a toddler by the hand. The brooding man with the icy blue eyes she'd seen at the CSA meeting was at their side. He must be Tillie's older brother. Just how many kids did they have?

"Thanks," Nathaniel said as the others smiled and nodded.

Mrs. O'Reilly motioned toward the young man. "This is our oldest son, Frank. Your mom struck up quite a friendship with our oldest daughter, Tillie."

"Oh yes, the books," Brynn said, then she remembered that her parents probably didn't know about the books. All eyes focused on her. "I'm sorry. I'm Brynn MacAlister. We met at a CSA meeting a few months ago."

"Yes, of course," Tillie's mom said.

"Tillie is a remarkable girl. She's helped me out a bit."

Mrs. O'Reilly's head tilted. "Really?"

There was something about the way she looked at

Brynn that made her squirm in her seat. "Yes, she's milked one of my cows a couple of times. She told me all about her music."

Tillie's mom smiled and nodded, then she stiffened. "We best be on our way."

After they left, Brynn shared a sympathetic look with Nathaniel. So it wasn't just Brynn who noted the brush-off. Was Tillie not supposed to help out neighbors? Did her family not support her music?

One thing was certain—it wasn't the first time Brynn's mouth had gotten her into trouble, and it probably would not be the last.

Chapter Ten

It turned out that the B&B had room for two guests, just not four. Nancy's family seemed forlorn, and Brynn invited them over before any decision was made about where they would stay.

Wes and Max helped Brynn in the kitchen as she prepared a cheese plate.

"Gram talked about you every time I called," Max said.

"Oh yes, the Earl Grey morning tea ritual," Wes chimed in. "You know, she didn't warm up to a lot of people. That says something about you to our family."

Brynn warmed and swallowed a lump forming in her throat. She nodded, unable to speak with the emotion welling in her throat. She kept her hands busy with the cheese. Granny Rose always said work was the great healer. What was that quote? "Busy hands, warm heart."

"We hate to put you out," Hannah said, as Brynn and the young men entered the living room. She held her phone. "There's no room at the any of the motels or hotels within a twenty-mile radius."

Brynn set the cheese platter down on the coffee table in front of them. "As you can see, there's plenty of room here. In fact, it used to be a bed-and-breakfast. You two can stay if you want. The guest cottage is just sitting there empty."

"Thanks for the offer, but our things are at the B&B, and I just feel the need for some space," Nathaniel said.

"I can see that," Brynn said, noting that the man looked exhausted and pale. "Have some cheese."

Soon after they finished the cheese plate, the couple left, after hugging and kissing their sons, and thanking Brynn, again.

The next morning, after tending to the cows and showering, Brynn learned that both of the young men were in the same college. Max was studying biology, and Wes was undecided.

"I guess I've not found my passion, yet. I've been thinking about business, but I just can't imagine myself as a businessman," Wes said, as he sat at Brynn's kitchen table with his brother, drinking tea, while Brynn popped blueberry muffins in the oven. The younger of the two, his deep brown eyes, reddened from his grief, held little hope. He was lost.

Brynn had often thought that for most people college came at the wrong time. "You'll figure it out. When I first went to school, my major was chemistry. Look at me now." She gestured. "I've gone from chemistry to cheesemaking. My parents weren't too happy about it."

"That's not too big of a leap," Max said, head tilting. "If you think about it."

"True." Brynn pulled up a chair and sat at the table. "I love the process of cheesemaking. It's chemistry of a different kind, I suppose."

Brynn thought about Granny Rose, who grew up on a small dairy farm in Ireland and had insisted on keeping cows, even once she was married and living in Virginia. Always Red Devon, the same cows she grew up with.

The room quieted as the three of them drank their tea, the sound of Petunia mooing every now and then.

"The other two cows don't like the noisy one," Wes said.

Brynn glanced out the window. Marigold and Buttercup were off to one side of the field grazing, and Petunia was alone. Marigold had become a little frightened of Petunia, and Buttercup was just disgusted.

"I think she's getting on their nerves. She's been kicking and trying to bite them, too."

"Whoa! What?" Max said. "Cows bite and kick?"

Brynn smiled. "Yeah, they have personalities. Which I didn't think about until I got to know one at cheese school. My granny kept cows, but by the time I came along, she only had one."

Granny's cow's name had been Eleanor Rigby, and she was playful and demanding. Brynn would never forget the first time Eleanor Rigby nuzzled her and gazed at her with those big eyes. It was as if her heart cracked open and her world shifted. She hadn't eaten a steak or a hamburger since.

"That's amazing," Max said. "You know, some people believe cows are sacred. In India, for example."

Brynn smiled. "I've read about that."

The room quieted again.

Max cleared his throat. "I'd really like to see where Gram's place was. She was so happy to be here." His voice cracked.

Brynn felt her throat tighten. "I'll walk you over there in a bit, okay? But how about let's finish our tea, and then you can help me find a Christmas tree? I could use two strapping boys like yourselves."

"I don't know how strapping I am," Wes said. "But I'm willing to help."

The three of them piled into her 2005 Subaru Outback and made their way to the nearby Christmas tree farm.

Bluebell Farm was humming with activity. There was free apple cider for the crowd. A lovely acoustic guitar rendition of "Silent Night" played in the background as they walked through the stands of trees. The scent of cinnamon, apples, and pine was heavy in the air. Kevin Ryder, the owner of the farm, approached Brynn.

"Hey there, looking for a tree?"

Brynn nodded and then introduced the young men to Kevin, who immediately expressed his condolences.

"Let me know if I can help you," Kevin said.

"Will do," Brynn replied as he walked off.

She turned to Max and Wes. Though they were only ten years or so younger than Brynn, she felt much older than them. "What do you think of this tree? Do you think it's big enough?"

Max shrugged. "I like that one over there better," he said, and pointed to a taller, thinner tree than the one Brynn had selected.

Brynn took it in, considering the spot she'd chosen at her house and imagining both trees sitting there. It was a big decision.

"Hmm," Brynn said. "I do like the shape of that one better. I'll take that one."

She looked around for Kevin. After she found him and told him what she wanted, she paid for the tree while Max and Wes dragged it to the car.

As she was paying, a voice sang along with the guitar music. It stopped her. The voice rang so pure, crisp, and true. It reached into the center of her. "Who's that?"

"Who?" Kevin said, distracted by counting money.

"Who's the singer? On the speakers?"

"Oh, that's not a recording. That's Tillie."

"She's here?" Brynn's heart raced in excitement. Tillie!

"Yes, she's inside the barn over there." He tilted his head in the direction of a big red barn.

"I had no idea. Her voice is . . ." She struggled to find the right word.

"I know, right?" He handed her change. "Shame about her family."

"What do you mean?" Brynn lowered her voice.

"Well, they're not exactly supportive of her music." He grimaced. "They put up with it. But barely. They're old school. You know, singing is frivolous, unless it's in church."

Brynn tucked her money into her purse. "Oh, that's too bad."

"Hey, you need help?" A young man approached them from somewhere between the trees.

"Yeah," Kevin said. "Tie that tree on the roof. Tie it securely this time, please."

"Okay, Dad," he said.

"We don't need any more trees slipping off vehicles," Kevin muttered.

Once the tree was secure, Brynn thanked Kevin's

son and tipped him. "Do you guys mind if we take a peek in the barn over there?" she asked her guests.

"Sure," Wes said.

The three of them sauntered into the barn, where a small crowd was gathered. The space was filled with sound.

Tillie sat in the corner on some bales of hay with a guitar in her arms and her strawberry-blond hair sweeping down over her shoulder.

As she sang "Green Sleeves," there was an edge of sorrow in her voice, a sorrow much older than her years. Brynn blinked back tears. She looked away from Tillie, as if it would stop the emotional on-slaught, but it didn't. Her eyes gazed over the crowd. She recognized some of the faces, noting that Tillie's parents were not there. She also noted the smitten look on Wes's face.

Brynn reached into her pocket for a tissue, as she caught herself thinking she wished she'd brought Nancy with her. Then she remembered, yet again, that Nancy was gone.

Chapter Eleven

After picking the perfect space for the Christmas tree and setting it up, Brynn stood back and took in her scantily decorated tree. "There's just not enough ornaments." She didn't know when she'd have the time to shop, so this might have to do.

"If you have popcorn and string, we can make garlands," Wes said.

"We also used to paint pine cones," Max said. "I noticed you have some huge pine trees near the driveway. I'll go and collect some. Do you have paint?"

Brynn thought a moment. "I don't think so. I have a hot glue gun, some glitter, and yarn. That's about it."

Brynn inwardly congratulated herself for keeping herself and her guests busy and thereby keeping their minds off Nancy. Nancy's grandsons were young and so full of life. And it was Christmas.

Brynn felt safer knowing the young men were there. She was not an easily frightened person, but she had to admit, the fire marshal's visit freaked her out. She was Nancy's closest neighbor, and they were both new to the area, both wanting to start again in the quaint community.

"Let's turn on some music," she said, realizing how

quiet it had gotten. She walked over to the stereo and slid a Dolly Parton Christmas CD in. Okay. It was time. She could handle Dolly. She wasn't going to let Dan take her love of Dolly, or her favorite holiday, away from her.

"I love her voice," Wes said. "But that girl at the Christmas tree farm was superb, wasn't she?"

Brynn nodded. "Her name is Tillie. She's delightful. She was quite upset about your grandmother."

He cocked his head. "Really? I didn't see her at the memorial service."

"No," Brynn said. "She stayed behind to watch her family's store. But she and your grandmother loved the same books. Tillie borrowed books from her."

His gaze dropped. "I guess all of her books, pictures . . . everything, is gone."

A pang of sadness tore through Brynn. She reached over and hugged him. Even though she'd just met him, hugging a grieving person seemed appropriate. They broke apart when Max came back into the room with a bag full of pine cones.

They set up a station at the kitchen table and made a garland of popcorn, and glitter pine cones. As they were doing so, Brynn's phone rang. It was Nathaniel.

"Are they giving you any trouble?" Nathaniel asked.

"No, they're being very helpful," Brynn said.

"Really? It's like pulling teeth to get them to help us with anything," he said. "I guess it's true what they say. Other people can get your kids to do things you can't. But anyway, I'm calling to see if the boys might stay another night. Our flight was canceled. We booked one for the next day."

"Sure. They can stay here. I've got plenty of chores they can do. Besides, the company is nice," she said. She'd never said that before; she'd always liked being alone. But now, though it was hard to admit, she was frightened and vulnerable here by herself, with no close-by neighbors and a possible arsonist and killer in the mix.

"Good," he said, and then paused. "Can I ask you something?"

"Certainly."

Wes and Max continued dipping pine cones in glue.

"Was my mom okay?"

"Yes, as far as I know. She was happy and excited about her plans. She had a hard time finding a contractor for the renovation, but other than that, she was fine."

Brynn remembered with a jolt that Nancy had tried to tell her something at the hospital. Either she'd said, "Paul the contractor" or "call the contractor."

"Well, I'm glad she was happy," he said, his voice cracking. "But the fire doesn't add up. She was so cautious."

"Well, the fire marshal is looking into it."

"That's right. What was his name again?"

"Mike Rafferty. Would you like his number?"

"It might be silly, but yes, I would. As I understand it, there was a terrible mistake. Mom should have been sent to Charlottesville immediately."

Brynn remembered hearing that a few times, yet she was uncertain if that would have made a difference at all. But if it made her son feel better, she was happy to oblige. She found Rafferty's card and read off the number to him.

By the time they hung up, Max and Wes were finished with the pine cones and were stringing the popcorn garland around the tree. Brynn decorated a few pine cones and surveyed the happy scene. Today was not the actual holiday, but the tableau brought her joy and gave her a slice of hope that she might have a decent Christmas.

She hung up the pine cones, and the three of them stood back and congratulated themselves on a job well done.

"So, Brynn, what do you think about the fire?" Max said, out of nowhere.

"What do you mean?" The memory of the raging flames was still fresh in her memory.

"Do you think someone set it?"

"I have no idea," she said after a moment. "I'm hoping that it was an accident."

Wes shrugged. "What does it matter? I guess all that matters is that Gram is gone. I just can't believe it."

"Oh, it matters," Max said. "If someone killed Gram, we need to find out and avenge her death."

"What do you mean by that?" Brynn said.

"I just mean we need justice for her. We need to find her killer and make certain they pay."

As if it were that easy. "Well, I have every confidence in our local law officials." Or at least she thought she did. She wasn't acquainted with them because she was so new here and hadn't really had any reason to get to know them—until now.

Chapter Twelve

Later, Brynn, Wes, and Max walked to the church where Nancy had lived. Max and Wes were braver than Brynn. They walked among the rubble while she stood off to the side. Nancy's grandsons walked down into the basement. Brynn didn't know if that was a good idea, but since they were family, she supposed it was fine.

"Brynn!" Wes called. "You should come down here."

Tendrils of fear, mixed with a sense of invading Nancy's privacy, poked at her. She didn't like this at all. "I don't know about that."

He walked back up the steps and poked his head out. "It's not burned here at all."

"What?" she found herself racing to the stairs. "What do you mean?"

"See for yourself," he said, pointing with his head.

She followed him down the stairs and took in the small apartment where Nancy lived. They were right, there was no fire damage here. The fire had been contained to the upstairs. The place was immaculate. Her futon was open and blankets lay on the floor, but other than that, her books were shelved, her dishes and pans were in place, and piles of paper were stacked neatly next to her computer.

"It reeks of smoke," Max said. "So most of her stuff is ruined."

"Not necessarily," Brynn said. "We should find out if there are ways of removing the smell. I think she'd love it if you could take her things back home with you."

Max wrinkled his nose. "Yeah, but only if we can get rid of the stench."

Brynn agreed. She'd only been in the apartment a few minutes, and her head was throbbing. She spotted Nancy's computer—her pride and joy. She had loved that thing. Brynn walked over to it and ran her fingers along the keyboard. She spotted a pile of papers next to it. Bills and bank statements and such. But a half sheet of notebook paper stuck out with its ragged edges hanging over. Odd. She pulled it out. When she saw what it was, she quickly slipped it into her pocket. She didn't want Nancy's grandchildren to see the horrific note:

Get out or die.

Her heart raced. It was true: someone had set the fire and wanted to kill Nancy. And they did. Nancy, her closest neighbor, who was also a new person to the area, just like Brynn. Who was to say they wouldn't come after her and her cows next?

She drew in a deep breath, trying to calm herself down.

Max came up beside her. "We need to tell Dad about this. I think he should be the one who goes through her things."

Brynn nodded. She wasn't sure if her mouth would even move, let alone form words.

"I found the spare key right where she always leaves it, under the closest rock to the front door," Wes said. "We need to lock this place up. Anybody could walk in here and steal her things."

The three of them left the basement apartment, closing and locking the door behind them. Brynn was so glad they'd come. Her fear of the note's threat turned to anger. How could someone do this? Why would someone do this?

She'd call Mike Rafferty first thing in the morning to find out. Obviously, they hadn't gone into the basement to check things out yet—or at least it didn't look like it. They probably had already been there and checked the place out. She hoped she and the boys hadn't tainted anything that might be evidence— except for the note in her coat pocket. She hoped she wouldn't get in trouble for lifting it.

The young men and Brynn walked across the field in silence. They were shaken by seeing their grandmother's place, full of her things, without her in it. Brynn understood. She was a bit shaken, as well. For more than one reason.

Just what had Nancy been trying to tell her in the hospital?

Were there any local contractors named Paul?

Brynn decided then and there to find out. She needed to know. She'd also tell the fire marshal about Nancy trying to communicate with her and what she said. Perhaps he'd consider it useful, along with the note, in helping discover who killed Nancy.

As they came down the hillside, the sun hanging low in the sky, Petunia let out a deep *moo*, which startled Max and Wes.

"What's wrong? Did we scare her?"

"No, she's depressed. She lost a baby," Brynn said.

Petunia rocked back and forth and mooed. Brynn walked over to her and rubbed her behind the ears. A look of pleasure came over the cow's face.

"Look at that," Max said. "I didn't know cows were like dogs or cats. She really likes the attention."

As they stood there, Buttercup sidled up beside Wes. "Uh," Wes said, backing up a little.

"Don't be afraid," Brynn said. "She's gentle. She wants to check you out."

As if on cue, Petunia dropped her head on Brynn's shoulder, and Brynn hugged her while rubbing her behind the ear. What could she do for her? She wouldn't muzzle her. She didn't think giving the cow antidepressants was a good idea either. What else could she do?

She remembered Willow's suggestion about an acupuncturist. She'd never given any of that pseudomedicine much thought. But she was getting desperate—and so was Petunia.

Chapter Thirteen

After the morning milking, Brynn headed back into the house to get her shower and some breakfast. As she entered the house, the scent of frying eggs greeted her. She rounded the corner to her kitchen, and there stood Wes and Max, cooking breakfast.

"Good morning," Brynn said.

"Good morning. Take a seat, we're making you breakfast," Wes said.

Warmth spread through her. Nobody had made her breakfast in years. She walked over to the sink to scrub her hands. "So thoughtful of you."

"I think I speak for the whole family when I say thanks for letting us stay here," Wes said.

"And," Max said. "Thanks for everything you did for our grandmother."

Brynn took a seat at her table, which was already set. She felt like a queen. A lazy queen. She'd done nothing out of the ordinary for anybody. Why were they fussing so?

"Nancy was my friend. It's the least I could do," Brynn said, with her throat burning. She swallowed.

"There's enough room in this house for your whole family."

"It's a big place, but it's very cozy," Max said, setting a plate of biscuits on the table. "Why did you buy it? It seems a little big for you."

"Max! That's nosy, don't you think?" Wes exclaimed.

"I don't mind," Brynn said. "Originally, I bought the place with my fiancé. But it didn't work out."

Her family had pleaded with her not to take this on alone. But she would not let Dan define her. This was her dream, and she'd pursue it without his cheating self.

"You must have dodged a bullet," Max said. "His loss, not yours."

If only Brynn believed that, deep down. If only she didn't feel like a failure in some strange way. Even though it was him who cheated on her, she figured she had a part in it. Had she been neglectful, becoming so focused on their wedding and honeymoon plans that she didn't pay enough attention to him?

A bubble of resentment rose in her chest. In her bones, she knew he had no excuse. She'd done her best. He just wasn't the one to share her life with. What if she'd gotten ill later in life? Or some other tragedy struck while they were married? Would he use that as an excuse to cheat? Just because her attention had been focused elsewhere was not an excuse for cheating.

After breakfast and her shower, Brynn sat on the edge of her bed and dialed Mike Rafferty.

"Rafferty."

"Mr. Rafferty, this is Brynn MacAlister. We spoke the other day about the fire?"

"Yes. How can I help you?"

Brynn ran her finger along the seam of the quilt that covered her bed. "Nancy's grandchildren are staying with me for a few days. They wanted to see the church, or what's left of it." The image of the white clapboard church's charred remains was fresh on her mind.

"Did you take them over there?" He sounded impatient, which made Brynn a little nervous. They should not have been poking around over there, and yet she couldn't prevent Nancy's grandsons from poking around.

"Her grandchildren insisted on going into her place, you know, the basement."

"Geez. Now, it's officially been declared a crime scene. Did they touch anything?"

"Not much, no. They think it's their dad's place to go through her things."

"Well, thanks for telling me about this."

"That's not really why I called."

"Why did you call?"

"At one point, the boys called me downstairs, and I went. While I was there, I found something disturbing. A threatening note."

There was silence on the end of the phone.

"It says 'get out or die.' I took it because I didn't want her family to see it. They are upset enough."

"I'll be right over, Ms. MacAlister."

Oh boy. How would she explain his presence to Nancy's grandkids?

She dressed and headed downstairs, where the young men had cleaned her kitchen to a sparkle. Where were they? They didn't seem to be anywhere in the house. She glanced out the window and saw them in her backyard field with the cows. The cows were as fascinated with the young men as they were of the cows.

Good. I hope they stay there.

Seeing Petunia out there rocking and mooing reminded Brynn she had another call to make. She sat at the kitchen table and dialed Willow.

"Hi Willow, it's Brynn."

"What's up, Brynn?"

"Can you give me the number of the woman you told me about? The acupuncturist?"

"Sure, but she's right here. I can send her over. Her name's Schuyler."

"I'm getting desperate. It's been two weeks, and Petunia is still distraught."

"Try not to worry," Willow said. "Schuyler can help."

Something about the way she said that soothed Brynn. Perhaps the acupuncturist could help. Brynn was getting tired of all the complaints about her cow. But more than that, she just wanted Petunia to be happy.

When the doorbell rang, she wondered which of her appointments it could be. She opened the door to Mike Rafferty, out of uniform, wearing a black leather jacket, unzipped, over a flannel shirt. He nodded. "Ms. MacAlister. May I come in?"

"I'd rather that you didn't. I don't want to alarm my guests."

His face fell, and then stiffened. "Okay, we'll talk later. But I want nobody else over there. Is that understood?"

"Yes, but—"

"It's a crime scene, Ms. MacAlister."

"They lost their grandmother."

He softened. "I understand, but I need a few days."

"I'll see what I can do." Brynn handed him the note she'd swiped from Nancy's desk.

"Thanks. You did the right thing by calling me. This might be nothing, but I need to follow up with it," he said. "I best be on my way."

"Thanks for coming," Brynn said as a tiny red car pulled into her driveway alongside Mike's truck.

"God, what's she doing here?" he muttered.

"Excuse me. What?"

"My sister, Schuyler."

"She's here to help with Petunia."

He tilted his head. "Your cow?"

Brynn started to explain, just as the petite redhead walked up her sidewalk.

"Hey, Mike," the young woman said.

"Hey," he said. "I'm on my way out."

There was something oddly powerful about Schuyler. She was small but moved with such confidence. She looked up at him and said, "Good." And she continued walking toward Brynn.

"Are you Brynn?" she said, smiling.

"Yes," Brynn said, extending her hand. She'd never shaken the hand of a person wearing a nose ring before. "Come on back and meet Petunia." As they came around the corner, a large furry, orange and gray, with black spots, floppy-eared dog bounded toward them.

"Where did he come from?" Brynn asked.

"She. I don't know where she came from, but she's been hanging around me," replied Schuyler. "Loves to ride in the car."

"Animals tend to find her. Always have," Mike said, from behind them.

"Are you still here? I don't need you breathing down my back."

The dog danced around them, going from one to the other, sniffing, tail wagging.

"Okay. I'll be on my way," he said, walking off to his truck.

Schuyler turned her attention back to the dog. "You need to stay here. You might scare Petunia."

The dog whined, but she sat.

"What kind of dog is that?" Brynn asked as she opened the gate to the field.

"A mutt. I think there's a little Saint Bernard in there and collie. Hard to say. I think she's young and will probably get bigger. I've tried to find her family, but so far, nada."

Schuyler wore a thick, cobalt blue, wool sweater coat, and a knit hat to match. As she approached Petunia, the cow took her in. Brynn thought Petunia might see that deep blue color and be curious.

Schuyler placed her hands on Petunia and rubbed her. "Poor girl," she said.

Brynn stood watching, wondering when the woman would get out her needles and start prodding Petunia.

"I can try acupuncture on her, focusing on just trying to relax her. But other than that, it's just going to take time. I'm not sure there's anything anybody can do for her. She's heartbroken."

Brynn wanted to cry. She knew exactly what heartbreak meant.

Chapter Fourteen

The wind chafed at Brynn's cheeks. She drew her scarf in tighter around her neck as she watched Schuyler.

"Can you distract her? I only want to place a few needles in her. I'm used to my patients moving around, but we at least have to keep her calm," Schuyler said.

Brynn hesitated when she saw her pull out the long, but very thin needles.

Schuyler frowned. "Are you okay with this?"

Brynn didn't want to tell Schuyler that she was skeptical of acupuncture. "I'll try anything for Petunia."

Schuyler nodded, with a look of determination. "If the needle bothers you, just look away. I'm stimulating her body to produce neurochemicals. When I place the needles in the tissue in a specific spot, biochemical changes happen. So, it's like signals travel up and down the spine."

Brynn rubbed Petunia's nose. "Pretty girl."

"So this also releases endorphins and hormonal chemicals—somewhat of a 'runner's high,'" she continued.

As Brynn stood there, watching the petite Schuyler

work around Petunia's bulk, she wondered how old the vet was. It was hard to tell with small people. They always seemed younger, just because of their height. Her sister, Becky, took after their mom and was small, and she was often annoyed with people treating her as if she were a child.

"So, how did you learn to do this?"

"School." She didn't say for Brynn to shut up, but her voice conveyed it. Schuyler was clearly not much for small talk.

As she moved around Petunia, she hummed a sweet tune. After a while, it lulled Brynn. She didn't know about the cow, but Brynn's eyes were heavy, and she was ready for a nap. Instead, she pet Petunia, whose eyes were opening and closing at a slower rate than before the treatment. Brynn glanced over at the other two cows, who were not paying a bit of attention to Petunia. Often when something was wrong with one cow, it flummoxed the others. But Buttercup and Marigold were leery of Petunia, as she had tried to bite and kick both of them over the past few weeks.

The wind was picking up, and the cold bit Brynn's face. The sky was mottled gray, and she wondered if they would get the predicted snow. She hoped it would hold off until Christmas morning. It was always so magical to wake up to snow, especially on Christmas.

"Let's leave the needles in there a few more minutes," Schuyler said with a low voice. Then she continued to hum.

Petunia was slowly reacting to the needles. She'd stopped mooing. How long would that last?

After the treatment was complete, Petunia lay down in the field in a state of bliss.

"You can close your mouth now," Schuyler said and laughed.

It was true; Brynn was standing there with her mouth open, like a ridiculous cliché.

"Thank you for helping her," Brynn said.

"You may not thank me when you get the bill," she joked.

They walked away from Petunia and out the gate where the dog was still sitting and waiting. Its tail wagged. Brynn reached down and rubbed the dog's soft head.

"Would you like to come in for some tea or coffee?"

Schuyler hesitated. "As long as my brother's not coming back."

"I don't think he is."

"What was he doing here, anyway?" She placed her bag in the front seat of her car and shut the door.

"He's investigating the church fire and Nancy Scors's death."

"He likes to make a mountain out of a molehill," she said, crouching down to pet the dog.

Brynn led her to the front door and opened it. "I don't think he's doing that in this case. Come on in."

Brynn was unaware of where Wes and Max had gone to—they were probably in the guest house, though she wondered if they were back at Nancy's. She lit the stove and placed the kettle on it. "What kind of tea do you like?"

"Herbal tea of any kind," she replied, and sat down at the kitchen table. "Nice view."

The kitchen window looked out over Brynn's backyard field and the cows as they grazed. Beyond that were the swooping hills and mountains of the Blue Ridge.

"I heard about the fire. A real tragedy. That church has been here forever. We used to play over there as kids. And poor Nancy. I didn't know her, but what an awful way to die." Her voice was thick with sympathy.

"Is mint tea okay?"

"Perfect."

Brynn sat at the table while they were waiting on the kettle to whistle. "You know, I saw her at the hospital. She was at Augusta, and then they placed her on a life flight to UVA."

Schuyler's head tilted in curiosity. Her eyebrows gathered. "They usually send burn victims directly to UVA Medical Center. That's strange."

"She tried to say something. It probably means nothing. She may have been out of it with pain meds." The kettle went off, and Brynn stood to ready the tea. She plopped the bags in her teapot.

"What did she say?"

"She said either 'Paul the contractor' or 'call the contractor.'"

Brynn brought the pot to the table along with the cups and poured the tea.

"Hmm," Schuyler said. "I happen to know a guy named Paul who's a contractor."

Of course she does.

Brynn stopped pouring and set down the pot. "Do you mind giving me his contact information? It's probably nothing, but maybe she was trying to tell me something important. She'd just hired someone from Lexington, because she'd had problems finding any locals to help her."

Schuyler picked up her cup of tea and breathed in the steamy scent. "I thought what she planned was cool. But many people didn't like the idea."

"Why?"

She sipped from her tea. "You have to understand. We love our history. That church was a part of us, just like the mountains and the air we breathe."

"But she was preserving it and was going to put it to good use."

"I get that. But some of these old-timers? They want nothing to change."

They must not be happy then, with all the many changes in their community. What some people were seeing as a renaissance of sorts, others saw as an imposition. Not for the first time since moving here, Brynn wondered what she'd gotten herself into.

Chapter Fifteen

When Brynn and Dan discovered Shenandoah Springs, they thought they would be a part of a community that practiced their values, as they made their way as micro-dairy farmers and cheesemakers. They never dreamed that some members of the community may not want them here.

Not that Brynn hadn't felt welcomed by most of the community, especially the members of the CSA. But there were definitely people who were making moving forward difficult.

Of course, Brynn's plans had gotten even more difficult—for she was one man down. Tending the cows, keeping up the barn and house, let alone the property, would have been much easier with Dan around. But she'd be damned if she would let this dream slip away from her.

She sat at her kitchen table as she pondered recent events. She'd found the table at a local secondhand store, and it was perfect for her kitchen nook. It was a small farmhouse table, handcrafted. Just looking at it brought her joy. But now, she sat there looking at Paul's phone number. Should she call him? What on earth would she say? She sat there formulating questions and wondering how the man would react to a perfect stranger calling and questioning him.

Just then, Wes walked into the room. He and Max had been out for a long walk around the neighborhood. "This is a gorgeous area," he said. "I've always loved it. It reaches right out and grabs you."

"I like it here, too," Brynn said.

"Petunia seems better," Max said as he came in behind Wes.

"Yes, she received an acupuncture treatment and responded immediately. It was amazing," Brynn said. "Can I get you some tea or coffee? Are you hungry?" They hadn't discussed dinner.

"Mom and Dad are coming to pick us up. They want to take us to dinner and would like it if you'd join us," Wes said.

"That's so kind of them. Of course, I'd love to join you."

"Our folks eat kind of early, so we'll be leaving in about an hour."

"Perfect. Then I should be back in time for the evening milking."

She left the room and headed upstairs to get ready for dinner. She'd yet to go out for dinner since she moved to Shenandoah Springs. She just didn't have the time. This would be a real treat for her.

After Brynn readied herself for dinner, she sat on the edge of her bed and dialed Paul Seeger, the contractor.

He answered the phone gruffly. "Seeger."

"Hello, Mr. Seeger. We've not met. I'm Brynn MacAlister. I live in the rectory of the old church?"

"Yeah?"

Brynn tried to sense whether he was put out by her call. But it was hard to tell. "Did you hear about the fire?"

"I heard about it. What a shame. And poor Nancy. How the hell did it happen?"

"They're still investigating it."

"Yeah?"

"The thing is, I went to the hospital to see Nancy, and she tried to tell me something before she was flown to UVA."

"What? What did she say?"

"I'm not sure, but I think she said, 'Paul the contractor.'"

Dead silence on the other end of the line.

"But," Brynn said. "It could've been 'call the contractor.'"

"So you're not sure what she said." There was a note of something like relief in his voice.

"Did you know her? I mean, she just hired a contractor."

"That would not be me," he said. "I'd be disinherited if I touched that church." He laughed.

"Why?"

He paused, then sighed into the phone. "Some people have strong feelings about it, that's all. And some of those folks are related to me."

Of course.

"I don't understand. Nancy was preserving the church and wanted to help the community by giving the farmers another place to sell produce."

"Yeah, I'm aware," he said. "But like I told Nancy, some people consider that place sacred. Just because it hasn't been used in a while, well, that means nothing."

So he *had* spoken with her about the renovation to the church. "How did she react?"

"She was disappointed. Our specialty is historical renovation. We're the best there is. She wanted us to do the project. But we couldn't for a couple of reasons. It basically boiled down to us being too busy."

"And the disinheritance?" Brynn said.

"Yeah," he said, and laughed.

"She hired someone from Lexington. Any idea who that could be?"

"There's a lot of contractors in Lexington. I have no idea who she hired," he said, sounding irritated. "Sorry, I can't help you there."

Well, of course, Brynn could find out. What Brynn really wanted to ask was where Paul was the night of the fire, but she couldn't bring herself to ask the question, after he'd been so forthcoming. After all, he wasn't working with Nancy at all. What reason would he have to kill her? And would a local man with obvious respect for the community and its history burn down the church? She doubted it.

"Thanks, Mr. Seeger."

"Surely. If you need any help with the rectory, give us a call."

As if she could afford any renovations. But she kept that to herself.

"Merry Christmas, Ms. MacAlister."

"Same to you."

Though she was trying to get into the spirit of the season, it was getting increasingly more difficult.

She'd gotten the Christmas tree and decorated it with her two houseguests, and her Petunia would be a part of the living nativity. But Christmas was about more than the outer trappings. She'd have to dig deeper to find that Christmas spirit—there was an arsonist and a killer in her new community, and she couldn't shake her fear.

Chapter Sixteen

Brynn learned three things from her dinner with the Scors family. One: Nancy had been a wonderful mother and grandmother, which didn't really surprise her. Two: the police would not allow anyone back into Nancy's place until after the investigation was over, which could take weeks.

The third thing she learned was she'd have to make Mrs. Rowe's Family Restaurant a part of her life. She loved the place, with its down-home, southern ambiance. Plus, they served the best coconut cream pie she'd ever eaten in her life. Biting into it was like biting into a piece of heaven.

"So, are you going to stay longer," Brynn asked, hoping they would, because she was enjoying having the young men as guests—just having them there made her feel safer, knowing there was a criminal out there, close to her home.

"We need to get back," Nathaniel said. "But the boys could stay awhile longer, if you don't mind? We'd like to have them back for Christmas, of course. But they're on break, and they love it here. Is it okay for them to stay with you?"

"We'll pay you, of course," Hannah chimed in.

"So kind of you to offer, but that's unnecessary," Brynn said. "I've got a few more chores around the place for them. They've already been a big help. Besides, I like having the company while this investigation is going on."

"I hear you," Hannah said. "You should get a dog. They're the best security system."

The image of Schuyler's huge, friendly pup came to mind, but Brynn shoved it down. She could not afford the upkeep of a dog, not along with the upkeep of three cows. Not to mention the responsibility. She already had her hands full.

Brynn stood next to the glass case full of cookies and pie while they paid their bill at the cash register, She reluctantly turned her head away from the sweets and followed the family to the parking lot, where they all piled into the car.

As they rode along, Brynn gazed out of the car's window. Snow flurries floated in the air—a whiff of them really, and not enough to lie on the ground. She hoped the weather held out for Nancy's family to be together for Christmas.

"Do they really think someone set Gram's house on fire?" Wes asked.

"Yes," Nathaniel replied. "I'm sure they'll find out who. Fire investigators are experts."

An image of Mike Rafferty popped into Brynn's mind. He did seem on top of things. She made a mental note to call him in the morning and ask what he thought of the threatening note—which she had kept from Nancy's family. They were deep into their grieving process and hurt over the fact that someone had set her place on fire. They didn't need to know, yet, that the arsonist may have deliberately set it hoping to kill Nancy. Brynn shivered.

Paul the contractor had nothing to do with it. Brynn wondered how to find Nancy's Lexington contractor. But did that really make sense? Why would a contractor set fire to a place he was set to renovate?

But it was the only lead Brynn had, and she needed to find out who that contractor was. He or she might at least be aware of something that could help them find the person who did set fire to Nancy's place.

It was a long shot, but Brynn had to try.

After Brynn, Wes, and Max exited the car, and after the boys said good-bye to their folks, she asked them if they wanted to help with the cows. They watched as Nathaniel and Hannah drove off, waving, then Wes and Max followed Brynn to the field. They brought the cows in, and she set up the milking stool and bucket.

"I guess I thought you used the machine for this," Wes said.

"I have one, and I do use it sometimes, but Petunia is sensitive, and she likes hand milking better."

"But what about the other two?" Max asked. "Why aren't you milking them?"

"I practice a different kind of dairy farming. I only milk one cow at a time and let the others build up their vitamins and stamina. There may come a time I'll need to use all three girls, but for now, Petunia is giving me just the right amount of milk for my cheese. Perhaps even more."

"That's interesting. You're kind to them. I like that."

A smile cracked Brynn's chilled face. "You can taste the kindness in the cheese. Or at least I like to think you can." *Such a Granny Rose thing to say.*

"Let me try," Wes said, and he sat on the stool, ready to pull. He easily found a rhythm, and Petunia responded well to his touch. You just never knew about these things, particularly with a sensitive animal.

After milking and storing the milk, the three of them headed inside the toastier house, and Brynn made them all hot cocoa. Her specialty. She served the real thing, with real milk from her girls, and added a little cayenne pepper seasoning to it.

"So delicious!" Max said.

"I agree," Wes said. "This is the life. Milking cows. A beautiful, fragrant Christmas tree. And a delicious cup of hot cocoa. What more could you ask for?"

What more indeed? Brynn took in the scene—the decorated, lit tree against the window, with flurries still coming down, and the two content young men. It looked, smelled, and tasted like Christmas to her. If only it felt like Christmas. But she suspected she'd not relax about Christmas, or anything else, until the investigation was over and they'd caught the arsonist.

Chapter Seventeen

The next morning, Brynn found a charming, sparkling fine snow on the ground. She stood a few moments and took it in as the sun rose. After milking and letting the girls out, she made her way back to the house where a delicious cinnamon scent hung in the air. The "boys" had been in her kitchen again.

Her nose and fingers were so cold, she thought they might fall off at any moment, but her stomach growled and warmed from the scent.

Wes turned from the oven as Brynn walked into the room. "Good morning. You two are spoiling me," she said.

"You opened your home to us. It's the least we could do," Wes said.

"Coffee is ready," Max said.

Brynn scrubbed her hands at the kitchen sink, and they all sat down to breakfast.

The baked French toast nearly made Brynn swoon—the eggy bread was doused in cinnamon and milk. She'd never made something like this for herself. Usually it was a bowl of oatmeal or fresh yogurt.

She should treat herself better. But in the meantime, she was enjoying every bite.

"You're a fantastic cook," Brynn said to Wes.

He glanced at his brother with a look of dismay. "So they tell me."

Max cleared his throat. "He wanted to go to cooking school. Our parents talked him out of it, so he could go to college."

"I hate college," Wes said, and then drank from his coffee.

"Oh, that's too bad," Brynn said. "I'm sure your parents are trying to do what's best for you."

"I'm sure," Wes said. "But when they see my grades, they might think again." He smiled.

"Let's not talk about that so early in the morning," Max said.

The three of them sat quietly eating and looking out over the field.

"I wonder how the investigation is progressing," Max said.

Which reminded Brynn that she needed to call and check in with the fire marshal.

She looked at her phone to see what was on the schedule today. She had a meeting with the CSA to discuss the plans for a headquarters of sorts. Willow had been exploring locations for a farm stand during the summer, which they'd manage along with their regular produce deliveries.

Also, Petunia had rehearsal tonight for the living nativity scene. Willow would help transport Petunia using her truck.

"I'm sure it's moving forward," Brynn said.

"Why would anybody do that?" Wes said. "I don't understand. Why would anybody want to hurt Gram?"

Brynn set her coffee down on the table. "It may have been an accident. They don't know yet."

"It sounded pretty clear to me it wasn't an accident," Max said. "It's unfathomable."

She agreed. She couldn't believe that somewhere in this bucolic, peaceful area, an arsonist-murderer was lurking. But perhaps that was just her naïveté. Her mother had always said that bad people and good people were everywhere.

A pang of missing Dan shot through her. If he were here, she'd feel safer. That is, the Dan from ten months ago, from before she'd known he was cheating. No, she didn't need him. She tamped that missing him emotion right down. Forget him.

After breakfast and a long, hot shower, Brynn phoned Mike Rafferty, the fire marshal.

He picked up after two rings. "Rafferty."

"Good morning, Mr. Rafferty. This is Brynn MacAlister."

"G'morning," he said. "What can I help you with?"

"I was just wondering if that note I gave you helped with the investigation."

"Not yet, no," he said. "If we find a suspect, then we can compare handwriting."

"What about fingerprints? I mean, can you send it to a lab somewhere?"

"Yes, several prints have been lifted from it. All Nancy's, unfortunately. We don't have to send out for fingerprints. We don't have the resources of city police, but we do have a fingerprint lab," he snapped.

Way to go, Brynn. "Sorry," she said.

"No worries, Ms. MacAlister." He paused before asking, "How's your cow?"

"She's doing much better. Schuyler really helped

her. I didn't believe it would work, but it did," Brynn replied.

After ending their conversation, Brynn was torn about whether to proceed with trying to find the Lexington contractor Nancy had hired. She didn't know anything about investigating a crime. She had no business doing it. What would she even ask the man? Where were you on the night of the fire? And why would he even answer her? She felt foolish even thinking about it now.

It wasn't as if she had nothing else to do. There was a barn to clean, a cow to transport to the church, and cheese to make. She had plenty on her plate. She needed to let this go.

In the meantime, she readied herself for the CSA meeting. She was starting to feel like the CSA members were her friends, and she looked forward to seeing them, especially Willow. She was more helpful than anybody. Brynn had a hard time remembering names, but she never forgot Willow, who actually looked exactly like a woman named Willow should look. Long and lean, with long, straight brown hair and big brown eyes. She was part African-American and part Cherokee and loved to talk about her ancestors—on both sides. Brynn loved to hear her stories.

Brynn was a few minutes late to the meeting, and all the participants looked up at her when she entered the room. "Sorry," she said.

The others went back to listening to what Tom was saying.

Willow smiled up at her as she sat.

"So, it's between three places. The old community center, Blackberry Hollow Farm, and the O'Reilly Apple Orchard."

"They always have a nice setup," Josh said. "Wouldn't be much work we'd need to do, except bring in bins."

"They also have quite a loyal following," said Willow, smiling at Frank O'Reilly, who was there representing his family, Brynn supposed, as none of the others were there.

"But Blackberry Hollow has more areas to park," said Tom.

Brynn's eyes went to Frank, who was intently watching and listening to the conversation around the table. But he didn't quite meet anybody's eyes. Was he shy like his sister?

"The community center is free," said Tom.

"Yes, but it lacks charm," Willow said.

"We could give it charm," Brynn said. "If it's free, there's no reason we can't charm it up."

Willow smiled. "It could be nice. The river and the trail are nearby. People could come and get their produce, and then take a walk by the river or have a picnic."

"But giving the place charm might cost us," said Tom.

Brynn looked around the table. "It doesn't have to cost a lot."

"Okay, then I move to table this discussion until Brynn can come up with some prices for us to consider. That way we can really weigh the options."

"Me?"

"I guess I should've warned you," Willow said, grinning. "If you open your mouth with ideas, you get the honor of pursuing them."

Chapter Eighteen

Petunia was one of the sweetest cows Brynn had ever met. And she'd met a lot. But the cow was not happy about going into the trailer pulled by Willow's truck.

"C'mon sweetie," Brynn said, pulling gently on her rein. Willow dangled a few more carrots in front of her. Petunia turned her nose up at them and mooed loudly.

Brynn saw her cow getting stressed. Petunia was going nowhere tonight.

"How about one of your other cows?"

Brynn had selected Petunia because of her good nature and love of people. The other two weren't quite as people friendly. But they weren't mean. Either one of them could certainly stand in for Petunia. Marigold was too shy. It would stress her out to be in a crowd of people.

"Okay, let's try Buttercup." Brynn led Petunia off the platform and into the gated field, and they made their way into the small barn. She slipped the rein off Petunia, who was still agitated and mooing.

"I hope she calms down for you," Willow said, coming up beside Brynn. "Schuyler said she responded so well to the acupuncture."

"She may just have gotten spooked by the trailer," Brynn said. Or the acupuncture treatment had worn off.

Buttercup turned out to be compliant.

Once the cow was situated, Brynn and Willow drove off in the truck, pulling the trailer. As they pulled out of the driveway, they saw a young man walking along the road. Brynn thought it was Tillie's brother. "Is that—"

"Frank O'Reilly," Willow finished. "Yes. He's a bit odd. Always has been."

Brynn noted he was heading in the opposite direction from her house. "Does he often go walking along the road like that?"

"I've seen him walking around before. I guess he likes it."

Brynn glanced at him in the mirror. She wasn't certain, but she thought he looked in her direction. Hard to imagine he was Tillie's brother.

Brynn and Willow were about ten minutes late for rehearsal. Reverend Ed Higard wasn't pleased.

"I'm sorry," Brynn said. "We were delayed. Petunia didn't want to come. So we brought Buttercup."

"Okay, fine," he said. "I take it she's still giving you problems. I guess a mooing cow like that would be a distraction to the other animals. The other folks are right around the corner." He waved in the direction where the others were gathering.

Brynn, Willow, and Buttercup walked around the corner of the church.

Brynn scanned the scene and the animals—a donkey, a sheep, and a camel. A camel? Who would have thought?

Brynn grinned. "Who owns a camel around here? Isn't it too cold for him?"

"He's a rescue camel from the zoo," Willow said. "Belongs to the Donohues. Some kinds of camels do fine in the colder weather. They're not all desert dwellers. Besides, people forget that the desert gets cold."

"He's a sweetheart," Ed said as he came up beside them.

The players who were portraying Mary, Joseph, and the baby Jesus, made their way over to the animals.

"I'm aware you all thought this rehearsal was ridiculous, but it works best if the animals are acquainted with the people and the other animals involved. And we are only a week away from Christmas Eve," Ed said.

All the animals and their people took places around the "actors."

"Okay, can you move the cow to the other side of Mary?"

"Sure," Brynn said. She wanted to help and be a part of the community, but she thought Ed was taking this way too seriously.

"Now, I want all the people with the animals to drop out of the picture," he said.

Brynn started to walk away, and Buttercup followed her.

"Sorry," Brynn said. "Buttercup, stay."

Willow placed carrots on the ground, which distracted the cow long enough for Brynn to slip away.

All the animal keepers clustered together in a group

and observed the scene. Brynn had to admit, the scene worked.

"The Bible doesn't even mention animals at all at the Nativity. It's totally fabricated," Willow said under her breath.

"Really?" Brynn said. "I had no idea." She had to admit she'd not given it much thought.

The baby who was playing Jesus fussed. His mother gave him a pacifier.

"They had no pacifiers in biblical times," Ed said. "But I guess it's better than a fussy baby."

As if we didn't know there were no pacifiers back then. He was so condescending. Brynn made a mental note to make sure she was very busy this time next year, too busy to participate in the Nativity, and so would her cows. Okay, maybe she was getting a little grumpy.

Once they were back in the truck, with Buttercup safely back in the trailer, Brynn exhaled. "I'm so glad that's over with," she said.

Willow laughed. "Not a fan of Ed, are you?"

"I've been trying, you know. I want to fit in here and be helpful, but he's just not very likable."

"He's okay," Willow said. "But like my daddy always said, 'All preachers do is lie and eat chicken.'"

Brynn laughed. "What's that supposed to mean?"

"I think it's just supposed to mean what it says," Willow said. "My dad is a kind of a matter-of-fact dude. No metaphors for him." She turned right onto Honey Pot Road. "But, needless to say, he doesn't like preachers."

"Speaking of preachers, do you mind if I ask you something?"

"Shoot."

"What happened to the Old Glebe Church? I mean, before the fire and everything. Why was it abandoned?"

"Well, there are two stories about it," she said, pulling into Brynn's driveway. "One is that, during the Civil War, the church was used as part of the Underground Railroad, unsuccessfully. So, for years after, people had bad memories associated with the place. And then, of course, most folks moved closer to town and went to church in Staunton."

Brynn exited the car. "What was the other story?"

"Just that the leaders of the church all died off, and nobody could afford to keep the place up," Willow said. "That's probably the truer story. I don't know. I've never really looked into it."

"In any case, it's a shame it's gone," Brynn said.

The two of them walked across the field as a full moon lit their way. Brynn opened the barn door. Inside, Petunia was still agitated, rocking back and forth and mooing.

"Poor girl," Willow said.

"Looks like I need to call Schuyler tomorrow."

"Good idea. It usually takes several treatments," Willow said.

Given that Petunia had responded so well to the first treatment, Brynn hoped the next one would be her last.

Chapter Nineteen

Brynn was tuckered out. But then again, she felt like exhaustion was the new normal for her. When her head hit the pillow, every muscle unwound, and she drifted off to sleep. She was deep in a dream when a tickle in her throat woke her. She coughed and coughed. Then she turned back over, and the tickle was still there. Then her eyes flew open. What was the odd scent? It smelled like chemicals . . . or gasoline . . . or lighter fluid. Where was that scent coming from?

She sat up in her bed, reached for her robe and ran downstairs, knocking over everything in her way. Gasoline meant fire!

Where was it coming from? She flicked on the outside lights, and from the corner of her eye, she saw a figure in her front yard—she couldn't say if it was a man or a woman. But when the light flicked on, the person dropped something and took off over the hill.

Brynn's heart thudded against her rib cage. She found her cell phone and dialed 9-1-1.

Someone had been in her yard. Someone was planning to set her place on fire just the way they had done to the church. Her mouth felt like sandpaper as she tried to explain it to the operator. "I live on Parson

Ridge, just off of Glebe, and someone just tried to set my place on fire."

She opened the outside door as she saw Wes heading toward it.

"What's wrong? I saw the light come on and smelled something odd," Wes said as he tumbled into the room. Brynn held up her finger.

"I'll dispatch a fire team over there right away," said the operator.

"There's no fire. I caught him. I mean, I didn't catch him. I saw him taking off over the hill and maybe through the woods," Brynn explained.

Meanwhile, Max came barreling into the house. The next thing Brynn knew, they were both gone.

"I still need to send a team. There may be dangerous chemicals lurking," the operator replied.

"Okay." Brynn took in a deep breath. Danger. Chemicals. Gasoline. Or was the scent turpentine? It didn't matter what it was, if someone lit a match, her place would go up in flames.

Wes and Max came back into the house several minutes later.

"We couldn't find anybody," Wes said. "Are you okay?"

"I'm fine," Brynn said, adrenaline still coursing. "I think someone was trying to set this place on fire." Could that be? Could it be the same person who set Nancy's place of fire? Why?

"We need to find out," Max said. "Whoever it was, took off out of here very quickly."

The sound of sirens erupted in the distance.

Why hadn't she seen it before? Whoever didn't like Nancy—another outsider—would also dislike another outsider living in a parsonage with a new dairy parlor.

Someone seemed to be against anything new. So against it that they were willing to destroy the very thing they sought to protect. Her face heated.

Someone wanted her dead. Now this situation had just gotten personal. She'd not stand still for it. No indeed.

She'd yet to look up the Lexington contractor. But she would in the morning. And she'd find Nancy's killer, as it didn't look like the local law enforcement was doing anything—at least not that she could tell.

"This is bizarre," Wes said. "I don't get it. This place seems so lovely, the people so friendly."

Brynn grunted. "That's what I thought, too."

After the fire trucks, police, and paramedics had come to investigate, Mike Rafferty arrived on the scene. From the window, Brynn spotted him talking with a firefighter who was taking soil samples from the corner of the yard where she had seen the person.

Flashlights were out and beamed across her yard. She wondered how the girls were taking all the commotion.

Rafferty came toward her door, and she opened it.

"We can't keep meeting like this," he said, and gave her a sideways grin.

"What?" she snapped.

"Never mind," he said, flustered. "Can I come in?"

"Of course." She led him to the living room where Wes and Max already sat.

"Nice tree," he said.

Brynn stood with her hands on her hips. "I don't care about my tree. I want answers, Mr. Rafferty. I want to know who was in my yard in the middle of the night, and what they were pouring onto my grass. And, I want to know what this has to do with the church fire. If you can't tell me that, I'll find someone who will. Or I'll do it myself."

The room silenced as they stood face to face.

"I'm sorry, Ms. MacAlister, I know you must be angry and scared," Rafferty finally said. "I don't have all the information you want, but I've got some of it. Please sit down." He gestured with his arm to the couch.

Brynn sat down, reluctantly, torn between her anger, fear, and embarrassment at speaking to Rafferty like that. She could hear her mother right now. "Brigid Elizabeth MacAlister, you weren't brought up in a barn. Where are your manners?"

"Whoever was here wasn't very serious about what they were doing, and you should be happy about that."

"What makes you say that?"

"There was just a small patch of grass doused with lighter fluid, but they built a circle of rocks around it so it wouldn't spread. I'd say it was a prankster or a warning." He sat next to her on the couch. "I'm sorry. As to the rest of your questions, I simply don't have any answers."

"A warning?" Wes said. "About what?"

"Someone wants me gone, just like they wanted Nancy gone." Brynn's voice was deep and low, barely recognizable to her.

"The question is why," Wes said.

"If we find out the answer to that question, we have our guy," Rafferty said.

"It must not have to do with the church specifically," Max said.

"You shared a property line. What else did you and Gram have in common?" Wes asked.

"We're both new here," Brynn said as she shivered. Someone had stolen Nancy's dream and her life. Now they wanted to do the same to her.

Chapter Twenty

Brynn tossed and turned beneath her quilt that night, as odd thoughts popped into her mind. What if there was something about the Old Glebe Church and rectory she didn't know? Would that point her in the right direction?

She and Dan had bought the place loving the idea of being a part of history, even though they were not particularly interested in the religious aspect of that history. Their house had only been lived in by preachers and their families—except in the 1990s when someone tried to turn it into a B&B. She and Dan were grateful for all the updates they'd made to the place, starting with the indoor plumbing. But when they left, the place sat idle for years before it was sold. Which was strange when you thought about it. She and Dan bought it, along with most of the furniture, on the spot.

She had thought it would be fun, to someday look up their place's history, along with that of the Old Glebe Church, but she hadn't had the time, what with tending the cows, and moving in, all without Dan. It seemed as if she had no time for any personal life at all, let alone historical research.

If she had more money, she'd hire someone to help in the barn, at least. Keeping the barn and the dairy parlor clean was of utmost importance to creating quality cheese.

After a fitful night, she arose at her usual time of 5:30 AM and slipped on warm clothes in order to make her way to the girls. The cold was biting. It was even unpleasant in the semiheated barn.

After milking Petunia and giving her extra rubs behind the ears, Brynn let the cows out and made her way back into the warm house, where Wes and Max were making breakfast.

"Good morning," she said.

"Good morning," Wes said, holding a plate of something that looked like doubled-up French toast. "I found this amazing soft cheese in the fridge, so I made stuffed French toast."

Brynn's mouth dropped. She'd never heard of such a thing. "I made the cheese last week," she said. "So it's fresh."

"You made it? It's delicious," Max said. "Do you sell it?"

"No, right now I'm just selling the hard cheese. It's more cost effective, easier to store and transport. But I did have plans, for later. Your grandmother planned a refrigerated section in the store."

They gathered at the table. Wes fussed over the placing of the plates, glasses of juice, and coffee. Finally, he settled down and sat.

Wes and Max would be flying back home later today. Brynn tried to relax and enjoy her breakfast, but she didn't really want them to go. They'd helped her in the barn, with the Christmas tree, milking, and had made these delicious breakfasts. All of which she could do herself, of course, but it was so nice to have help. And to have company.

"What happened last night was wild," Max said. "I mean, what the hell was that about?"

Brynn sighed. "I don't know, but I'm going to get to the bottom of it. Nobody will scare me away from this house and land. It's mine. I bought it fair and square."

Just then, a knock came at her door.

"Who can that be so early in the morning?" Brynn asked.

She made her way to the front door and opened it to several members of the CSA, standing there holding dishes and bags in their arms.

"Oh God, are you okay?" Willow said.

"What—"

"News travels fast around here," Willow said, beaming. "We all brought you some food, so you don't have to worry about fixing anything over the next few days. You've got enough on your mind."

Brynn's heart cracked and soared. How lovely. "Please, come in."

The group followed her into the kitchen where Wes and Max were still eating at the table. Brynn introduced everybody.

"Would you all like something to eat? Some coffee?" Brynn asked.

"We've all eaten already. I could use a cup of coffee," Josh O'Connor said, handing her a jar of his honey, along with a tin, which, from the way it smelled, held biscuits. Even though Brynn had just finished eating, her mouth watered.

"Coffee sounds good," Willow agreed, as she placed several bags full of food on Brynn's counter.

"I agree," Kevin said, handing Brynn a casserole dish with what looked like scalloped potatoes inside.

"You all sit in the living room," Wes said. "I'll make a fresh pot of coffee and bring it in to you."

"Well, that's nice," Willow said, smiling.

The group made their way into the living room, and Brynn suddenly realized she'd just been in the barn and looked, and probably smelled, like it.

"So, what happened?" Kevin said.

Brynn explained everything that had happened overnight, and the three CSA members sat as if in disbelief.

"I'm flummoxed," Willow said. "Like, what's going on here? I've lived in Shenandoah Springs my whole life and can't remember anything like this ever going on."

It occurred to Brynn that maybe one of the three of them would know something about the history of this place. "Do any of you have any idea why someone would burn down the church, then try to warn me off? Is there something I don't know?"

"I'm not sure I follow," Kevin said.

"Like, I don't know, buried treasure or something."

"There've been a lot of stories about this place and the church over the years, as I told you yesterday," Willow said.

"I wouldn't be worried about history right now," Josh said. "I'd be worried about getting a good alarm system."

Alarm system? An expense Brynn hadn't counted on.

"Maybe you need a dog," Willow said.

A dog might be cheaper than an alarm. And it certainly would be more fun.

"I'll look into getting a dog," Brynn said, as Wes and Max brought in cups of coffee. Tendrils of fear ran through the center of her. She couldn't believe she had to worry about burglar alarms and guard dogs in a place like this. Rural communities were safer, weren't they? Or maybe that was just another false thing she had believed in her whole life. Just like so many other things.

Chapter Twenty-One

After her guests had coffee and left, Brynn showered and dressed in clean clothes. Then she sat down at her computer to search for a contractor in Lexington. It wasn't much, but it was the only lead she had. Even if it didn't make much sense for a contractor to burn a place down, she had to try.

Willow had offered to do a little historical research on the church and house. Brynn was eager to hear about those results. Even if it led them nowhere on this investigation, it would be interesting to know the history of this place.

She keyed in "contractors in Lexington," and a slew of them popped onto her screen. She read over them and their specialties. There were only three who mentioned historical renovation as part of the services offered. That meant there were only three contractors she needed to call. Not bad.

She dialed the first on the list. No answer, so she left a message. She dialed the second on the list.

"Grady Renovation," the voice on the other end of the phone said.

"Hi, this is Brynn MacAlister in Shenandoah Springs.

I was wondering if you could answer a few questions for me," she said.

There was a pause on the other end of the phone. "What are you selling?"

"Oh, nothing. I'm just looking for a contractor."

"What kind of project do you have going on?"

She wasn't doing a great job of this. "None. I'm sorry. What I'm looking for is a contractor who might have been working with Nancy Scors on the Old Glebe Church renovation."

"That's not us," the voice on the other end of the phone said. "Ms. Scors talked to us, but she didn't like our pricing."

"Okay. Thanks so much for your time."

One more contractor to call. But her thoughts were interrupted by her doorbell ringing. Must be Schuyler.

By the time she made her way down the stairs, Wes had opened the door and was letting someone in— Tillie!

She looked around Wes and smiled at Brynn. "Hi, Ms. MacAlister."

"Tillie, how wonderful to see you! Please come in," Brynn said.

"I was so sorry to hear about what happened last night. My parents sent you some apple butter and homemade bread," she said.

She followed Brynn into the kitchen and a flummoxed Wes followed behind her. Max grinned at Brynn, and she wondered what that was about. What was she missing?

"Looks like other people have been here," Tillie said, as she set her stuff on the counter.

"People have been very generous," Brynn said.

"I'm so touched. Thank you, Tillie, and please thank your parents for me."

She gave a brief nod. "Hey, I noticed that Petunia is still agitated."

"Yes, unfortunately. But Schuyler is coming over to give her another treatment. It helped last time."

Tillie strained her neck and looked over at Wes, who was standing there, gaping at her. "What gives?" she asked.

"Uh, I . . . I don't know," he said, and shrugged. "I really liked your singing from the other night. You have a gorgeous voice."

"Thanks," she said. "I wish my parents were on board with it. They think unless you're praising God with your voice, it's irrelevant."

"Wow, that's too bad," he said. "I get it, though, my parents don't get my wanting to be a chef. That's why I'm in college."

"That bites," Tillie said.

"How about some hot cocoa?" Brynn asked.

"I was hoping you'd ask. Your hot cocoa is the best I've ever had." Her dimples framed her smile.

"Why don't you and Wes and Max go into the living room, and I'll bring it to you when it's ready?"

"Okay. I guess."

The three of them left the room, and Brynn brewed her hot cocoa with fresh thick heated cream. She stirred in cocoa and chopped baking chocolate, which melted in dark brown streams in the frothy brew. She added in cinnamon and cayenne pepper. Laughter erupted from the living room. It was a good sound in this old place. It was a sound she missed. A sound she needed more of. She didn't want to dwell on all the horrible happenings—and she wouldn't. But she felt compelled to get answers.

Brynn fetched her tray from the cupboard, placed four cups on it, and poured the thick liquid in. The scent of cinnamon, chocolate, and cayenne pepper was so strong that it nearly overwhelmed her. Well, if you had to be overwhelmed . . .

Brynn walked into the cozy scene of the three young people sitting on the couch opposite of the Christmas tree and window.

"It's snowing!" Max said.

Brynn sat the tray down on the coffee table and turned to see big fluffy flakes landing on the grass.

"It's snow that might stick," Tillie added.

As the four of them sat, drinking their hot cocoa and watching the snow, Brynn nearly pinched herself, for this was a moment straight out of Hallmark. Enjoyable company. Good drink. Beautiful white scenery, with a lovely Christmas tree in the room.

It was wonderful enough to almost make her forget about everything else. Almost.

Max and Wes's phones both pinged at the same time. Max looked at his. "Just what I thought. Our flight has been canceled."

"Mom and Dad will not be happy about this," Wes said.

"I'm sure they want you home. But they want you safe, most of all." Brynn set her drink down on the table. "Besides, their loss is my gain." She grinned. "I love having you two here."

"Thanks. I love it here," Wes said.

"I like it here, too, but it will be Christmas next week, and I'd like to be home for it," Max said.

"I don't care if I ever leave," Wes said.

"Speaking of parents, I need to go. Mine will be looking for me." Tillie stood. "Thanks so much for the cocoa."

They stood and walked her to the door, all of them stepping out onto the front porch for air as Tillie walked off, waved briefly, and then disappeared over the hill. Max walked back inside. Wes stood with a forlorn look on his face. "I love this place. It's so beautiful, and the people are wonderful. I feel so close to Gram here."

"I know exactly how you feel," Brynn said, leading him back into the living room. Brynn missed Nancy's company, but having her grandsons here felt right, almost as if Nancy herself had planned it that way.

Chapter Twenty-Two

The snow was coming down in great big flakes at a rapid pace. Brynn, Max, and Wes watched the cows from the window. Even though Petunia was still rocking and mooing, she lifted her head and looked around, as if charmed by the snow. Buttercup and Marigold were frolicking. Actually frolicking. Marigold would run through a drift and Buttercup would circle around and come at the drift in another way.

The three of them were enjoying the sight when Brynn's phone buzzed. It was Schuyler.

"Hi Brynn. I don't think I can make it today. I'm sorry. How is she?"

"She's still rocking and mooing, but she's distracted by the snow."

"Well, a little distraction never hurt a depressed cow," she said. "I'm hoping the roads will be clear by tomorrow. It's pretty icy. I figured it was best to stay home."

"You're probably right. My houseguests' flight was cancelled, as well. Better safe than sorry," Brynn said.

"Hey, I'm sorry to hear about what happened last night."

The grapevine in Shenandoah Springs was short and quick. "Thanks."

"Are you okay?"

"Honestly, I'm a bit shaken." Brynn walked into the kitchen and placed her cocoa pan in the sink to rinse out.

"I would be, too, because of the church burning down. It seems too coincidental."

Brynn squirted dishwashing fluid into the pan, filled it up with water, and scrubbed it out with a brush. "My thoughts exactly. Do you know anything about the history of this place? Or the church?"

"Not really. People used to say the church was haunted, cursed, the usual thing with abandoned places. As kids, we used to play over there. We loved to read those gravestones. But they were too old and worn."

Brynn imagined Schuyler as a girl playing among the tombstones. "Sounds like fun."

Schuyler laughed. "I'm more afraid of live people than dead people. I always have been. In fact, I prefer animals."

"Now there's something we have in common."

"I'll see you tomorrow," she said.

Brynn finished cleaning up the kitchen. She then filled a pan with saltwater and made her way into her makeshift cheese cave, aka cellar, where several round circles of cheese awaited washing. It was extremely important to clean the cheese to keep the flies and any kind of harmful bacteria away. Two of her cheeses were over a year old. She poured the saltwater into a large pie pan and took her round brush—made specifically for washing the cheese—dipped it into the saltwater, and washed the hard cheese with circular motions, making certain to clean around the edges.

"What are you doing down there?" a voice came traveling down the stairwell.

"Washing the cheese." Her voice echoed a bit.

Wes and Max came down into the cellar.

"This is cool," Wes said. "Look at all the cheese. And in nice little neat rows."

"It's kind of creepy," Max said. "And it smells bad. Like cheese."

"That's what it should smell like, idiot."

"I have more brushes," Brynn said, and handed them each one. "This is how you wash cheese." She demonstrated how to do it, and each of them followed her lead.

Max looked as if he might throw up.

"Is it that bad?" Brynn asked.

"I'll be okay," he said.

"I've been researching the church," Wes said as he scrubbed. "And you can only get so far."

"What do you mean?"

"There are no online records before, like, 1910."

"So what did you find out? Anything useful?"

"The church officially closed in 1955. There were only a few families living in the village. Most of them had moved into Staunton, Lexington, or even Roanoke. So it made little sense to keep it open. Nobody had the money to keep it afloat."

"Nothing odd about that. They abandon churches in rural areas a lot. People need to work, and farming never made it easy." Brynn moved on to the next round hunk of cheese.

"There was one thing I found odd."

"Get to it," Max said, looking up from his cheese scrubbing.

"Well, a lot of the names were the same as the names of people I've met since I've been here. Higard. McNeil. O'Reilly. Andrews."

"That would be odd, except that most of these families have been here, in this area, for generations. Some of them may have moved to Staunton, but they are still around."

"Imagine staying in one area your whole life. I couldn't wait to get out of our town," Max said.

Silence permeated for a few minutes—except for the sound of washing.

"I think it's actually kind of nice," Wes said, breaking the quiet. "Your family would always be around you, the people who appreciate and love you would be around, kind of looking out for you. Nice," Wes said.

"That's one way of looking at it," Max said. "But the other way is that they'd always know your business. I don't like that."

"What does it matter if you have nothing to hide?"

Out of the mouths of college students.

"This area is full of friendly, kind, and good people. Check out all the food they brought me. It's just so lovely," Brynn said. "But there is something . . . off. That's all I can say about it. I mean what happened with Nancy . . ." Her voice trailed off as a shiver crept through her.

Chapter Twenty-Three

Brynn thought about the two brothers as she placed a few casseroles in the oven for a late lunch. They looked very much alike, but Max was taller and darker. Wes was small framed for a man and had huge, beautiful expressive eyes, framed in dark lashes. But the two seemed different from one another. Which she shouldn't find surprising, since she and her sister differed from each other as well.

Becky was into hair and makeup and made her living as a cosmetologist. Her goal was to own her own shop someday. Her daughter, Lily, was the light of Brynn's life. Oh, how she wanted to see them for Christmas. There was nothing like watching a little one open gifts on Christmas morning.

Brynn had never been into any of the "girly" stuff her older sister was into. She was a scientist, an explorer. As she grew up, she collected plants, rocks, and any stray animal that happened along. She wanted to identify what made things tick, and then what things were made of. Hence, chemistry became her passion.

"I like chemistry, too," Becky always said. "But the kind that makes you pretty."

Next year, Brynn vowed, they'd be together for Christmas.

"Are you sure I can't help you?" Wes said as he walked into the kitchen.

"I'm just heating up a couple of those dishes people brought by today. The green bean casserole and the scalloped potatoes. So there's not much to do."

Wes sat down at the kitchen table and looked out at the snow. "She must have been so scared."

Brynn knew exactly who he was talking about.

He continued. "She was the best gram ever. I wished she could have died peacefully in her sleep. It seems so callous and unfair for her to die like that."

Brynn's heart ached as a slice of longing ripped through her. If she could only see Nancy one more time. "I wish the same thing. But, unfortunately, that's not what happened." What could she tell him that would bring him peace? "She was very high on pain medication when I saw her at the hospital. So, you know, she wasn't feeling any pain."

"She would have preferred bourbon to pain pills, but I guess she didn't have a choice."

Brynn laughed. "True."

"Why would someone burn down that church? Want to hurt her? I don't understand."

Brynn sat down at the table with him. "I don't understand either. But evidently, there's something going on here that we don't know about."

"Either that, or there's some crazy fool out there burning things just for the heck of it," Max said as he walked into the kitchen.

"I read about arsonists last night," Wes said. "Sometimes people set fires with criminal intention, like to kill someone, or to cover up a crime. Or sometimes they are actual pyromaniacs. You know, it's a mental disorder. Well, wait. What did they call it? An impulse-control disorder."

"Remember Randy Jenkins? I wonder what happened to him," Max said, and laughed. "He was this kid we grew up with. Always had matches in his pocket. Got caught so many times setting things on fire."

"There was that time in school when he set the art supply room on fire!" Wes said. "I remember." He quieted. "You know, it's disturbing. After reading a bit about it and thinking about Randy, it makes sense. They set fires to relieve tension and stress. That kid had it rough."

"Wasn't he the boy who we found out was homeless? His family had abandoned him?"

"Yes, it was awful."

"Makes me wonder even more who set the fire at Gram's house."

The three sat in silence as the kitchen filled with the scent of creamy scalloped potatoes and green bean casserole.

"The fire marshal is investigating the fire. He'll find out what happened," Brynn said, trying to sound hopeful. She recalled she hadn't heard from the other contractor in Lexington. Nor had she phoned the third contractor yet. She'd do that after supper, before she brought the cows in. She wasn't sure any of that would help, but she had to try.

"The church had an interesting history. I wasn't able to get to any primary sources, but I found articles suggesting it was used in the Underground Railroad," Wes said.

"Someone mentioned that to me as well. But if that

were the case, wouldn't it have been on the historical register?" Brynn asked.

He tilted his head. "Yes, but there's no mention of that anywhere."

"It takes a lot of money and attention to get something listed as a historical treasure," Max added.

"I suppose we'd have to go into town and study records on the church there," Brynn said.

"That would be the thing to do," Max said, and then glanced out the window. "But not today."

After eating, Max and Wes had a long Skype session with their parents, who were concerned about them getting home for Christmas. Brynn made her way to her room to make a few phone calls. She still needed to learn which contractor Nancy had hired. A contractor in Lexington wouldn't have the attachment that a local one would. But Brynn couldn't figure why any contractor would set the place on fire, especially one that had just gotten work from Nancy.

But Nancy thought it was important enough that she tried to communicate about it before they whisked her off on the helicopter.

Brynn dialed the contractor. It was late in the day. Perhaps there'd be no answer. It surprised her when he picked up on the second ring.

"Flannery Contracting. How can I help you?"

"Hello, Mr. Flannery. I'm Brynn MacAlister. I live in the old rectory at Shenandoah Springs."

"Yes?"

"Have you heard about the church burning down?"

A pause. "Yes. Very unfortunate." He let out a long breath into the phone. "We planned to work with Nancy. We'd just signed a contract with her three days before it burned down."

Bingo! Brynn's heart beat faster.

"I was looking forward to it. It was going to be a great project. She had wonderful ideas."

"Do you have any idea who'd burn down the church?" Brynn asked.

"Do they think someone set the fire on purpose?"

"Yes."

"Hard to believe." He sounded genuinely surprised. Perhaps he was a good actor. Some people were good at lying.

"Any ideas?" Brynn asked again.

"Let me give that some thought, Ms. MacAlister. If I can think of any reason, I'll let you know."

"Thank you," Brynn said.

"Did you say you live in the rectory?"

"Yes, I moved here about three months ago. I have a few cows, and I make cheese."

"Wonderful," he said. "I always wanted to see that place lived in, you know? Seemed like an awful waste to have it sitting there. Like the church. It would finally be used . . ." His voice trailed off.

"Thanks so much, Mr. Flannery. You've been a big help," Brynn said, and they said their good-byes.

So the plot thickened. Nancy had hired Flannery to help with the renovations only three days before someone burned it down. Could it be an odd coincidence? The man seemed genuinely upset and concerned.

So why was Nancy going on about a contractor? Was it the drugs messing with her mind? Nancy's last words were seared into Brynn. She was not willing to let it go.

Chapter Twenty-Four

The next morning, the snow had melted, and Wes and Max checked in with the airline. Their flight had been rescheduled, and they were soon ready to leave for the Shenandaoh Valley Regional airport.

"I really hate to go," Wes said, as they stood in the lobby of the small airport.

"I wish you both could stay, but I'm sure your parents would like to see you for Christmas."

"I felt so at home at your place," Wes said.

"You're welcome to come back anytime," Brynn said.

She stood and waved them off as they disappeared into the security area.

As she drove home, she mulled over the whirlwind of the past week. The church fire. Nancy's death. Her unexpected houseguests. A fire almost started in her front yard. Curls of fear traveled through her. She hated to feel so frightened, so vulnerable.

It would scare anybody, wouldn't it? Someone was out to get her. Unaware of why, she contemplated her next move. She briefly toyed with the idea of calling Becky and pleading with her to come for a visit. Then she thought of her parents. *No. Darn it, I can do this. I can make this place my own, make this business flourish. I can.*

As she pulled into her driveway, a car pulled in behind her. A flicker of fear grabbed at her, then she realized it was Schuyler. She parked, and Schuyler parked next to her, with the dog in the back wagging its tail.

"Hey there," Brynn said as she exited the car.

Schuyler and the dog were already out of the car, Schuyler with a bag in her hand. "How's Petunia?"

"Same. Unfortunately."

"Acupuncture is not like Western medicine. It's more like building up to healing. You know? It may take several treatments."

The dog pranced around, now coming over to Brynn, who reached down to pet her. The dog stood on her hind legs and placed her front paws on Brynn's hips to make it easier for Brynn to rub her.

"Sorry about that. She's a little exuberant."

"It's okay," Brynn said. "Have you found her owner?"

"No, unfortunately," she said, moving toward the gate, bag in her hand, ponytail swinging down her back.

Brynn followed her.

"Stay," Schuyler said to the dog. "Sit."

She whined, but she obeyed.

"Sometimes dogs can stress out large animals, particularly sensitive ones, like Petunia."

But Petunia had come over to the gate and had stopped mooing, while she was checking out the new creature who was being very good, sitting there, as the cow took her in.

"Looks like Petunia is curious," Brynn said.

"Okay, Freckles, up," Schuyler said.

"What did you say her name was?"

"I've been calling her Freckles. She seems to like it.

When you look at that snout with all of the little red flecks, it looks like freckles to me."

"That was the name of my Granny Rose's first cow!"

Freckles approached Petunia at the gate and looked up at what must have seemed a huge creature to the dog—even though the dog was pretty big herself. Petunia slowly blinked a few times then nuzzled the dog with her nose. Freckles's tail wagged.

"This is . . . interesting, right?" Schuyler said.

"Sweet," Brynn said, her heart beating quickly. Perhaps Petunia just needed a new friend. Maybe that would calm her. She'd read about cows and other animals becoming friends, but she'd never seen it with her own eyes. "May I borrow Freckles?"

"Borrow? Heck, you can adopt her. She's had all of her shots and is very healthy."

The dog and cow appeared enamored. And having a dog around, especially one as big as this one, would deter any unwanted visitors.

Freckles pawed at the fence gate. Brynn opened the gate and watched as the dog and cow frolicked. "It looks like I don't have a choice."

Schuyler nodded. "It certainly doesn't."

Petunia's depressed demeanor had vanished. She was charmed by Freckles, and it was the same with the dog. In the meantime, Buttercup and Marigold barely noticed the dog.

"Well, I don't think Petunia will need that treatment. I think we found her cure."

A hot, stinging rush of tears swelled in Brynn's eyes.

"Oh, now," Schuyler rushed to her. "I didn't mean to make you cry." She dug in her pocket and handed Brynn a tissue.

"It's just that . . . I've been so worried about her. I'm just so relieved. So happy that she's fine."

Schuyler took her in. An expression of respect came over her face. "If only everybody cared about their animals the way you do."

Brynn gathered herself. "Do you have time for a cup of mint tea?"

Schuyler grinned. "I believe I do, since my patient doesn't seem to need me."

The two of them settled at the table in Brynn's farmhouse kitchen, and the conversation naturally turned to the incident in Brynn's front yard.

"Freaky, right?" Schuyler said. "What are your thoughts about it?"

"I think your brother was right. Someone was trying to warn me off or scare me. And they succeeded at scaring me. But I'm not going anywhere."

"That's good to know," she took a sip of her tea. "Any idea who did it?"

"None at all. The only lead I have is the contractor thing. I found out who Nancy hired. Flannery out of Lexington."

A red-faced Schuyler almost choked on her tea. "Are they still in business?"

"Evidently. Why?"

"It's just that their son was in a whole lot of trouble last year. Drugs. And between his drug money and legal fees, he pretty much wiped them out. Or so I thought."

Imagine that. The local vet-acupuncturist seemed to be aware of everybody's business. But then again, it seemed like nobody had any real secrets in Shenandoah Springs, at least not for long.

Chapter Twenty-Five

So Flannery had money trouble. Bad money trouble. Didn't they always say when investigating a crime to "follow the money trail"? Or was that just on TV and in the movies?

She needed to meet Flannery in person and assess him. It was easier to lie over the phone than in person. She'd heard there were "tells" if someone was lying. What were they?

Brynn sat down at her computer and searched "tells in lying." She read over the information:

A change in voice.
They try to be still.
Direction of their eyes. Sometimes people who are not
    telling the truth may glance to the left because they
    are constructing answers or imagery in their head.
Covering their mouth or eyes.
Unusual gesticulating.
Taking that hardline pause.

Brynn didn't know if she could remember all of that, but she'd try to keep it in mind when she spoke to Flannery in person. But the question was how to make their meeting seem legit. What could she ask him to fix or expand? To at least give her an estimate for? She'd have to mull that over.

A sudden round of barking came from Freckles, who was still outside with Petunia. The dog seemed jubilant to be in the field with Petunia and the other two girls.

Brynn hurried downstairs and out the door to see what was bothering her.

A vehicle had parked in the driveway. And a man was standing with his hands in his pockets, looking out over the field.

"Can I help you?" Brynn said.

He turned toward her. It was Tom Andrews, from the CSA, the man who told her she should muzzle Petunia. The man who went on and on about the church—and Nancy.

"We heard about your trouble," he said. "My wife and I, that is." His weight shifted, and he looked toward Petunia. "Your cow seems to be better."

"Yes," Brynn said. She didn't need to give him details. She wasn't quite sure she liked him.

"Anyway, there's a bag of food in the truck. I'll get it for you. My wife, you see, she's a good baker, and, well, she's known for her pies. She made you a few."

Brynn felt awkward because the pies were still in the truck, but he wasn't, and he showed no signs of going to get the pies. "That's so kind of her." A few awkward beats. "Ah, would you like to come in for some coffee? Tea?"

"Nah, I best be on my way," he said as his hand came up to his ball cap and adjusted it. He walked toward the truck, opened the door, and handed her a brown paper bag filled with three pies. Three pies! What would she do with three whole pies?

"Thank you," she said, and took the bag.

"I like what you're doing with the place," he said, with an odd note in his voice. It was as if it rose a decibel, and then stuck in his throat as he forced it out.

Perhaps it was because Brynn had only just read about liars, but she felt certain he was lying. He *didn't* like what she was doing with the place. And he had said at the CSA meeting that he didn't like what Nancy had planned to do with the old church.

"Welp, I've got a meeting with the historical society. I'll catch you later," he said, and slid into the car, started his engine, and drove off, leaving Brynn holding her bag of pies.

Brynn looked over at Freckles, who was standing near the gate with Petunia. "Good girl. Do you want to come inside?"

She whined and sat down on the ground. Evidently not.

Chapter Twenty-Six

Brynn placed the containers on the table and peeked inside to see what kind of pies Mrs. Andrews had baked for her. They were labeled APPLE, EGG CUSTARD, and SHOOFLY. Shoofly? She'd heard of it, but had never had the desire to eat something called "shoo fly." A cinnamon and molasses scent wafted from it. She supposed she'd have to give it a try.

She sliced into the shoofly pie. It was denser than most—almost like a cake. She sliced again, fashioning a small slice, just enough to try it. She scooped the pie slice onto a plate and tucked in. As she chewed it, the flavors mingled in her mouth. Molasses, yes, cinnamon yes, but most unpleasant. She ran to the trash can and spit it out, gagging, and trying not to retch. Her stomach waved and rolled. Until then, she had never met a pie she didn't like. But as she steadied, she threw the whole thing into the trash. What an awful waste of pie.

She slid the other two pies onto a shelf in her refrigerator. Maybe she'd feel like tasting a few slices tomorrow, but for now, she couldn't look at pie. Thinking about her growing waistline, she thought perhaps it was a good thing.

Is this what shoofly pie really was? Or did Tom ask his wife to make something terrible for her to be spiteful and mean? She'd gotten the idea he didn't like change. He was definitely of the old-school population Willow had told her about. After all, one pie was more than enough. But three was an overkill.

What had Brynn become? Here she was suspecting a man and woman who'd been kind to her. Sure, he was a tad surly, but that didn't mean he was trying to get rid of her, or that he'd set a fire to a church that had been a part of the landscape for generations. He'd mentioned he was a part of the historical society, and that probably meant he respected the area's history. Why would he burn a part of it down?

She needed to get a hold of herself. She didn't like what the fire was doing to her. She suspected everybody.

She shuddered.

So far, the dog seemed to be a good watchdog. Perhaps she would be good company as well. The house seemed empty since Wes and Max left.

Her cell phone buzzing interrupted her thoughts. It was her sister, Becky.

"Hey, Becky."

"I'm just calling to check on you. How's everything going with you?"

Brynn paused.

Becky seized on the pause. "What's going on?"

Brynn took a breath and told her sister what had been happening—everything from the church fire to the fire in her front yard. It was Becky's turn to pause.

"I don't like the sound of any of that. Maybe you should hire someone to tend the girls and come home for Christmas."

"I can't do that," Brynn said. "We're in the local living nativity scene."

"What? That doesn't sound like you."

"I'm not doing it again. I've decided I don't like the pastor. But understand, church is very important in a community like this. It's more than a religious thing. It's social. And I want to succeed. In order to do that, I have to be a part of the community."

Becky grunted. "Isn't being a part of the CSA enough?"

"The CSA is great, though it's not without its issues. You reminded me, I'm supposed to be researching ways to give the community center some charm. Now that the church is gone, we're counting on it."

"I don't like you being alone there. You said it was a friendly place. It doesn't seem like it to me." Worry edged her voice. "Perhaps we should rethink a visit."

Brynn's heart skipped a few beats. "That would be awesome. But if you can't afford to come, I don't want you to worry. I have the girls, and, oh, I have a new dog, Freckles."

"That's great. What kind of dog is she?"

"She's a Saint Bernard mix of some kind."

"Aww. That reminds me of Rhiannon." Rhiannon was one of their childhood dogs, named after the popular Fleetwood Mac song.

The name of the dog prompted a song from Becky, and the two of them signed off laughing—Becky was notorious for flat singing, which had become a family joke. None of them could sing well at all, but Becky was the worst of all of them.

As Brynn's thoughts turned to singing, she thought of Tillie and her ethereal voice and Willow saying Tillie's family didn't approve of her music. And, evidently, her family didn't approve of some of her reading either. When she thought of Tillie, it was with a mix of emotions. Such potential. And not just with her music. She was bright, warm, and so composed for one so young. Of course, her family had a lot to do with that. Why were they so against her growing intellectually and musically? One of these days, when she knew Tillie better, she'd ask.

Brynn slipped on her coat and boots and walked out to the field to bring in the cows. They followed her as they usually did. This time, she had one more creature in the small herd—Freckles, with the ever-wagging tail and huge bark.

After milking and storing the milk, Brynn whistled at the dog. "C'mon girl. Into the house."

The dog sat down and whined. She didn't want to leave Petunia.

"Okay then," Brynn said. "I'll bring your bed out here and your bowl, too. Okay?"

She crouched down to pet Freckles, and the dog rose on her hind legs, her front paws on Brynn's shoulders. The dog's liquid brown eyes seemed to look directly into Brynn's soul. She hugged the dog. One more creature to love.

As she hugged the dog, she felt a sudden tension. Freckles lurched away from her and growled. Brynn turned to find Frank O'Reilly standing in the doorway. She nearly jumped out of her skin.

He held out his hand, which held a piece of dried meat. "Dog treat," he said. Freckles looked up at Brynn.

"It's okay," Brynn said, and the dog took the treat.

"I love dogs," he said with a silly, crooked grin.

Brynn's nerves were ragged and frayed, and even

though he'd done nothing wrong, she wanted him to leave. It was late, and he really had no business here.

"Mom and Dad sent more food for you. I left the bag on your front porch."

"Oh, well thanks for bringing it. And for the dog treat. Freckles seems to like it."

They stood for a few awkward beats.

"I need to lock up, so . . ." She gestured with her hand for Frank to exit through the door.

"Oh, okay," he said, and exited the barn door. Brynn followed closely behind.

She locked up and turned around to see him still standing there, hands in his pockets. "Good night then," she said, and walked away.

"Good night."

When she arrived at the front door of the house, Brynn lifted the bag of food and turned to find him walking over the hill.

Chapter Twenty-Seven

The next day, after milking the cows and feeding the dog, Brynn drove to the old community center to take some photos. She needed inspiration to come up with some solid ideas to share with the CSA. And she also needed specifics. Studying the photos would provide a touchstone. She stood back from it and examined it from afar, snapping a few photos from different angles. The community center resembled an old barn. She couldn't figure out what other people had against it—she thought it was perfectly charming with its old barn wood and wooden beams.

Her first thought was that it would be lovely to place some benches along the path to the river. She could also imagine hanging baskets of flowers around the entryway. But there needed to be something to hold the produce. Huge bins? Rustic tables? And they'd need to be easily covered or moved inside at a moment's notice.

Well, that was beyond her skills. Flowers and benches were one thing, but moveable bins were another. She wondered if there was a kitchen inside. She made a note to ask. It would be convenient to have a spot to clean produce right before displaying it. She needed to ask Willow about a key. And she needed to find someone to answer questions. Someone . . . like a contractor.

She'd call Flannery when she got home. This was a perfect opportunity to check him out. Was he lying when he said he thought using the church as a place to sell local products was a great idea?

At this point, he was the only person that Brynn could think of who had any stake at all in the church—except for the other local farmers, artists, and crafters. But he had more of a stake because he would've been paid to renovate it. It absolutely made no sense he'd want to destroy it. Unless it was something like insurance fraud. But Brynn doubted that any kind of insurance would be in place on a project just three days after signing a contract.

Brynn pulled her scarf in closer around her face. The wind was picking up. She walked down the path toward the river. When she arrived at the river bank, she admired the landscape. Most folks loved blooming, full trees, but she found bare trees beautiful. The way they reached up and grabbed at the sky, the way their silhouettes twisted, and the way they held insular energy and promise.

The hills beyond the river, spotted with snow patches and surrounded by leafless trees, were a blue winter solace. Dan was right about this place. It was gorgeous.

But it was the only thing he was right about. He thought she'd forgive him for his indiscretion. Then when she didn't, he thought she'd not pursue this dream, that it would be too hard for her. Maybe he was right, who knew? But for now, she was managing.

Her phone buzzed. "Yes?"

"Ms. MacAlister?" said a voice she didn't recognize.

"Yes, that's me." She turned to head back to the car.

"This is Pete Hoffman from Hoff's Bakery. We received your basket of cheese, and I gotta tell you, it's some of the best cheese I've ever had."

Brynn warmed in the cold Shenandoah wind. "Thank you."

"We'd be happy to carry some of your cheese here. We have a small refrigerated section. Stop by and let's chat about what we can do."

Brynn's heart was bursting. "Sure. When would you like me to stop by?"

"How about tomorrow? I've got ideas I'd like to run by you. Really. This cheese is amazing." Excitement seeped through his voice.

Brynn sifted through her schedule in her mind. "How about eleven-ish?"

"Sounds perfect. See you then."

Brynn's steps felt lighter as she made her way to the car. She may not know much, but she knew how to craft an excellent cheese. Her cheese sold itself— once tasted.

She turned the radio on in her car and sang along with the Christmas songs. It was perfect music for the scenery—spreading fields, sweeping hillsides, farmhouses, barns. She pulled into her long driveway and parked her car. First, she checked on her girls. All three, plus Freckles, were in the field. She did not understand who that dog thought she was, but she fancied hanging out with cows.

When she approached the house, she noticed something on her front door. Something black and feathery, tinged in red. Her heart leapt into her mouth. Someone had nailed a dead crow to her door. She turned her head quickly and took refuge inside her car. Why would someone do that to an innocent animal? Why would someone put it on her door? Tears flowed down her face. She allowed herself to sob, to get it out of her system. What was going on here?

As soon as she calmed herself down, she phoned the sheriff, then Mike Rafferty. Both men were there in a matter of minutes.

Mike rapped on her car window. She rolled it down. "You can come out now. It wasn't what it looked like."

"What do you mean?"

"It was a dead bird all right. But it had been dead a long time. It was a stuffed bird. Fake blood. Taxidermy."

"Do you mean that someone just wanted to scare me with a stuffed bird?" Brynn shook with anger.

"Are you okay?"

She blew her nose. "Depends on what you mean by that."

A crooked grin splayed across his face. "Okay. What can I do to help you?"

What Brynn wanted was him—or anybody—just to hold her. Some human contact would help. But she turned her head, then looked back at him. "Will you please find who did this?"

"That's a little out of my jurisdiction, but the sheriff will make inquires."

"What's going on here? First the church and Nancy.

Then the attempted fire in my yard. Now this! Have you gotten anywhere on your investigation?"

"I can't discuss an ongoing investigation with you."

Frustration tore through her. "No, but you can let me and my place be sitting ducks."

Chapter Twenty-Eight

After milking Petunia and settling the animals in for the evening, Brynn plodded back to the house where she thought about cooking supper, but then thought again. She didn't think she could eat anything. As her gaze shifted along her counter, where a few of the pies sat, she thought if she couldn't eat pie, she couldn't eat anything. Waves of nausea rolled through her as she paced.

She walked into the living room, flipped on the Christmas tree lights and waited for that peaceful Christmas feeling to come over her. She waited and waited.

A knock at her door made her jump. She was letting all of this get to her, she scolded herself. She needed to get a grip. She took a deep breath and answered her door. She opened the door to Willow and Schuyler.

"Mike told us what happened," Willow said. "I just can't believe someone would do that to a bird! I never understood taxidermy, but then to nail it on your door? Douse it in fake blood? Outrageous."

"I'm furious. We need to find out who did this," Schuyler said. Her sweet face hardened with anger.

The Shakespearean quote "Though she be but little, she is fierce" came to Brynn's mind at that moment.

"Please come in. Get out of the cold," Brynn said, gesturing with her arm. "Let me take your coats."

Willow and Schuyler walked into her kitchen and sat at the table. They both had been here before and knew their way around.

"Can I get you something to drink?"

"I hear you make a mean hot cocoa," Schuyler said.

"I do," Brynn said, beaming.

"Is that pie?" Willow asked.

"Yes, Tom Andrew's wife sent it over. If you want some, help yourself."

As the three of them sat at the table, drinking hot cocoa and eating custard pie, Brynn picking at hers, snow started to fall.

"So, you were only gone like an hour?" Schuyler said.

Brynn nodded. "I drove over to the old community center to check things out and take pictures. I'm in charge of coming up with ways to make it more charming. We may use it for the CSA farm shop."

"Now that the church is gone," Willow said.

"So it had to be someone who knew you were gone," Schuyler persisted.

"Or someone who was watching for their opportunity. Like watching this place," Willow said.

"My driveway is a bit long. But you can see the place now, in the winter with the leaves and foliage gone," Brynn said. "I'm at a loss. First, the church and poor Nancy, then what happened in my yard, and now this."

"It has to be connected," Schuyler said.

"You must be so scared," Willow said after a moment. "I would be."

"I'm not sure if I'm more frightened or angry."

"Those emotions come from the same place," Schuyler said.

Brynn mulled that over. "I can see that. Hey, Schuyler, remember what you told me about Flannery?"

"What? That he's broke because of his troubled son? Yes. It's true. It surprised me to learn they're still in business. They sold their farm."

Willow cleared her throat. "What are you thinking, Brynn?"

"I may be crazy. But could he have something to do with all of this? It keeps nagging at me. First, I thought, why would the contractor who just got the job burn down his project? Then I wondered, if he's so desperate, could it have something to do with insurance?"

Schuyler sat forward. "You mean like business insurance? It seems to me the only one who'd have benefited from the place burning down, as far as insurance goes, was Nancy."

"Or Nancy's family," Willow said.

"Well, they live too far away to be involved in any of this."

The three of them sat in silence.

"I just remembered that you were going to research the history of the church," Brynn said to Willow.

"Yes, I'm still sifting my way through all of it. But the church was built in the 1800s. Back then, it was a big deal to have an actual church. There were still a lot of traveling preachers in these parts. But Shenandoah Springs was becoming a booming place," Willow said.

"Until the interstate took most of the traffic out of here," Schuyler said.

"That and Staunton, Lexington, and Waynesboro had all the good-paying jobs. Farming is difficult. Few families survived, stayed here. But a lot of them are still in Staunton," Willow said. "Anyway. Legend says the church was used in the Underground Railroad. But I haven't been able to find any proof of that. Neither has the historical society."

Schuyler dropped her hand on the table with a slam. "Those people don't know what they're doing. Armchair historians. They think the world revolves around Shenandoah Springs, like history happened nowhere else."

Willow's eyebrows arched, and she grinned. "If you want an opinion, Schuyler always has one."

Brynn laughed. It felt good to laugh. A few hours ago, she thought she would have a nervous breakdown. Now she was sitting and laughing with two women who might be her friends.

"I'm going to ask Flannery to help me out with the old community center," Brynn said. "I need to meet him and get a feel for him, see what he knows."

Willow looked at Schuyler. "Let me be with you when that happens. Or Schuyler. Keep in close touch. Two or three heads is always better than one."

"I doubt he had anything to do with this, but if he did, we'll find out," Schuyler said. "And he'll be sorry. We'll make sure of it." Her voice had the edge of anger. Brynn didn't know her well—but she was glad Schuyler was on her side.

Chapter Twenty-Nine

Brynn gave up on falling asleep. She tossed and turned until she couldn't do it anymore. She arose from her bed and padded downstairs for a Tylenol PM, which usually helped her to sleep. Then she padded back upstairs, sat at the desk in her room, and turned on her computer. She'd just surf the web until she felt woozy enough to sleep.

She keyed in "Flannery Contracting." A slew of items came up on the screen. First, she clicked on their website, which was nicely done. She looked at their family pictures and wondered which one of their two boys was the drug addict.

Drugs were a problem everywhere, she was aware, even in the bucolic Shenandoah Valley. Not only did they ruin the lives of the addicts, but often, also of the families. Financial devastation. Broken lives. OxyContin. Crack. Heroine. All of it led to devastating circumstances. Well, it said a lot about Flannery that he had at least tried to help his son. Sometimes parents cut off their kids completely. Sometimes they ended up homeless because of it. Brynn's heart broke when she thought about it.

She clicked around a bit more. She stopped dead

when she noticed the Flannery company logo. It was a crow! Could it be a coincidence? She clicked on "About Our Logo."

> *Our family logo stretches back to ancient Celtic times. Our family's heritage is in the West of Ireland. We were caretakers and embalmers. The crow is the bird associated with our family because of its role as a bridge between the worlds of life and death. Today, we hold on to our heritage, but now are only caretakers of houses and barns, bringing them new life.*

It didn't seem like a very friendly motto. A chill traveled along Brynn's spine. Was it too coincidental that someone placed a dead, stuffed crow on her door, and the contractor who Nancy hired used the crow as the symbol of their business?

If it was them, what were they hoping to accomplish? And why be so obvious in using a bird associated with their family? A calling card, of sorts?

Brynn turned away from her computer. Her mind was on fire, but her eyes were beginning to feel heavy. She'd have to call the sheriff and Mike tomorrow to let them know what she found out. She was eager to know their reaction. She was also eager to find whoever left the crow, burned down Nancy's house, and almost set a fire in her own yard. Someone wanted them both gone, but why? Why would Flannery—or anybody—care what they were doing?

Nancy had planned to add something of value to the community. And Brynn was just here to make cheese. She hadn't stepped on anybody's toes. There weren't other cheesemakers around, were there?

Even if there were, cheesemakers were not usually competitive people. There was always friendly competition. But cheese was like wine, in that it relied heavily on taste. If you liked one kind of cheese, it didn't mean you liked all cheeses. Taste was highly specific. So what was the point to nasty competitiveness between cheesemakers?

But still, it nagged at her, even as she lay back down beneath her quilt. She'd look into some of the bigger dairy farmers in the area. And she'd also look into any of the cheesemaking operations. Perhaps she had missed something when she researched the area. Even if there was cheesemaking going on at the other farms or even bigger places, she couldn't imagine that someone would be angry enough at her to be so destructive and nasty. She made small-batch artisanal cheese. She could never compete with the big farms and big cheesemakers. And she wouldn't want to.

She'd faced a moral dilemma when she decided to buy her own cows, so she could control the cheesemaking process from start to finish. She didn't like being part of the dairy industry, which was not known for its compassionate treatment of cows. But she decided that she would do things differently. She'd be as compassionate of a micro-dairy farmer as she could be. So far, so good. And the more she'd gotten to know some dairy farmers, the more she learned not to believe everything she read about them. Just like everything, there was good, along with the bad.

The next morning, after milking, and after breakfast, Brynn called Sheriff Matthew Edge.

"What can I help you with, Ms. MacAlister?"

"I've been trying to figure out why someone would leave a crow at my door."

"It was probably just kids, being kids."

Sparks of anger shot through her. "And how about the fire almost set in my front yard? Kids, too?"

"It's a good possibility. Now, Ms. MacAlister, we're working on finding out who did both of those things, along with setting the church fire."

"Obviously they're all related," Brynn said.

"We don't know that. Don't leap to any conclusions, and leave the investigating to the pros."

Shame and embarrassment filled her. Was she butting her nose in where it didn't belong? She needed to be careful. She was new to the community, and she was a businesswoman with a reputation to consider.

"I'm sorry to bother you, Sheriff," she said, and hung up. She kept what she found out about Flannery and crows to herself, along with anything else she'd learned. She had no business investigating any of this, but the local authorities were moving too slowly for her. She was a woman alone on a farmette with only a dog for protection. She needed to take control of the situation before something else happened—something worse.

alone along the side of the road. What an odd young man. Tillie was so friendly and nice; he was brooding. An interesting family, to be sure.

She drove by what used to be the center of the village, the old town square. Some of the locals were tending to it, and it now had a Christmas tree, along with a couple of park benches. A sign for an old hardware store still hung above one of the empty storefronts. With the huge home improvement stores less than twenty miles away, Brynn guessed nobody needed a small one close by. Mom-and-pop hardware stores were a thing of the past.

As she drove along, she noted the two new businesses, places that had recently been painted. One was a coffee shop, which Brynn had been meaning to check out, and the other was some kind of herb shop called "Misty's Herbs." The shop was painted bright yellow. Now that looked like a place Brynn might like to investigate, as well.

She drove along, taking in the scenery, and she felt her stress give way just a bit. Someone was interested in her cheese. She clung to that thought, instead of all the others rambling around in her brain. Like her failed relationship. Like her lonely Christmas.

When she pulled into the parking lot of Hoff's Bakery, it surprised her to see so many cars. The Hoff's business was lively. She found a place to park, and, as she stood at her car with the door open and gathered her things, she overheard raised voices. She flushed and tried not to listen to what was obviously a personal argument.

She grabbed her things and walked into the bakery. As her face turned to make sure she'd closed the door against the cold winter air, she spotted Tom Andrews

Chapter Thirty

Brynn readied for her meeting with Paul Hoffman. After showering and dressing in a pair of black pants, a turtleneck, and a blazer, Brynn glanced at herself in the mirror. Yes, she looked professional and friendly. She swept her long hair up in a bun, then decided against it.

She made her way to the kitchen and scooped the fluffy crème fraîche into a small plastic container, repeated the process with the *fromage blanc*, and filled a paper bag with the samples for Mr. Hoffman. She brought along her soft cheese as well. Perhaps Wes was correct—these soft farm cheeses had potential. And Mr. Hoffman said they had a refrigerated section in their bakery.

Brynn gathered her handbag and her bag of cheese samples and was on her way. She shoved a pang of fear deep inside, hoping she'd not find any more surprises at her place when she returned from her meeting.

As she drove along, she was once again awestruck by the beauty of Shenandoah Springs, with its fields and mountains, dotted by houses and barns. The sky was winter blue, with not a cloud floating in it.

Once again, she spotted Frank O'Reilly walking

in the parking lot with a woman, who she assumed was his wife. Brynn wanted to thank her for the pies, but she turned her head back quickly. Tom was arguing with his wife. He was a man with a hot temper.

Heavenly scents filled Brynn's nose when she entered the bakery. Cinnamon. Bread baking. And warm sugar. The counter traffic was lively. Behind the counter were neat metal shelves stacked with loaves of fresh-baked bread. Brynn stood and drew in the scent.

"Can I help you?" asked a woman coming up beside her.

"Yes, I'm Brynn MacAlister. I'm here to meet with Paul about my cheese."

A grin spread across her face. "Fabulous. I'm Paul's wife, Sheila. That's some delicious cheese you make."

Brynn warmed. "Thank you."

"Follow me into the back, where his office is. He's expecting you."

She was a tiny woman with the sinewy arms of a baker. In Brynn's experience, bakers were a hard-working group. She had the utmost respect for them.

Brynn followed her back, past huge bins of sugar and flour. They passed by the huge ovens, where men and women dressed in white were scurrying, tending to the baked goods—sliding them in, taking them out, or placing them on display pans. It was like a symphony for the eyes and a feast for the nose.

"Hey, Paul," Sheila said, knocking on the door, then opening it. "Ms. MacAlister is here."

He turned from his desk with a stiff smile. "Ms. MacAlister. Thanks for coming." He stood and shook Brynn's hand. His hands were large and clammy. Perhaps it was because of the cold temps in the office.

"Thanks for having me. I'm so excited about the possibilities."

"I'll leave you to it," Sheila said, and left the room.

"Please have a seat," Paul said.

It struck Brynn that he was much friendlier on the phone than in person. Perhaps he was just tired. There was an air of unease about him.

"I brought you some samples of my soft cheeses," Brynn said, and placed the paper bag on his desk.

He brightened momentarily. "Thanks," he said.

An awkward silence filled the room.

"So, yesterday you called and said you had ideas about carrying my cheese, maybe offering some exclusive cheeses here?"

He nodded. "Yes, I did." He groaned. "I'm sorry. That was before . . . before I had a good look at the books. I just don't think we can come to any arrangements right now."

Brynn's smile gave way. "What?"

"You've got a fine product. It's just not right for us right now. Maybe some other time." He looked away, then looked back at Brynn. "I'm sorry to drag you all the way here. I'm sure you have things to do."

What was going on here? Brynn didn't understand. He called her out of the blue yesterday, with accolades and opportunities, and now he was trying to get rid of her. She tapped down the hot threads of anger zooming through her. She was a businesswoman, in a new place, with a reputation to mind. She couldn't afford a tantrum.

"I'm happy to explore other arrangements. You could sell my product, without paying me up front for it. Sort of a consignment arrangement," Brynn said.

"We prefer not to work like that. Too much can go wrong. So, no. Let's table this discussion until the spring."

She stood. "I'm sorry to have troubled you. Please keep the samples. If you change your mind, you know where I am."

She started to walk out of the office.

"Ms. MacAlister?"

"Yes?" She stopped and turned back to face him.

"Merry Christmas."

She nodded, then continued on her way.

When she walked out of his office and through the rest of the place to the front of the store, all she could concentrate on was not crying. The hot sting of tears threatened to embarrass her in front of all the customers.

Sheila was occupied filling a bag with bread, but she looked up and waved. Her eyebrows knitted briefly, as if something confused her, then her attention shifted back to her customers, and Brynn exited the shop.

She couldn't drive away fast enough as tears ran down her face. What the heck had just happened? Okay, calm down, she told herself. It was just business, nothing personal. He said he looked at the books. It was a financial decision.

But Brynn couldn't shake the feeling it was indeed personal. Then she told herself to stop it. The man had never met her before. What could he possibly have against her or her cheese?

Chapter Thirty-One

Brynn drove home and called her sister after she poured herself a big glass of wine.

"What are you doing?" Brynn asked.

"Wrapping a multitude of Christmas gifts."

All of Brynn's gifts were already wrapped and sent. But perhaps she should give Willow and Schuyler a small gift. They had been so kind to her. She'd also like to give Tillie a gift, but she was uncertain how her parents would take that gesture.

"What's wrong?" Becky asked.

"The oddest thing just happened."

"Another odd thing? One more thing, and I will insist you move out of that place."

Brynn decided to keep the bird story to herself.

"This wasn't scary. It was just strange. I'd like your opinion." She then relayed the story of how Paul Hoffman had called her out of the blue and wanted to explore ways in which they could carry her cheese in the shop. And how when she arrived, he'd completely changed his mind.

"It's not your cheese," Becky said. "It can't be. Something must have happened between his call and your arrival."

"I'm confused. He's been in business for years. Why wouldn't he be aware of how he was doing before he called me?"

"Well, not all business owners are as astute as you are—or as small as you are. It's easy for you to keep track of things in your head. But if it's a big business, it could be harder. You know?" Her voice softened. Brynn knew Becky was trying to calm her and herself. She appreciated how much this move and this business meant to Brynn.

Brynn breathed in and out. "Maybe you're right. I'm just on edge because of all the other stuff that's happened."

"That must be it. Listen, Lily will be home from school any minute, and I've got to hide these gifts before she gets here. So, I better go."

"Okay. Talk to you later."

The idea of Becky hiding Christmas gifts and playing Santa lifted Brynn's spirits. It must be a lot of fun to have a child at Christmas. As an aunt it was fun, too.

She hated keeping the bird incident from Becky, but it was best she didn't learn about it at this point. It would only worry her, and there was absolutely nothing she could do.

She took her glass of wine and moved into the living room, turned on the Christmas tree lights, and some Christmas music on the stereo. She sat down on the couch and enjoyed the view. Her field outside through the window. The tree lights and the tree decorated with things Wes and Max had made. She sipped from her glass. It was okay to be alone. She would be fine. After all, Christmas was just another day. That was her mantra.

She set her glass down on the coffee table and

curled up on the couch. She missed her niece and sister, and her mom and dad in Richmond. Next year, she hoped they would all be together. Perhaps by then, she could hire someone to look after the girls while she visited her parents in Richmond.

A draft chilled her, and she reached for an afghan, pulled it over her shoulders, and closed her eyes. It would be okay. She didn't need a house full of people on Christmas. Not this year. She certainly didn't need Dan, the cheating fool of a man. No, indeed. She was more than fine without him. She drifted off in a lovely soft nap and dreamed of cheese.

When Brynn awakened from her nap, hunger pangs demanded her attention. She sat up and folded the afghan and made her way to the kitchen. She still had several casserole dishes from friendly concerned people in the community. She just needed to heat them up. She slid a cheesy, broccoli-rice casserole into the oven, along with a vegan meatloaf, which intrigued her.

As she waited for her food to heat, the scents filled the room, and she warmed, recalling how friendly most people had been since she'd arrived. Which made all the other stuff more intriguing.

She'd phone Flannery tomorrow and set up a time to meet him at the community center. He'd have ideas, and she'd brainstorm questions to ask him, questions she hoped he'd answer in such a way that she'd find her answers about the church, Nancy's death, the incident in Brynn's front yard, and the bird on her front door.

The next morning, Brynn had a hard time getting out of bed, even though she looked forward to Freckles greeting her every morning with her tail wagging, looking at her with that grin on her face. Petunia was a much happier cow these days, now that she had a new friend. Who would have imagined a dog would be the one key ingredient for Petunia's happiness?

Freckles seemed happy, too. Brynn had wanted a house dog—but this dog was so happy in the barn, with her dog bed and her best friend in the same area. It was as if the two had fallen madly in love with one another. It was one of the sweetest things Brynn had ever witnessed.

Marigold and Buttercup seemed unfazed by the dog, for the most part, though Buttercup was curious. Brynn had witnessed her sniffing around the dog, and once, even nuzzling her with her nose. It would take a lot longer for the shy Marigold to warm up to Freckles.

After milking and letting the cows and the dog out into her field, Brynn walked back into her house, showered, and ate breakfast. She planned to call Flannery today, but first she needed to figure out some questions to ask him. Questions that might implicate him in the murder of Nancy, plus the multitude of other incidents.

What exactly did their contract cover? The whole project? Or just part of it?

Did he have insurance? And exactly what kind of insurance was it?

She stopped, sighing, unclear how to ask these questions without him figuring out her suspicions.

Maybe she should use them as part of her questioning for the project she was pretending to consider him for. Yes, that's it. She'd ask these questions, along with others about the project, so he wouldn't become suspicious of her. That's all she needed. She didn't need her place to be the next one to burn down.

Her stomach knotted as she considered it. All of her savings, plus all the money her grandmother left her, had gone into the cows and this property. If she lost it, it would break her heart. And it would give Dan something to gloat about, no doubt. She wouldn't let that happen.

She dialed Flannery.

"Flannery Contracting. How can I help you?"

This was a different voice than before. A younger voice.

"Yes, hello. This is Brynn MacAlister. I spoke to someone the other day. I think it was the older Flannery."

"Yes, that would be my dad. How can I help you?"

"I might need help and wondered if he could fit me in."

"What kind of project did you have in mind?" The voice held the edge of hope.

"Well, it's not that big of a project. The CSA is looking for a place to sell our goods, and we're considering revamping the old community center. I'm in charge of adding charm, but when I went over there to look at it, I thought I could use help. Perhaps from a contractor. Nancy had hired him, and I know how she was so picky, so I . . ." Brynn was rambling.

"Oh, I see," the man said. "Hold on."

Brynn's heart raced. Was Flannery the guilty party? If he was, could this arrangement be slightly dangerous? She then recalled that Willow and Schuyler wanted her to bring one of them, if not both, along to their meeting. Perhaps they knew something she didn't.

"Looks like he can meet with you tomorrow morning. Is that okay?"

"Certainly. Let's say eleven?"

"How about ten-thirty?"

"Okay. And please tell him to meet me at the community center. I may have some others with me."

"Others?"

"Other CSA members. But I'm uncertain who."

He hesitated. "Okay. I'll tell him."

"Thank you."

"Merry Christmas, Ms. MacAlister."

Why did people keep saying that? She didn't want Christmas to be right around the corner. And there would not be anything merry about it.

"Same to you," she said.

After they hung up, she phoned Willow, who said she'd happily meet Brynn and Flannery. She also said she'd call Schuyler to see if she was available.

Freckles barking madly shook Brynn out of her revelry. She moved to the front door and peeked out the window. It was the sheriff. Odd.

She opened the front door before Sheriff Edge had the chance to knock.

"Ms. MacAlister," he said.

"Yes, how can I help you? Why don't you come inside? It's freezing out here."

He nodded. "Thank you."

Wiping his feet and taking off his hat, he entered Brynn's home.

"Can I get you some tea or coffee?" Brynn asked.

"No, thank you. I'm not staying long, really. I just have a few questions for you."

Why did the law make her so nervous? She'd done nothing illegal in her life. Okay there may be illegal cheese she'd eaten—but that's it. She'd often had a friend in England ship her some unpasteurized Stilton, and another friend in France ship her *Bleu d'Auvergne*. In return, Brynn sent her farmstead cheese to them.

"How well did you know Nancy?"

Brynn's heartbeat sped up. "She was my neighbor. We chatted almost every day. But our relationship was on a surface level. Meaning, Nancy didn't open up much to me. I knew about her family. She talked about the church renovation." She paused. "We also talked about food."

Sheriff Edge nodded thoughtfully. "She ever talk about her past?"

"Not much, no."

"She ever say why she came here?" He shoved his hands in his pockets.

"She said land was cheap. She and her husband had driven through here once and fell in love with the place. When she saw the church for sale in some magazine, she felt as if it was a sign. She jumped on it."

"Hmph," Sheriff Edge said. He scratched his chin. "She ever talk about Tillie?"

"Tillie? No. In fact, I wasn't aware that they knew one another until after she passed away."

"Do you know anything about their relationship?"

Brynn's brain sorted through everything she knew. "Well, I take it that Tillie borrowed books from her. Unfortunately, the books may have been ones her parents didn't want her reading."

"Did Tillie tell you that?"

"Yes, and someone else mentioned it. Kevin Ryder. The Christmas tree farmer. It came up because I was over there buying a tree, and she was singing. Have you ever heard her sing?"

"Of course I have. Everybody has," he said.

"So talented, right?"

"She surely sings beautifully."

Was Tillie in some kind of trouble? That couldn't be.

"Tillie seems like a good girl, too," Brynn said. "My cows love her, and that's always a good sign."

Sheriff Edge grinned. "Sounds like something my dad would say. Dairy farmer. Long gone."

"Sorry," Brynn said. "Is everything okay with Tillie? Is there something I can do?"

"Nah. I'm just trying to get a handle on everybody Nancy spoke with the last few days of her life, and what her relationships were. Her relationship with Tillie seemed odd. That's all."

"It seemed odd to me, as well. But, evidently, they got on."

"So they say," he said noncommittedly.

After he left, Brynn considered calling Tillie, but she didn't want to worry her. Poor girl. Her family didn't support her music, and, evidently, didn't want her reading certain books. Brynn didn't know much about raising kids, but none of that sounded good to her at all.

Chapter Thirty-Two

Brynn and Willow pulled into the gravel parking lot of the old community center. They were a bit early. Schuyler couldn't make it because someone's horse was ailing, and she needed to take care of it.

They sat in the warm car, listening to Herb Alpert's rendition of "Jingle Bells" over the radio and looking out over the mountains. Brynn's spirits were lighter. She was certain she was getting closer to finding answers about Nancy's death. Even though she was nervous about meeting a possible killer, she felt better with Willow there. She had a soothing nature.

Soon enough, a van with a crow logo and FLANNERY CONTRACTING printed in big letters on the side came into the parking lot and parked next to Brynn.

She and Willow exited the car.

A man exited the van and walked around to greet them. "You must be Ms. MacAlister. I'm Zach Flannery." He held out his hand, and she shook it.

"Yes, pleased to meet you."

He stiffened. "Willow. Good to see you."

Willow shifted her weight from one leg to the other. "Nice to see you, too."

He was a tall man, big boned, and had the weathered

look of a man who'd spent a lot of time outside, working with his hands.

"Let's get to it, shall we?" Brynn said, holding the keys up and jiggling them. "So, the CSA is looking for a place to sell our goods. We still plan on making deliveries, but another outlet for our produce would benefit everybody."

Brynn unlocked the door. Each of the CSA members had keys to the place And now Brynn had her own, thanks to Willow. "One thing I wondered about was huge rolling bins or shelves. You know, so we could take them outside."

He looked around the space. "You might be better off with stationary shelves lining the walls. Could be done really cheaply. And then one big table here, where you could make a nice display."

"What about outside?" Willow asked.

"Same thing, but with sturdier wood that could handle the weather."

Brynn sighed. "Okay. I really wish we didn't have to do this, and that the church hadn't burned to the ground. That place oozed charm."

Flannery's face fell. He cleared his throat. "Nancy had big plans. It would have been perfect." He walked away from them and knocked on the nearest wall. "Just what I figured. These walls are solid. It's a shame this place hasn't been used much over the years."

"The new one has better heat and is shinier," Willow said. "Plus, it has bathrooms."

"We could take care of this for a relatively small fee, Ms. MacAlister. It would be my pleasure to help. We have a lull in our schedule now because we cleared everything for the church contract."

"That's too bad," Brynn said.

"How odd you signed a contract, and three days later it burned down," Willow said.

"It's not any odder than a lot of the things that happen in life. What do they say? God works in mysterious ways." He looked her straight in the eye, which was a sign he was telling the truth.

Brynn couldn't catch a vibe from him. He seemed polite, friendly, and knowledgeable. But if he was desperate for money, who knew what he—or anybody— would do?

"So, I've never hired a contractor before," Brynn said. "Would we sign a contract? Would that include some kind of insurance?"

The three of them walked back outside.

"Well, first, I'll come up with an estimate. If you agree with that, we'll get a contract together. I do have insurance, which covers incidents on the job, like if anybody gets hurt, or any property is broken or destroyed while we're working. That kind of thing."

Then burning down the church would not have helped with his money situation. In fact, it was probably just the opposite. Unless they had already started work on it. Nancy would have said so. But perhaps not.

"That sounds good," Brynn said. "Please do that, and I'll take the contract to the CSA board, and we'll see if we can get this project rolling."

Snow spit from the sky, which was moonstone gray and looked as if it would let loose with more snow any minute.

They walked back toward their cars, but Brynn stopped. "Did you have time to start anything on the church before it burned?"

Flannery looked off to the side. If Brynn remembered correctly, that was a tell, a sign he was getting ready to lie. "Why?"

"Oh, no reason," Brynn said, trying to keep her voice light. She caught a glimpse from Willow, her eyebrows knit and arms folded. "The thing is, well, Nancy and I were friends. And I'm just trying to sort through what happened the last few days of her life. I don't know why that's important to me, but it is."

"Well, if it will put your mind at ease, we didn't get started at all. We were planning to start the very next Monday." He opened the door to his van. "I had special equipment I needed to order. You'll be hearing from me soon."

He slid into his van, and the engine roared as he drove off.

"Well, that wasn't very helpful at all," Willow said.

"I'm not sure, but I'm certain he was lying."

"Why do you say that?"

"He looked off to the side when answering the question about whether they'd gotten started over there. I'm betting they were working there already."

Brynn and Willow walked to the car and got inside. Brynn turned on the engine and cranked the heat full blast.

"How would we prove that, now that everything has been burned to a crisp?"

"Not everything," Brynn said. "Nancy's stuff that was in the basement apartment was spared."

"Well, a lot of good that does us. We can't go inside her home."

"Can't we?" Brynn said. She pulled out of the parking lot and drove straight to the burned church. While driving over to the place, she phoned Nathaniel for permission to enter the house. With his approval, they exited the car.

Brynn and Willow stood overlooking the burned rubble of the church. Brynn choked back tears. "Perhaps this wasn't such a good idea."

"But we're here now," Willow said. "Might as well go in."

They stepped over charred debris and headed for the basement. Brynn's heart raced faster with each step downward. She slipped in the key and opened the door. It was like a tableau, in that it was exactly as she and Wes and Max had left it.

Emotions rushed through Brynn, but she swallowed them down. They had work to do.

"Okay, let's get what we came for and get out of here," Willow said.

"Agreed."

They both walked to her desk where there were piles of papers and files. "I'll take this pile. You take the other," Willow said.

Brynn sorted through her stack—medical bills, electricity bills, auto bills.

"Here it is, a contractor file," Willow said, and laid it down on the desk. The two of them hovered over it.

"And there are a bunch of Flannery papers clipped together."

They both turned at the sound of a cry from the far corner. Willow's eyes widened. "What was that?"

It came again, and it was moving toward them. A yellow, furry creature, looking a little sooty.

"Here, kitty," Brynn said. The cat walked right over to her. "This must be Romeo. I'd forgotten about him."

"Nancy had a cat?"

"No, the cat had her. He's a stray, but he hung out and ate here. She never knew when he'd stop by and visit. Her family probably didn't know about him either." Brynn smiled as she stroked the cat's back. Its purr had gotten loud. "Poor thing must be hungry."

"Has he been here all this time? Why didn't you see him the last time you were here?"

Brynn mulled that over. "I don't think he was here before. Someone must have let him in without realizing it."

"Which means that someone else was here."

A cold chill traveled up Brynn's spine. "It was probably the police."

"Let's hope so. Does it look like anything is missing?" Willow glanced around while Brynn continued to rub Romeo.

"Not to me." Brynn stood. The cat wrapped itself around Brynn's legs.

"Let's take the file and the cat and get out of here. This feels like we're invading Nancy's privacy, and I don't like it," Willow said, after a few beats.

"Agreed. But hopefully the file will help us figure out what happened to her. So invading her private space will be worth it." Brynn scooped up the cat, and Willow took the file, and they left Nancy's basement apartment, beneath what was the newest part of the Old Glebe Church. Built in the 1920s, the expansion housed a religious education hall. The basement was built then, as well.

Brynn thought maybe the cat wouldn't allow her to hold him, but he seemed to like it and snuggled against her coat, purring all the while.

As they walked back to Brynn's place, leaving her

car behind because of the cat, they heard a cow mooing loudly. Odd. Petunia hadn't mooed like that since Freckles came along.

As they walked up over the hillside and down the other side, all three cows were standing at the edge of the fence facing the hillside. Petunia, rocking and mooing.

Where was Freckles? "Hold him, please," she said to Willow, and handed her the cat. Brynn trotted toward her field, opened the gate, and walked inside. "Freckles?" She whistled. "Freckles." She ran inside the barn. "Freckles?"

The dog was gone. How could that be? Why would he run off? Brynn thought he loved it here.

Willow came into the barn, holding and rubbing the contented cat. "Where do you think she's run off to?"

"I have no idea. She seemed to love Petunia, the farm, well, all of it." Brynn wanted to cry. She was beginning to love that dog—and so was Petunia.

"Let's give the cat some milk and call Schuyler. She may have an idea about where she ran off to."

After the cat drank some milk, Brynn opened a can of tuna and fixed a plate for him. While he was happily eating, Willow phoned Schuyler.

"She has no idea where he could be," Willow said when she hung up. "She's shocked he would run off. She says to give it a day or two, and he may come back."

"A day or two? He could be dead by then. Or hurt."

"Okay, calm down. Animals do amazing things, come home after months of being away, survive all kinds of things," Willow said with a soothing note in her voice. "But in the meantime, Schuyler suggested we drive around a bit. Stop the car and call out for her. Not very far, just sort of around the neighborhood. And alert the community about her going missing."

"Okay." Brynn knew she was on edge. It was just so odd that Freckles had left after finding a good home. With all the strange things that had been happening, another thought came to the front of her mind. "You don't imagine someone took her, do you?"

"Why would someone do that?" Willow said, smiling, trying to reassure Brynn. "Taking a dog is tricky business and wouldn't be easy. I'm sure Freckles wouldn't go off with just anybody."

"That's probably true. It's just that so many odd things have been going on. I don't know. Maybe I'm not thinking clearly."

"Okay. Let's get started on our search for Freckles. Perhaps she's around and will be tucked into her bed in the barn by milking time."

"Maybe," Brynn said. But her gut was telling her otherwise.

Chapter Thirty-Three

Brynn and Willow drove throughout Shenandoah Springs and stopped the car in several different places to call for her. They drove past the apple orchard, and Brynn briefly thought she saw Freckles, but it was just a cement statue in a yard. She'd never seen so many statues in yards as she had in Shenandoah Springs. Mostly of deer, which often startled her as she drove around town.

The car snaked along the narrow roads as dusk was coming on. A live deer popped out from a bank. Willow gasped as she slammed on the brakes. "It's a bad time of year for them. Look how skinny she is."

"Poor thing," Brynn muttered. She was giving up hope she'd ever see Freckles again.

The frail-looking doe made her way to the other side of the road, only briefly glancing their way.

They continued driving into what remained of Shenandoah Springs. It used to be so much more, from Brynn's understanding. But there were clusters of homes around this part of the area—homes of people who were not farmers. They were all lit up with Christmas lights. One house was decorated in all blue lights. Another had a projector of sorts projecting glittery snow against the house. If Brynn wasn't so worried about Petunia and Freckles, she would enjoy the displays a lot more.

They swung around to head back out to the rural area of town. They'd approach it from a different way. They stopped at the pull over at the bridge over Buttermilk Creek and called for Freckles. The only returning sound was the rush of the creek.

"Okay," Willow said. "Let's keep going a while longer, but it's getting dark and we should probably get home soon." Her face was stiff with concern.

"You're right. Besides, I have to call around to see if anybody's seen her."

"We'll find her soon. Freckles is a such a scrappy dog. Who knows where she even came from? She was probably let out of a car, you know, dumped along the road."

The two of them got back inside Willow's truck. "That's awful. Why would someone do that?"

"It's crazy, right? But people have this idea that if they can't handle their animals or they don't want them, they can drop them off in the country and they will survive. Once, I found a box of kittens along the road. It's a definite problem here."

"Why don't they take them to the SPCA?"

"It costs money, and they ask too many questions, I guess."

Willow drove on in silence as Brynn watched out the windows, hoping for a glimpse of Freckles somewhere. Anywhere. *Oh, Freckles, where are you?*

What they did find was Frank O'Reilly walking the road. Willow stopped the car.

"Hey, Frank," she said.

"Hey, Willow." He stopped walking.

"Have you seen a stray dog, half Saint Bernard?"

His eyebrows knitted. "Ms. MacAlister's dog? No, I haven't seen her. Run off on you?"

"Yeah." Willow lifted her foot from the brake. "Thanks, Frank."

He didn't respond, just walked farther down the road.

"What's his story?" Brynn asked.

"He's just an odd duck. I think he's been in some kind of trouble before, but he's younger than me, so I don't know the scoop."

"He comes from a good family," Brynn said.

"That he does, but these days, I'm not sure that matters." Willow drove on in silence, each woman engaged in their own minds.

Later, once she was back home, after milking Petunia and calling all the people she was familiar with in town to ask about Freckles, Brynn fell into bed. Every bone in her body ached. Usually, she could deal with the weariness of taking care of the farm herself, but it was getting to her. A fleeting thought of hiring someone to help came into her brain—but she couldn't afford it yet.

As she tossed and turned, with Freckles and Petunia on her mind, she remembered the file she had downstairs—Nancy's "Flannery" file. How had Brynn forgotten about that? She'd see to that first thing in the morning. Well, after milking and feeding the cows, letting them out, and cleaning the barn.

Brynn woke up to a frosty morning. Even with the heated barn, it was still uncomfortably cold. Her cows didn't mind the cold one bit. In fact, they liked the cold more than they did the heat. Heat stressed them out.

It was so cold, she decided to wait until it warmed up later in the day to clean the barn. She'd planned to make a batch of crème fraîche later today, bottle it up, and give it to her neighbors for Christmas gifts. Her milk stores were piling up. She'd planned to brew up a batch every other day, but it was proving increasingly difficult to keep up with that schedule.

After tending the girls, she took a nice, long, hot shower and thawed out. She rubbed moisturizer on her dry, chapped hands. She examined them—they'd aged twenty years since she'd been here. She sighed. What did it matter, anyway?

Her cell phone buzzed. She saw on the screen it was Schuyler.

"Good morning, Schuyler."

"Have you found Freckles yet?" No pleasantries for Schuyler. She got right to it.

"Nothing."

"I don't understand. She loved it there. She loved Petunia. She loved you. It doesn't make any sense. Unless she was sick."

Brynn's heart squeezed. "Sick?"

"Sometimes when animals are sick, they will just go off by themselves to die."

"You said she had all of her shots, right?"

"Yep. You better believe it. But perhaps she ate something bad. Or got bit by something. If it were a different season, I'd say a snake. But it's winter."

Brynn sighed. "I hope she's okay."

"How's Petunia?"

"She's back to rocking and mooing." Brynn rubbed

more lotion on her hands. It didn't seem to make a difference at all. What a waste.

"Perhaps I can stop by today. No promises. I've got a tight schedule."

"I'd appreciate it if you can. The neighbors might complain again about my loud cow."

"Really? Tell them to—oh, wait a minute, hold on, I've got another call coming in."

Brynn waited, sitting on the edge of her bed. She ran her fingers along the edges of the quilt pattern while she waited for Schuyler to come back on the line.

"I need to go Brynn. Hope to see you later."

"Okay, good-bye." But Schuyler had already hung up.

Schuyler was an odd one, mused Brynn, but she couldn't help but like the petite, spunky redhead.

Brynn dressed and headed downstairs for breakfast—oatmeal in the microwave and a pot of coffee. She sat at the kitchen table and fingered the pages of the Flannery file she'd snatched from Nancy's apartment.

She read through the papers, which included estimates, drawings, and payment plans. Nancy had already made one payment. And Flannery Contracting had been to the place twice to prepare for the project.

Brynn's heart sped up. Flannery had lied. He said they hadn't started working there, and they had. What if the fire was caused by something they did? Or worse yet, what if he or one of his workers intentionally set that fire, hoping to collect insurance money?

Could it be? Was preparing considered working? She thought so.

One thing Brynn saw in black and white was that they *had* started working, which meant Flannery was lying.

Brynn dialed Fire Marshal Mike Rafferty.

"Rafferty, how can I help you?"

"Hi Mike, it's Brynn."

"Oh, hello, what's up?"

"I'm just checking in with you to see how the investigation is going." Brynn was sitting at the kitchen table and looking out the window at her backyard field with its three Red Devon cows—one rocking and mooing.

"We have a few leads. Things are moving kind of slow because of the holiday," he said. "Why are you asking?"

Brynn thought that should be obvious. "Have you looked into the contractor Nancy hired?"

"They check out. Flannery Contracting is legit," he said. "They're a licensed business."

"Licensed businesses have accidents all the time, I imagine," Brynn said.

"Brynn, you're misunderstanding something."

"What's that?"

"This fire was set intentionally. It wasn't an accident."

She was aware of that. "Perhaps Flannery set it." There, she said it.

There was silence on the other end of the phone. "Mike?"

He sighed. "Why would they set it? That makes little sense. She was a paying customer."

"I have her file and saw how they had already prepped to work," Brynn continued. "But I wondered the same thing. Then I thought about insurance. Would they be able to collect some kind of insurance since they had already started working there?"

"That's unlikely. But it is a possibility," he said. "I'll look into it. But please keep this to yourself. Rumors can kill businesses. I know this family, and I find fraud hard to believe. If a whiff of this suspicion gets out, it would destroy them."

"What? I wouldn't want that." She paused. "But if they set the fire that killed Nancy, they get what they deserve."

"You're a hard woman, Brynn MacAlister."

Damn straight.

She didn't know this Flannery family. She had no history here. But perhaps that meant she could see things more clearly than the others.

"Please inform me about what you find out. I'm certain whoever set that fire has been messing with me, too. I'd sleep better knowing."

"But you have Freckles, now. Right? Dogs are great for keeping strangers away."

"Freckles is missing. When I came home yesterday, she was gone. Willow and I drove around and looked for her, and I called around last night to alert people to look for her."

"She's just gone?"

"Yes. We all think that's strange. But she was a stray, remember? Perhaps she wandered off again." Brynn kept telling herself that. She didn't want to consider that someone had taken Freckles—or that someone could be keeping her or hurting her. That didn't seem logical.

"I hope you find her soon," he said.

"Me too," Brynn said before signing off.

Brynn sat at the table mulling things over. A part of her desperately hoped Flannery was innocent. It seemed as though he and his family had been through hard times. But if Flannery didn't set the fire, who did? She'd sleep better at night knowing who the culprit was. And she'd also sleep better with Freckles back.

The Old Glebe Church had been abandoned for years. Why did it matter so much to some of the locals? Why would it matter to Flannery?

Local history was interesting, and even Willow, who was a local, was having a hard time getting answers about the mysterious church. Parts of its history were shrouded. Brynn wished she had the time herself to do a little research. But she needed to get working on her next batch of *fromage blanc*. The milk wouldn't keep forever.

She planned to package it in small jars with drizzles of honey and almond slices. She'd give this to her new friends in Shenandoah Springs. She'd made it before, of course, and it always impressed—even though it was one of the simplest things she crafted. In fact, she found that as a general rule, keeping things simple worked better for her—and her customers.

She poured the thick, light yellow cream into her huge metal pan and started the burner. As the milk heated, she breathed in the sweet scent and stirred.

One reason she and Dan had selected the gentle breed of Red Devon cattle was that their butterfat content was high—just like a Jersey or a Guernsey. But the amount of milk produced was not nearly as high as the others, which were bred specifically for dairy. The Devons were perfect for her small batch, artisanal cheese.

Her phoned buzzed, and she wiped her hands on her apron, picked up her phone, and pressed the button. "Hello?"

"Hi Brynn, it's Wes."

"Wes! How nice to hear from you. How are you doing?" She picked up her ladle and stirred the thickening milk.

"I'm fine, though my parents aren't thrilled with me right now."

"Oh?"

"I flunked almost every class first semester," he said with some hesitation.

"I'm sorry to hear that," Brynn said, setting down the ladle and picking up the thermometer. She dunked it in the cream. It wasn't quite warm enough.

"So, after a lot of drama, they've finally accepted that I don't want to go to college. I wanted to go to cooking school, but now I wonder."

"About what?" Brynn said, leaning against the counter.

"I'd like to learn to make cheese."

Brynn's heart skipped a few beats. She always loved it when a person's cheesemaking passion sparked. "How fabulous!"

"I looked into schools, but then I wondered, why would I go to school when I know you? You could teach me."

"Wait. What?" Brynn hadn't ever considered teaching. She was busy actually making cheese and taking care of the cows and farm, along with the house.

"Think about it," he said. "I'd like to come and stay with you. I could help out with the cows and farm and everything, and you could teach me how to make cheese."

Brynn hesitated. "I can't pay you."

"You're misunderstanding," he replied. "I'd work for free in exchange for lessons. How does that sound?"

Having a young guy around would certainly help with some of heavy labor on the farm. And it would also help with keeping the harassers at bay. She wanted to make a go of this business on her own, but when she'd formed that goal, she hadn't imagined someone would murder her neighbor and harass her. She hated to admit it to herself. But perhaps she needed Wes's help as much as he thought he needed hers.

Chapter Thirty-Four

Brynn recalled being young and confused. She agreed to allow Wes to come and stay with her in exchange for his help. She hadn't thought about teaching cheesemaking before, but now that she had, she wondered if she might teach classes on the farm. It might be a way to earn extra money—and to spread the word about her Buttermilk Creek Cheese.

Some kids realized what they wanted to do with their lives and pursued it. Some thought they knew what they wanted to do—like she did. She thought chemistry was it. She wasn't certain what form that would take—whether she'd be working in a lab or somewhere else. But she loved the magic that happened with the mixing of chemicals. But the academic competition and stress became intense. She needed a break and talked her parents into allowing her to spend a year abroad in Great Britain. Which is when her life changed.

She'd responded to an ad for a helper at a cheese farm—a farm that bred Ayrshire cattle and made cheddar cheese. As she thought back on it now, her sidetrack became a clear pathway. Perhaps it would be the same for Wes.

The sound of a car coming up her long driveway brought her mind back to the present. She wasn't expecting anybody. She turned down the heat on her milk.

She walked to her front door and opened it. It was Schuyler. She waved and turned the engine off. A dog's ears popped up from the passenger side.

Was it? Could it be?

Brynn rushed to the car and peered inside.

"Freckles!" She opened the door to the dog, who leaped out of the vehicle and nearly knocked Brynn over. "What happened?" she turned to Schuyler after their lovefest.

"I'm not sure," she said. "But she will be fine."

There was a wariness to Schuyler's voice that Brynn hadn't heard coming from her before.

Brynn rubbed the dog's head as she whimpered, tail thumping.

"She checks out okay," Schulyer said. Her jaw set firm. "But she was found on a cliff ledge up on Harmon Mountain."

Brynn felt as if her chest might explode in rage. Air whooshed out of her lungs. "How did that happen?"

"I have no idea. I've given her some medicine, which should help with any kind of infection she may have picked up overnight."

"Thank you. Do you have time for coffee?"

"No. I wish I did." There was something else in her voice. Brynn couldn't place it. They watched the dog walk over to the gate. Brynn followed and let her in.

Brynn and Schuyler watched the happy reunion

between cow and dog. That the dog had been gone overnight didn't seem to matter one iota to either animal.

Brynn turned to look at Schuyler. "What's on your mind?"

"I don't know how to say this."

"Just spit it out." Brynn wanted to shake her. Nerves frayed, head spinning from all of this, she was losing patience.

"I'm almost one hundred percent certain Freckles was placed on the ledge. It would be too tricky a spot for her to get to on her own. Where were you yesterday?"

Brynn's heart was pounding so hard she wasn't sure she could answer. "I was with Willow. We were meeting with Flannery about the new farm shop renovation of the old community center."

Schuyler's head tilted in interest, and her eyebrows gathered. "Who knew you would be gone?"

Brynn thought a moment. "Flannery, Willow, you, and all the CSA members."

She grunted. "That narrows it down."

"What makes you think this was on purpose and not an accident? I mean, I have to tell you, I brought up that possibility to Willow yesterday, and she reminded me of how difficult it would be to steal a dog."

"Not if you have food," Schuyler said. "Freckles is very trusting. Especially for a stray. If someone offered her some good food, she might go along with them. Or at least get into the car."

"Once she was in the car, anything could've happened," Brynn concluded.

The two women stood and watched as Petunia nuzzled her friend.

"If I were you, I'd make sure someone is here next time you go offsite. Or just don't tell anybody you're leaving."

"I have another nativity rehearsal tonight. Anybody who's involved with that will know I'll be gone."

"What time is the rehearsal?"

"Seven."

Schuyler pulled out her cell phone from the pocket of her long sweater and flicked her finger along the glass. Then she slipped it back into her pocket. "I'll be here." Her jaw firmed up once again. "If I find anybody skulking around here, they'll be sorry."

Brynn shivered. She believed it.

"What do you think is going on here?" Brynn asked. "Why would someone take Freckles?"

"I've given up trying to figure out people. But in this case, I think it's clear. Someone wants you gone. The question is why."

Brynn agreed with her assessment. She needed to find out why anybody had a stake in her being here—or not. She was certain that it was the same person who set the church on fire.

Brynn nodded. "Don't worry, Schuyler. I'm not going to leave Freckles or my cows alone until we find the culprit. I'm beginning to think I should ask for police protection." She was only half joking.

But Schuyler was dead serious. "As if that would do you any good," Schuyler said as she walked away toward her van.

Between her obvious negative feelings for her brother, Fire Marshal Mike, and the last statement that Schuyler made before leaving, Brynn figured she

didn't like authority figures. Well, Brynn had been
there. But now, most of the time, she found comfort
in them. Still, she couldn't quite shake the strong
feeling she'd gotten from Schuyler's statement. She
wasn't a small talker. It seemed to Brynn as if each
word mattered when it came out of her mouth, and
she couldn't help but like Schuyler, whose kindness
toward animals spoke volumes.

Brynn took a seat in her living room with her
laptop, looking up occasionally to watch Freckles and
Petunia in the backyard.

Brynn researched the "Old Glebe B&B," which was
the name of her house when the previous owners had
tried to make a go of it. It went belly-up fairly quickly.
Which, on the face of things, seemed to be very
strange, because this was a perfect spot for a rural
B&B. Perfect for people who wanted to get away from
the crowd and noise of the city. And the house, even
though it was old, was simple yet beautiful, had been
updated, and was large enough for a small B&B.

She read over the reviews, which were all good. The
food was rated high. The relaxing atmosphere was
noted, as well as the layout and beauty of the land. So,
if it wasn't bad reviews that put them out of business,
what was it?

Brynn bought the place through a Realtor and had
never met the previous owners. She wished she had
asked more probing questions when she purchased
the place, but she was so excited to buy it that she
wasn't thinking.

Oh, it could be any number of things. Maybe a mis-
management of money. Maybe the owner had simply
gotten bored. Or overwhelmed. She'd been warned
about being a new business owner, how important it

was to play it conservative and ease into the business, earning a profit before expanding. But expansion thrilled Brynn as she thought about the many ways she wanted to use her cream. Yogurt. Buttermilk. Ice cream. All made with raw milk. Flavored by the grass, herbs, and flowers from the Shenandoah Valley.

She wondered if the B&B owners were still around here. She keyed in their names "Tony and Dori Sollitto."

A string of results came up on Brynn's screen. She scrolled through them and saw that the Sollittos now owned a booming B&B in Rocky Mount, North Carolina. They'd been running it for fifteen years. It had been named the best in the area on several occasions. It had gotten awards for its farm-fresh food.

Brynn sat back into her couch, glancing up at the cows and Freckles. The Sollittos evidently knew what they were doing. Could it be that someone scared them off like someone was trying to scare Brynn off? A pang of self-doubt struck her. How silly. Why would someone want to run her off? Why would they want to run the Sollittos off? It was the stuff of cheap mystery novels and B movies. *Get a grip, Brynn.*

Still, it was odd the house hadn't been lived in since then. And there'd been a long stretch of time before the B&B that it had sat empty. At one point, the church and its clergy owned it and lived here. But the church community had folded. It had gone bankrupt, and nobody cared to save it. Which was odd in a community like this—where almost everybody's social life revolved around their church, if not their farm, food, or craft.

She dialed Willow.

"Hey there," Willow answered. "What's up?"

"Freckles is back."

She gasped. "Fantastic!"

"Schuyler brought her back. Found her over a cliff."

Willow paused. "Is she going to be okay?"

"Yes, she's perfectly fine. Maybe she just got confused and lost. But with all the other stuff that's been happening, Schuyler agrees that someone wants me to leave the area. I think it's the same person who set the church on fire and killed Nancy. Tell me I'm crazy."

There was dead silence on the other end of the phone.

"And I've looked into the previous owners of this place, who turned it into a B&B, and I can't quite understand why they left. They're doing well running a different B&B in North Carolina. They must have business acumen."

Willow sighed. "That was before my time," she said. "I was a little girl then. But if you want, I can ask my parents about it." She paused again before asking, "Do you think they were run off?"

"I have an inkling. It would help if I knew why, then maybe we can figure out who's doing this. Has someone been doing this for years and getting away with it? And why? Now, they've actually killed someone," Brynn's voice caught in her throat. Poor Nancy.

"Why don't you call them?"

"How awkward would that be?"

"Very. But they could at least give you some answers," Willow said. "I'm still picking you and Buttercup up this evening, right?"

"Yes, and Schuyler will stay here. She doesn't think it's a good idea to leave the animals alone until we get this thing under control."

"Wow. Schuyler must be seriously concerned."

"We both are. I mean, there's the almost fire in my yard, and the dead stuffed crow on my door, and now probably someone took my dog. That's the last straw."

"Have you talked with the sheriff about Freckles?"

"No. Should I?"

"Probably. Just to let him know. Ask if he could swing by your place every so often."

Willow wasn't as down on the local law as Schuyler. Duly noted.

"Okay. I'll give him a call."

But first, she needed to strain her cheese, still on the stove, and then call the Sollittos.

Chapter Thirty-Five

Brynn tried to call the Sollittos but the phone number listed on their website wasn't working. Perhaps a snowstorm or something was messing up the lines. She focused back on her laptop and clicked on the B&B's website. She sent them an e-mail through the "Get More Information" form.

There. She hoped she'd hear back soon.

In the meantime, she made her way to the kitchen to check out her cheesecloth bags of draining cheese, which looked good. Her kitchen was warm and smelled milky. She sat down at her table to take it all in. Here she was, in Shenandoah Springs, the place she wanted to be, with three lovely cows and a dog, several burgeoning friendships, and maybe a cat, if she could keep track of him. Even with all the weird stuff going on, she felt like this was where she belonged. She refused to be run off.

A ring came from her doorbell. She got up to answer it and saw it was the UPS deliveryman, with several boxes for her.

"Thank you," she said, as she scooted her boxes inside her entryway. She tore open the first one. It was the custom labels she'd ordered. Gold oblong circles, rimmed in black, with the words BUTTERMILK CREEK FARM CHEESE. And there was space allowed for writing in the specific type of cheese.

Another box contained small, round cheese forms. She mostly used plant-based cheese forms because they were the most environmentally friendly, but with some cheeses they didn't work. The other package contained the special rennet, or binding agent, she used. She refused to use animal rennet, which came from the lining of calves' stomachs. She used only vegetarian rennet. The kind she preferred was the same kind used by the farm in England she'd first trained at; it was made of thistle. And it worked beautifully.

One lone package sat ready to be opened. She picked it up and saw it was addressed to Nancy. Brynn's heart sank. The delivery guy must not have known what to do with it, so he just left it with Brynn. What should she do with it? Should she open it? Or send it to Nancy's son? Yes, that's exactly what she'd do.

Still, a feeling of dread came over her. Nancy, of course, had had no idea she'd perish from smoke inhalation, and took care of her business as usual. That's what we all do. If only she'd known, would Nancy have done anything differently? Was Nancy being harassed, like Brynn was? If so, why hadn't she mentioned it?

Though Nancy had mentioned how odd she thought some of the locals were, she'd offered no specifics. So who knew what she actually meant?

Brynn placed Nancy's package under her Christmas tree. It was the only one there, since she'd already sent her packages off to her family, and she'd yet to receive hers.

She glanced at the clock and realized it was time to

get Buttercup ready for her trip to the local church for another rehearsal of the living nativity scene.

She slipped her coat on and made her way to the barn for Buttercup's harness.

As she prepared Buttercup, she heard the crunch of gravel beneath tires. Freckles barked a bit then settled down. It was Schuyler, who'd come to babysit her crew.

Soon after, Willow came along with her truck and trailer for the cow. Willow and Schuyler stood there chatting as Brynn led Buttercup through the gate and toward the trailer.

They all exchanged "hellos" and "how dos." Schuyler helped Willow open the back door to the trailer and pull down the loading platform. Buttercup was in a compliant mood and walked right up the platform and took her spot.

"What a good girl!" Brynn said, and stroked her. She turned to Schuyler. "Thank you so much for coming to watch my crew. I'll feel so much better knowing you're here."

"It's a sin and a shame you even have to worry about it," Willow said.

Schuyler nodded. "It's my pleasure. I love Freckles and don't want to see anything else happen. She may have just run off. Maybe we're making too much of it."

"I don't know," Willow said. "So many other things have happened."

The three women stood in the cold, their breath puffing out in smoke circles.

"Must be something to do with the house," Willow said.

"And the church," Schuyler said. "I was thinking

the same thing. Like maybe there's buried treasure there."

Willow laughed.

"I'm serious," Schuyler said. "Someone is after something on your property. Or wants to keep it a secret."

"More likely there're bodies buried there," Willow said.

Brynn gasped.

"I mean, metaphorically. Like someone is keeping a secret, and it's related to this property."

"Oh," Brynn said. "Thank goodness. I'm not sure I could live somewhere where there're bodies. You know, like on top of a cemetery or something."

Buttercup mooed impatiently.

"Why? It's not dead people you have to worry about, you know. It's the living ones," Schuyler said somberly.

"Agreed," Willow said. "Now let's get going. We have a nativity scene rehearsal to attend." She rolled her eyes. "I'm sure the animals appreciate all the rehearsals."

"Is she always so serious?" Brynn asked Willow after the two of them had gotten in the truck.

"You're unaware of what happened to her," Willow said. "Someone attacked her when she was in high school. It changed her a lot. She'd always loved animals, but they became her life. At one point, she didn't want anything to do with people. She's gotten over that, mostly. She's a black belt in karate and let's just say that mentally and spiritually, you couldn't find a stronger person."

Brynn played over in her mind how Schuyler had hummed as she was treating Petunia, and the calm that came over the cow, and Brynn. "It's kind of odd. She seems at one with the universe on the one hand, yet kind of suspicious and mad at it."

"Exactly," Willow said. They drove by Hoff's Bakery. Brynn felt a pang of regret.

"The oddest thing happened," Brynn found herself saying, and then spilled her guts to Willow about the episode at the bakery.

Willow pulled the truck into the church parking lot as Brynn told the story. Her mouth dropped. "Pete is a great guy. That doesn't sound like him at all. I don't get it."

"I don't either. I guess I've got no choice but to accept what he said."

The two exited the cab of the truck and walked to the back to let out Buttercup. Just then, Tom Andrews pulled up.

Willow whispered, "Wouldn't you know it? Creepy old Tom Andrews."

Brynn remembered what she'd seen in the parking lot of the bakery when he was arguing with his wife. She also remembered how he felt about the church being renovated. "Creepy" certainly seemed like the right way to describe Tom.

Chapter Thirty-Six

The Baby Jesus was going to have his way. It was the pacifier or screaming.

"I'm sorry," his flustered mother said to Ed. "He's teething." The woman playing Mary was dressed in the appropriate robes, but as she stepped forward, Brynn spotted a pair of jeans underneath.

"There were no pacifiers in Biblical times," Ed snapped.

The baby's father stepped forward. "Listen, Ed, maybe you should find another baby."

"At this late juncture? I don't think so."

Brynn stood near the snack table. The women of the church had provided cupcakes, chips, and a veggie tray. "I don't think you should worry about the pacifier."

Ed turned to look at Brynn. Her face heated.

"I mean, a lot of this isn't historically accurate," she stammered. "We need to keep the baby quiet."

His head tilted. "What do you mean? Historically inaccurate?"

She looked down at her feet, then at the table. "There were no cupcakes or chips and salsa, either." She grinned, and the group laughed, including Ed.

"Okay," he said. "Let's not worry about the pacifier." He laughed, again.

After the rehearsal, which went better than last time, Brynn and Willow chatted in the truck on the way home. Brynn admitted she still didn't like Reverend Ed Higard. And Willow filled Brynn in on Tom Andrews. He had taught history at the high school since the dawn of time, apparently, and was known for being harsh and unforgiving, and for being caught several times with his eyes glancing places they shouldn't be. And everybody adored his sweet wife, Elsie, and felt for her at having to deal with him.

"You know, I overheard them arguing the morning I stopped by the bakery," Brynn said. "I didn't listen to what they were saying."

"Sounds like him," Willow said, as she pulled into Brynn's driveway.

The two of them settled Buttercup into the barn, Freckles welcoming them with a wagging tail. Then they went into the house to see Schuyler and were surprised to see that Schuyler had a friend with her— Tillie.

"Look who I found skulking around the barn," Schuyler said, with a grin.

"I hope you don't mind," Tillie said. "But we milked Petunia for you."

"Mind?" Brynn said. "Heck no. Thank you both. How are you doing, Tillie?"

She shrugged and reached for her backpack. "I'm okay, I guess. Today was the last day of school for a week. That makes me happy. I hate school."

"You do?" Brynn sat down beside her on the couch.

"You're a bright girl. I know you like to read. Why do you hate school?"

"School isn't about learning. It's about passing the tests," she said. "I learn more at home on my own."

"Well, I need to go," Schuyler said and stood. "Do you need a ride?"

"Sure," Tillie said.

"Thanks so much for watching my crew tonight," Brynn said as she walked them to the door.

"I can't believe someone took Freckles!" Tillie said in an impassioned voice. "If I find out who did it . . ."

"We'd all like to find out who did it, believe me," Willow said.

"No, wait," Schuyler said. "We don't know that's what happened. Let's not jump to any conclusions."

"Schuyler is the voice of reason?" Willow said and laughed.

Schuyler grinned. "We're all in trouble then."

After the two of them left, Brynn turned to Willow. "How about a snack before you leave? I've just finished a fresh batch of *fromage blanc*."

"Mmmm. I can only stay for a little while, but that sounds fabulous."

The two of them sat in the living room with the lit Christmas tree, each with a glass of wine and a plate of the soft white cheese with crackers. Brynn had drizzled honey and sprinkled almond slices on the cheese.

"This is so good! It really makes a difference when it's fresh," Willow said.

"And raw. You can almost feel those microbes popping in your mouth!" Brynn held up her glass of wine and then drank from it. She was content sitting here with Willow, listening to Dolly Parton's

Christmas tunes, and gazing at the tree. But she had to admit, she'd be happier if they could find out who had been vandalizing her, and who had set fire to the church. No matter how content she was, there was a layer of fear and worry, just beneath her skin.

"Have you found out anything more about the history of this place?" Brynn asked.

Willow set her glass down on the coffee table and scooped more honeyed cheese onto a cracker. "Well, as far as I can tell, there doesn't seem to be any truth to the rumors that the church was used as a part of the Underground Railroad. It's just hearsay, I think. None of the national registries have any churches in this area listed at all."

"And what would that have to do with someone burning the church? If it was important to the Underground Railroad, it would have been protected. I mean, there'd be a plaque or a marker or something, right?"

"Not necessarily. There's a lot of history around here that doesn't have markers. I think that's one of the things the historical society is working on. But there's a lot of red tape." She drank from her wineglass.

"I imagine. I called the Sollitto family, but the phone number I had was disconnected. I tried to e-mail them, but I haven't heard back."

"You mean the family that ran the B&B here? Why?"

"I know it sounds crazy, but I wondered if someone ran them off. You know, like someone is trying to get rid of me. Perhaps they succeeded with the Sollittos." Brynn half hoped Willow would tell her she was crazy, that it made no sense, that in this day and age, people didn't run people out of communities. But she didn't.

"You know, I love this place," Willow said. "I grew up here. Left. Came back. For the most part, the people here are good, salt of the earth sorts. But there is still an element here who maintains a kind of fear of out-siders. It runs stronger in the mountains, I suppose. It pains me to admit that you might be right."

"When Dan and I responded to the ad in the mag-azine, it seemed like it was too good to be true, sort of like an organic, artisanal dream come true. This com-munity resurging with healthy farming techniques and food. What could someone have against that?"

"I'm not sure." Willow popped another cheesy cracker in her mouth. "But I'll keep my ears to the ground."

Even though she was still frightened and angry, Brynn had at least one friend on her side.

Chapter Thirty-Seven

A light dusting of snow sparkled at daybreak as Brynn made her way to the barn. The sky was pink and blue, hues of color that made her feel as if she were walking in a snow globe. Snowflakes floated around her. According to the weather on the news, the snow would be gone by noon as the morning warmed.

Freckles greeted her with a wagging tail and a happy hello dance. Brynn crouched down and hugged the dog.

"Are you hungry?"

Brynn fed Freckles and moved on to Petunia, who was ready for milking. She'd been hand-milking her as much as possible, while the cow was still grieving, but now that Freckles was back, and Petunia seemed fine—and it was bitingly cold—she figured the milking machine was the way to go.

She placed the milking cups onto Petunia and turned on the machine. Within minutes her first filtered bucket was full, and she replaced it. As her cow was being milked, she poured the thick creamy milk into a huge jar and placed it in her freezer. She kept the morning milk there for three hours before testing it to make sure it was clean and free of coliform and aerobic plate counts, which basically means: coliform shows if there are any coliform colonies in the milk. It's all about cleanliness of the milk.

Brynn wanted a proper milking parlor and hoped she could build one soon. But for now her barn with a built-in freezer would have to do—along with the makeshift lab in her make.

After milking and placing her jars in the freezer, Brynn walked back to the house, took a shower, and ate breakfast.

She opened her laptop as she spooned corn flakes into her mouth. Breakfast sure was better when Wes and Max had been around, she mused. She glanced over her long string of e-mails, including one from the Sollittos.

She clicked on it and read:

Dear Ms. MacAlister,

Thanks so much for reaching out to us. We often think of the place and wonder how things are going.

You mentioned that you had questions. We're happy to answer any you may have, although we've not lived there for quite some time. But we'll do our best. Please call our new phone number at the bottom of the e-mail.

We look forward to chatting with you.

Best,
John and Dori Sollitto

Brynn glanced at the clock. It was 9:30 AM, probably too early to phone them. She'd give it another hour or so. In the meantime, she had promised herself to sort through some of the many bills she'd been getting, and pay what she could online. If there was one thing she hated, it was sitting in front of a computer for a long period. She couldn't figure out how people did that every day. She needed to be moving around, outside, making cheese.

She'd just finished paying her last bill when Becky called. "How's it going?"

Brynn ignored the impulse to spill her guts to her sister. She had an inkling that Becky would come running if she understood half the stuff that had been going on. But she also knew Becky couldn't afford to do that. "Fine. How's it going with you?"

"It's getting crazy with the whole Santa thing. Trying to keep things hidden from Lily is getting harder and harder."

"Still, it must be fun." Brynn shut the lid of her laptop and stood up to heat water for tea.

"It is fun at times, but stressful. It would be easier if I had a helper. Are you sure you can't come and spend Christmas here?"

Brynn mulled it over. The idea appealed to her—being with her family would help her frayed nerves. At the same time, she couldn't leave the farm. "I can't do it. I wish I could. Now, this time next year, maybe. I've got a young guy coming to stay here to help out."

"Really? That's fabulous. It will free you up a bit. But did you say he's going to live with you?"

Brynn fetched a cup from the cupboard and sat it on the counter. "Yes. This place is big enough for an army. He's going to stay here in the guest cottage and work for free. At least, until I can start paying him. He wants to learn how to make cheese."

"Well, I have to admit. That sounds perfect."

Brynn placed a bag of Earl Grey in her cup. "It does. I think it's going to work out."

"Have things calmed down for you?"

Brynn didn't want to lie to her sister, but at the same time, what good was it going to do to worry her? "Well, everything is fine for now." That statement was true enough.

Becky said nothing.

"I've tried to contact the previous owners of this place to see if they can shed light on the locals." Brynn hadn't planned to tell her that, but Becky was using the old silence techniques on her. Brynn had to fill the silent spaces with conversation. Her sister understood that.

"That's a good idea. Sounds like other stuff must be going on?"

"Well, nothing for you to worry about. I've got it under control. No worries." The teakettle whistled, and Brynn's heart jumped. She took it off the burner and poured the hot water into her cup.

"Right," Becky said. "You're hiding something from me."

Brynn bobbed her tea bag in and out of the water, the scent of Earl Grey filling her nose. "It's just that it's clear someone doesn't want me living here. I'm trying to figure out why."

"That sounds like something out of a book or movie. Are you sure it's not your imagination running overtime?"

"Yes. Willow and Schuyler, two local women I've met, also suspect something strange is going on. Once we figure it out, I'll fill you in."

"Are you in danger?" Becky's voice raised a decibel or two. "I mean, someone *killed* Nancy! Are you next?"

Brynn's heart thudded against her rib cage. Was she? Absolutely. "I . . . ah . . . ah . . . I don't think so."

"What's that supposed to mean?" Exasperation poured through the phone.

"It means I've been the butt of some serious pranks, but I doubt anybody is trying to kill me. Just warn me off." At least that was her hope, but her guts told her otherwise.

"You don't think? Honestly, Brynn! What happened to Nancy? Was someone trying to warn her off, too?"

Brynn recalled their last conversation. Nancy had said some locals had behaved strangely to her. Is that what she meant? Brynn had assumed she meant contractors. But maybe Becky was right. Maybe Nancy had also been warned away—but she didn't heed the warning.

Chapter Thirty-Eight

"Hello, Mrs. Sollitto? This is Brynn MacAlister. I e-mailed you."

"Yes, please call me Dori. You mentioned you were having problems at the house. I remember we had some problems with a little water getting in the cellar from time to time, but other than that it was a sturdy place. What can I help you with?"

Brynn had poured herself a second cup of Earl Grey, and breathed in the scent. "Earl Grey, hot." Captain Picard from *Star Trek: The Next Generation*'s favorite command played in her mind. "Oh no, nothing like that. The Realtor had warned me about the cellar. We've fixed the issue. I love the house."

"Well then, what is it?" Dori's voice held the edge of impatience.

"It's that, well, were you aware the Old Glebe Church burned down?"

She gasped. "No!"

"Unfortunately, the woman who was living there died."

"How awful." She paused. "I'm not sure what this

has to do with us. We haven't lived there in fifteen years or so."

"It may not have a thing to do with you. It's just that I've been harassed, sort of warned away. And I wondered if you had the same kind of troubles." She drank from her tea.

"We had troubles all right, but not that kind of trouble. There were a lot of drugs in the area then, and our son got involved with the wrong crowd. What was his name? Flannery. Jacob Flannery."

"He must be Zach Flannery's son. I heard about that."

"No, his father wasn't Zach. I remember, because a few years later I read that Jacob's dad died, and his Uncle Zach took him in. I can't remember the father's name. Sam? Stan? I can't remember. . . . Jacob is a few years older than Zach's son."

"All I know is that the family went broke trying to help their son," Brynn said. "I just have to say, I'm shocked about the drugs in the area."

"I was too. But they've cleaned it up a bit since we were there. I read they've gotten a grant to support local small farmers, and it's really helped to revive the community. It was dismal then. We were a part of a group trying to help the community by investing in our individual businesses, but the tourism thing just didn't work out. People wanted to get away from it all, but mostly they wanted to get away from it all while still having modern conveniences like Wi-Fi and McDonald's. No thanks."

Willow had mentioned that time to Brynn. The community had theorized pushing tourism was the way to revive the dying community. But it didn't work.

"So we sold the place to a Realtor and cut our losses."

"That's too bad. This place would have been a great B&B."

"So we thought."

After the two of them finished their conversation, Brynn mulled over what she had learned. So there were three Flannery men. Zach, the father, who happened to be a volunteer firefighter and a contractor; his son, Sam Flannery, who nearly broke the family with his addiction; and Jacob Flannery, who, according to Dori, was a nephew of Zach's—and a troubled person. Brynn had wanted to get familiar with and be a part of this community, but this sure wasn't what she was counting on. Drugs? She'd steered clear of them her whole life. She certainly didn't want them or the drug culture anywhere around her. She hoped that Dori was right, and that the community had cleaned up its act.

Brynn recalled the things that had happened and the people she'd met. She'd only been here three months and couldn't discern if her judgments were accurate. Most of the locals had been kind to her, especially after the attempted fire in her front yard. She still had a fridge full of food the locals had brought to her in the wake of it.

But there were some prickly sorts—like Tom Andrews and Reverend Ed Higard, both older men stayed in their ways, she supposed. And then there was that odd business with Hoff's Bakery. He had been so enthusiastic about her cheese, and then within one day changed his mind, citing that it was a low time in his business, yet the place was brimming with people. She figured she should let that go, but it stuck in her craw.

The thought of business reminded her that she had calls to make, to follow up on the cheese samples she had delivered to local restaurants, coffee shops, and bakeries. She flipped open her laptop, opened her spreadsheet, and made the first call.

After her calls had been made, Brynn had a list of potential customers to call on after Christmas. Nine local businesses of out the fifteen she'd visited. Hoff's Bakery be damned.

She gazed out of her kitchen window and to her backyard field, where the grass was more brown than green this time of the year. But her girls were eating what there was available. They would only be grass fed. She planned on meticulous care of her north field over the summer, so she could use it for next winter's feeding. She had purchased some hay to get the cows through the winter, which she fed to them intermittently.

The sky was as blue as she'd ever seen it, and huge white clouds blew across the skyline. In the distance were the Blue Ridge Mountains, more visible to her in the winter because the trees were bare. This patch of land was hers, and she sighed with contentment. She wasn't going anywhere.

But she needed to feel safer, needed to find out what was going on. Who killed Nancy? Who tried to set the fire in her front yard, who nailed the stuffed bird to her door, and who took Freckles? She wouldn't feel safe until the authorities found answers. But with Christmas in two days' time, she doubted anybody would investigate much more. People were settling in for their family holidays. Most people. Not her. No. Not this year.

Brynn rehashed her conversation with Dori Sollitto.

She hadn't known how many Flannery men there were. Just how thick in this valley were they? She made a mental note to ask Willow or Schuyler about them.

Zach Flannery had his hands full if the boys he was taking care of had gotten involved in drugs. Poor man. He seemed so nice. Worn and tired. But nice. It was hard to imagine that he'd harm anybody. But people were complex and Brynn didn't really know the man.

Just then, her phone buzzed.

"Hi Brynn, it's Willow."

"What's going on?"

"I found out an interesting thing about the church. There are unmarked graves over there."

Brynn's stomach flipped. "What do you mean?"

"They're graves for people who didn't have the money for headstones, or people who died before they were baptized. You know, one of the churches in town has a section for babies who died before they were baptized. Isn't that awful?"

"Yes, but I don't think unmarked graves could be a reason to burn the church and kill Nancy, could it?"

"I have no idea. I mean I can't even imagine *any* good reason to do something like that. Can you?"

Brynn thought a moment. "Whoever did it was twisted. Logic can't apply at all. Perhaps I should take a walk around the cemetery this evening to see if there's anything strange going on over there."

"Oh no, I wouldn't go alone. You should never walk in a cemetery after six, especially not alone."

Was she serious? "What?"

Willow laughed and snorted. "No, but seriously, I'll come with you. You don't know what's going on over there. Don't go alone. After I finish canning this last batch of pickled beets, I'll be over."

Even dressed in her coat, hat, gloves, and boots, Brynn was freezing cold. She was no fan of the cold. But it didn't seem to bother Willow at all. Her cheeks had taken on a pink cast that spread across her nose. They walked across Brynn's backyard field and up the hill, across the field to the church. Between the church and the woods was a little cemetery. The stones were so old that much of the wording had rubbed off.

Brynn shone her flashlight around the headstones but saw nothing out of order.

"Look over here," Willow said. "Along the edge of the woods." She kicked away some leaves and pointed to slight depressions in the ground. There was even a brick lodged in the ground.

Brynn felt a little foolish being here. What were they even looking for? "It's sad. Unmarked graves. Although once you're gone, what do you care?"

"True," Willow said, and shined her flashlight farther along the edge of the woods. "Wait. That's odd."

She moved forward toward the woods. "There are some weird pieces of wood there."

Brynn followed her. Brynn swept away a pile of frosty leaves, to find a long piece of wood set in the ground. "What the—"

Brynn bent over and peered as closely as she could. "It's a box in the ground."

Willow turned, eyes wide. "You mean like a coffin?"

"It's not big enough for that. Open it."

"No way." She stood and brushed off her hands.

"Okay, I will," Brynn said.

"Are you sure you want to do that?"

"Absolutely. I mean, what could be inside? Aren't you curious?"

"A bit. More scared, I think." Willow paused. "Okay. You open it."

Brynn squeezed her fingers between the cold ground and the wood and pulled. She blinked. And blinked again. Cash was stacked in neat little piles. She slammed the lid closed.

"What is it?" Willow said.

"Money," Brynn said as her heart thudded against her chest. Adrenaline coursed through her, and she stood. "We need to get out of here."

Willow's eyes widened. "And leave the money? Why?"

Brynn nodded furiously. "Yes. Let's go." She swooped leaves over the box and grabbed Willow by the elbow.

As they walked away, Brynn swore she could feel someone's eyes on her, but she couldn't see anybody. The farther they walked away from the woods and the church, and the closer they got to her house, the better she felt.

"Maybe Nancy had a stash. Maybe that was her savings. We should inform her family," Willow said as they walked.

Brynn hadn't imagined that. She hadn't imagined anything, except that if there was money hidden in a box in the ground, it couldn't mean anything good. "That doesn't sound like her. She was sophisticated with her money. She had stocks and bonds and played the stock market. Does that sound like someone who'd keep a stash in the cemetery?"

"Should we tell the police?" Willow asked.

Brynn nodded, even as exhaustion rolled through

her. She felt each muscle unwinding. She was home now, and she was warm. And tired. "Yes, let's call the sheriff first thing tomorrow. What's your schedule look like?"

"I've only got a bit more canning to do, and it can wait. I can come by around ten. Is that okay?"

"Sounds good. I'll call the sheriff and ask him to come by then."

"Sounds like a plan." Willow started to leave but turned back as she opened the door. "Don't forget to lock the door."

"Ha! Don't you worry about that!"

Chapter Thirty-Nine

Brynn's thoughts raced as she tried to sleep. What had they stumbled on? The only reason to hide cash like that had to be criminal. Just exactly what was going on in the graveyard at the church? One thing was for certain—they'd journeyed there trying to figure out what could have led to all the trouble, and they had found it. But what was the money for? Was someone being paid off to keep quiet about something? Was the money real or was it fake? Had someone placed the money there for safekeeping? She'd never seen so much money in her life.

Brynn moved about her chores slowly the next morning. She'd barely slept. Everything took more effort. Her gaze kept traveling toward the half-burned church and the graveyard. The sheriff and Willow would be here soon. She brewed a new pot of coffee and thawed some cherry-cheese Danish she'd made a few weeks ago from a batch of her own farm-fresh cream cheese. It wasn't as fancy as it sounded. It was the simplest Danish recipe she'd ever run across, but when she placed them on a mint-green plate, they looked festive with their glistening red cherries in the center of the square.

She knew the secret ingredient that made these Danish so good—the fresh cream cheese. It made a difference most people couldn't quite identify. They just discerned it was better.

After Brynn, the sheriff, and Willow had situated themselves with coffee and Danish at her table, the sheriff took a bite.

"Dang, this is good," he said.

"Thank you."

"Now that you've plied me with the best cherry-cheese Danish I've ever eaten and some good coffee, you better tell me what's going on."

Sheriff Edge continued to enjoy his Danish—and even helped himself to another—as Brynn and Willow told him what they'd found last night.

"We'll walk over there in a minute," he said between bites. "But what I want to know is what prompted you to go over there in the first place."

Willow and Brynn glanced at one another, and Brynn cleared her throat. "I'm aware it must sound silly to you, but we've been wondering if someone is trying to run me off."

"And?" He slurped his coffee, with a look of satisfaction that reminded Brynn of a cat after drinking the best cream it had ever had.

"It seems like there must be something about this property. This and the old church. As if someone is hiding something." Willow sat forward in her chair. "I'd been reading about unmarked graves over there, and we wanted to take a look around."

"I see." His bushy blond eyebrows shot up. "And you found more than you bargained for."

"Indeed." Brynn tried to assess his reaction, but he was a pro and wasn't giving away much—except the fact that he was enjoying his midmorning snack.

"So what do you think?" Willow asked, impatient.

"First, you two need to leave the investigation to the law. I've told you that before, Brynn. I'm wondering if you don't understand plain English."

Brynn's face heated, and her mouth dried. She reached for her coffee, noting her trembling hand.

"Okay," Willow said. "Let's just say we weren't investigating anything. But we were just walking along and spotted it. Does that make you feel better? Geez. Who cares why we found it. We found it. What is it? I mean, it was a lot of money."

He sat back in reaction to Willow and tilted his head as he seemed to consider what she said. "Okay. But I want you two to stop this nonsense immediately. Do you hear?"

Tension hung in the air.

Brynn felt a nervous bubble forming in her chest and working its way up through her mouth. But she bit her lip. Easy for him to say. He wasn't being harassed. His neighbor hadn't died. He'd not found a bird nailed to his door. And his dog wasn't stolen.

She nodded in agreement.

Willow crossed her arms.

"The problem is, you two could get hurt. We wouldn't want that to happen. Would we?"

Brynn wanted to break the tension. "More Danish?"

"No, thank you. I've had enough. I say we need to take a walk over there, and you show me this stash of money." He stood, the leather from his belt and holster squeaking as he did so.

There was something about his tone that made

Brynn realize he didn't quite believe them. Well, time would tell.

She and Willow slipped on their coats. As they walked across her field and over the hill toward the Old Glebe Church, Brynn was a mix of emotions. Embarrassed. Ashamed. Frightened. And annoyed.

But more than anything, she was curious to see the sheriff's reaction to all that money. That would show him. Wouldn't it? There was something going on here. Something that shouldn't be ignored.

They walked along the edge between the woods and the cemetery and easily spotted the area where they'd found the half-buried box. Willow crouched down and opened it. Her mouth dropped. The sheriff leaned in and smirked.

"What is it?" Brynn asked.

"I don't know what you ladies thought you saw last night. But all I see is two books."

"Books?" Brynn couldn't believe she heard him right. What had happened to the money? Where did the books come from?

Willow reached in and picked the books up for Brynn to see. "Book of Mercy" and "The Flame," both by Leonard Cohen. She leveled a look at Brynn but didn't say a word. They both recognized that Leonard Cohen was one of Nancy's favorites as she frequently quoted him—and that she'd turned Tillie onto him, much to her parents' dismay, according to Tillie.

"Leonard Cohen," the sheriff said. "Never heard of the guy."

Which didn't surprise Brynn at all.

"Believe us. There was a stack of cash in that box," Willow said as they walked back toward Brynn's place.

"If cash was in there, it's gone now. I only saw a

couple of books in there. Which is odd enough in any case. But there's nothing illegal about any of it. If there *was* money in there, it'd be suspicious but not illegal. So, I'm not sure what you want me to do."

Brynn couldn't pay attention to their conversation. She wanted him to leave. He'd asked about Tillie a few days ago, as if she were a suspect. But he wasn't familiar with her literary tastes. If he were, chances are his mind would change quickly about the importance of the box in the ground. But Brynn couldn't imagine that Tillie had anything at all to do with the fire or any of it. It was way too easy to blame problems on troubled youth. And frankly, Tillie's troubles had more to do with her family. Not her.

But, even as she recognized Tillie was innocent, she also had a feeling of dread. The girl might be innocent, but she grasped more than she was telling. Maybe she was in some kind of trouble. Remembering back to when she was sixteen, Brynn thought she knew everything, but was deep down easily frightened.

Her heart went out to Tillie. How could she help? Would Tillie even be honest with her? Would she allow her to help?

She and Willow waved the sheriff off before Willow turned around, eyes wide, and placed her hands on Brynn's shoulders. "Let's call Tillie."

Willow walked toward the house.

Brynn followed. "We need to talk before we call her." She reached for the door and opened it.

"What's there to talk about? She must know something. Hell, maybe she even has all that money."

"I hadn't thought of that possibility. But I agree that she knows more than she's telling. But I think she's probably scared." Brynn remembered Tillie's odd behavior the day of Nancy's death and the few days after. She had shrugged it off as Tillie just being an awkward teen. But evidently, there was more to it than that.

Willow slipped out of her coat. "We need to call her immediately."

"I agree."

She followed Willow into the kitchen. Willow reached for her handbag and pulled out her cell. She looked up the O'Reillys' number and then placed the phone to her ear.

Brynn turned and filled the teakettle with water. She was so cold, she didn't know if she'd ever warm up. It was only December, and the cold was already getting to her.

As she flipped on the burner, she overheard Willow. "Okay, thanks," she said, then set the phone on the table.

"She's not home," Willow said. "She's on winter break and her mom doesn't know where she is, but she figures she'll be home before dark."

"Why did you call her family and not her?"

"I don't have her number."

Brynn had it, she was certain. But she still felt they needed to ease into their questioning of Tillie because she was a minor. So she decided not to mention it.

"I can't imagine being sixteen and running into a box filled with money. If she has the money, she and her friends are probably having a great time," Willow said, and sat down at the table.

"I can't imagine her being so flippant," Brynn said, reaching for cups. "What kind of tea would you like?"

"Do you have mint?"

Brynn nodded. "Tillie seems very much together for a sixteen-year-old." The teakettle whistled, and she poured the water into the cups. The steam comforted Brynn. Warmth. That's what she needed.

"I agree. But let's not forget she is only sixteen, and no matter how together she is, she's not an adult, with an adult view of the world. She's still immature to an extent."

Brynn brought the steaming cups to the table and set them down. "She was with me when I found out that Nancy died, and she took it in a very strange way. I wasn't aware she was friends with Nancy then. But looking back, I see that she was hurt and upset, but didn't want me to see it."

"She probably didn't know how you would take her reading Nancy's books. Her family is so odd that way. Like something out of the eighteenth century. Blows my mind the way they are. But still, she's their child. They're Mennonite, and they're just trying their best, I suppose."

"I thought Mennonites dressed differently, like the Amish."

"Some of them do. Those are the old-order Mennonites. Most of them are just like the O'Reillys."

The two of them sat for a few moments in silence. The idea of Tillie being involved in anything untoward was like a weight on Brynn's heart. The girl had the voice of an angel, and Brynn's cows adored her. Brynn figured she was good people.

"I think I have her number," Brynn finally admitted.

Willow perked up.

Brynn went off to find her bag and pulled out her cell phone. Her sister had called twice. Odd.

She scrolled through her contacts. Yes, there was

Tillie. She slid her fingers around on the screen and placed the phone to her ear.

"Hello?" Tillie's voice came on the line.

"Hi, Tillie, it's Brynn MacAlister. How are you?"

"Fine. What's up?"

"Can you stop by the house? I've got something to run by you." She wasn't exactly lying, was she?

"Sure. I'm with friends up at Massanutten. I won't be getting back until late. Can I stop by in the morning?"

Massanutten was the closest ski resort. Perhaps she had taken the money and taken her friends on an impromptu ski trip, Brynn thought.

"Certainly. See you then."

Brynn turned to find Willow standing behind her. "And?"

"She's going to stop by in the morning. She's up at Massanutten with friends."

Willow leveled a look at Brynn. "Massanutten? That place is expensive."

"My thoughts exactly."

Chapter Forty

Brynn's morning had put her in a foul mood—especially when she reflected on the sheriff. He was so condescending. Was it because she and Willow were women? Or was he like that with everybody? Or was he maybe just annoyed because they had called him to check out a box in the woods with nothing but Leonard Cohen books in it? Heck, she was annoyed by that. Why didn't she just take the money last night? She hadn't imagined it would be gone by morning.

And she didn't think that Tillie knew anything at all about that box.

The phone interrupted her thoughts. It was Wes.

"Hi Brynn, it's Wes. How are you?"

She considered telling him how she really was, what was really going on, but reconsidered. There had to be a perfectly logical explanation—other than that Tillie was involved with the fires and all the other stuff. "I'm good."

"I had been planning on moving in on the second of January. But now I'm thinking about the twenty-sixth of December."

Brynn's heart skipped a beat. That was in a few

days. "You can move in any time. What made you change your mind?"

He laughed. "Cheap airfares. Mom and Dad are still put out with me, so I figured I'd try to save them some money."

"Score points with your parents, hey?"

"Yes, but I wanted to run it by you first."

"Thanks for that." Brynn sat down on her sofa and gazed at the Christmas tree that Wes and Max had helped her decorate. It seemed almost a lifetime ago, but it was only a week ago.

"Is everything okay?" he asked.

"Just the same as usual," she said. "Weird stuff is still going on. It's like someone wants me gone. But I can't figure out why."

"Chances are Gram knew why," he said. "I don't understand why she never mentioned it to anyone."

"If she knew something, she may not have taken it seriously."

"It seems outlandish. The idea of someone wanting her to leave so badly that they set the church on fire and killed her." He breathed into the phone. "Knowing her, if she was threatened, she'd have laughed it off."

Which prompted a smile from Brynn. "True." But what if she hadn't had time? What if she'd stumbled on someone or something and didn't even have the chance to mention it to anybody? Brynn shivered.

"How's Petunia?"

"She's fine. She's adopted a dog."

"Come again?"

Brynn recapped what had happened with Freckles. As they were talking, the dog was barking. Brynn slipped on her coat and walked outside to see the commotion. A car was parked in her driveway.

"I need to go. I have a visitor."

"See you on the twenty-sixth."

"Okay."

A woman exited the car. Freckles stood at the fence at barked. "It's okay, girl," Brynn said, turning to the woman. She looked vaguely familiar. "Hi. Can I help you?"

She moved forward. "Hi Brynn, I'm Sheila Hoffman. Remember me?" She extended her hand, and Brynn shook it.

Hoffman? As in Hoff's Bakery? Yes. This woman was Hoff's wife, the woman she'd seen at the bakery. "I remember you."

The woman stood awkwardly with her hands in the pockets of her coat.

"Would you like to come in?"

"Thank you, but no. I need to tell you something."

Brynn's stomach churned. What was going on here?

"Okay."

"My husband and I love your cheese. We really wanted to work with you."

Brynn's stomach waved. She had been trying not to recall that day. Instead, she was focusing on the more positive responses she'd gotten for the samples of cheese she'd sent to other local businesses.

"But I understood that your husband changed his mind."

The woman nodded. "He did. I didn't. He never consulted with me. The bakery is half mine." Her jaw tensed.

"Oh," Brynn said. So articulate. She didn't want to get involved with what now appeared to be marriage problems.

"But here's the thing. He's easily influenced. Too nice of a guy."

"What do you mean? I don't understand."

"It's the good old boy network. I despise it." She lifted her chin up. "Someone's gotta tell you, and it may as well be me. Tom Andrews came into the store and asked us not to carry your product."

Brynn felt the air whoosh out of her body. "What? Why?"

"I wish I knew why. All I can imagine is that you're a woman in business, and some guys hate to see a woman succeed." Her jaw tightened.

Brynn couldn't believe she was hearing these words. What was this, the eighteenth century? "That's kind of ridiculous."

"Don't I know it? I've been reflecting. I've been angry my whole life about some things. I'm tired of being mad. I decided to start sticking up for myself and other women whenever I see or hear something like this."

Brynn thought she saw a tremble in Sheila's cheek. Was she cold? Or nervous? This wasn't easy for her.

"Tom Andrews assumes he's the cock of the walk. We need people like you if we are going to save our community. He needs to get over himself. So does my husband. Andrews loaned us some money awhile back and figures he can tell us how to run our business. That's going to stop."

Brynn crossed her arms to warm herself. She didn't really want to know any of this, but was glad she did. It all made sense. Tom Andrews and his wife were in the parking lot the day she stopped by the bakery. Shards of anger ripped through her. How dare he?

"Thank you so much for telling me," Brynn said.

"Are you sure you won't come in for a cup of tea or coffee?"

She cracked a smile. "Thank you, but I best be heading home. But I'll take a rain check."

She started to open her car door, then turned to Brynn. "I hope you'll give us another call. You have my word we won't run you away this time."

"Good to know." Brynn watched as the woman drove off.

An immense welling of respect bloomed in Brynn's chest. Women like Sheila were the backbone of this country. They may not be out marching for women's rights because they couldn't step away from their shops, bakeries, and jobs, but they were digging deep, taking breaths, and changing things in their families and communities. It was one thing to write books and give speeches, but it was quite another to make changes in your own community and family.

At the same time she was feeling respect and gratitude for Sheila, Brynn's stomach was roiling. Tom Andrews had a lot to answer for. She was aware he wasn't happy about Nancy's plans and didn't like what she was doing with the church, even though he'd lied and said he did. Now she realized he'd been going behind her back and telling people not to do business with her. Could he be the person vandalizing her? She considered calling the sheriff. But then thought again. Tom obviously judged her a silly woman. Well, she'd show Tom Andrews. And she'd do it to his face.

Brynn knocked on Tom Andrews's door. And she knocked again. A car pulled into the driveway, and she realized he and his wife were just getting home.

As she turned to watch them climb from the car, the view astounded her. The Andrews place sat up on a knoll, and it looked out over a small valley which included Buttermilk Creek Farm. Tom Andrews had a perfect view of her house and of the burnt church. She shivered.

"Well, hello there," Mrs. Andrews said as she walked up the sidewalk. "I don't suppose we've met."

Brynn extended her hand. "Brynn MacAlister. I've been meaning to thank you for those pies."

She smiled and shook Brynn's hand. "I'm Elsie Andrews. Come in."

Tom sidled up to them. "What's up, Brynn?"

Brynn crossed her arms. "You tell me." Her eyes met his.

"Oh dear," Elsie said. "Please come in and have tea. I've got more pie inside. Christmas pie. It's an old Amish recipe. Parts of my family were Amish, you see." The words "Christmas pie" rang in Brynn's mind. She had to admit it sounded interesting, probably downright delicious.

"Okay, I'll come in. But don't you go anywhere." She nodded toward Tom. She didn't want to be rude to Elsie, who was kind enough to offer her pie. "I want to talk to you."

"Well, it's always better to talk over food," Elsie said, and opened the door.

Brynn and Tom followed her inside, through the simple "four rooms upstairs and four rooms down" farmhouse. It was the same with most of the old places along Buttermilk Creek. But this place was a bit bigger than most and simply decorated, almost austere. Most of the furniture was Amish style, and the paintings were simple and primitive. Brynn immediately felt safe and peaceful. How odd.

The scent of cinnamon plucked at her nose.

They all three sat at a hand-hewn block table that almost ran the length of the small dining room. A painting of *The Last Supper* was the only one in the room.

Tom helped Elsie bring in plates and the white, fluffy pie. As Elsie cut the pie, Brynn wished she could cut the tension in this room as easily as she did the pie. The Andrews both understood why she was here. What could they possibly say to make it any better?

"Tom," Elsie said, after scooping the pie onto plates and sliding Brynn's plate toward her. "You owe Brynn an apology."

Tom grimaced. He picked up his fork and looked at Brynn. "I am sorry. It's just that it's hard on an old coot like me to see change coming so fast."

"Fast?" Elsie said. "I'd say it's about time."

He took a bite of his pie and chewed thoughtfully before answering. "I like my life. I've worked hard for it. And I like my view. The next thing you know, there will be skyscrapers and car fumes. I don't like it."

"What makes you think that by my having a good business those things will happen?" Brynn said.

"You've already made changes."

"I've tried to keep the integrity of the design and the land as much as possible. I want you to understand I've got no plans for skyscrapers in my fields." Brynn couldn't imagine he actually thought that, but she understood what he meant.

"It starts small." A winsome look came over his face. "I love this place. I know I come across as an old fart. But I hate to see growth that's not properly planned or well thought out." He took another bite of his pie, which smelled good and tantalized Brynn. But her stomach was churning. Brynn wanted to change the subject. "You do have a gorgeous view. I had no idea. You can see right down on my place. No wonder you're concerned."

"We wish we could see more," Elsie said. "Not very helpful with the fire."

"Yes, but you sent pie." Brynn smiled. "You're forgiven." She wedged her fork into the pie and brought the bite to her mouth. Her taste buds popped and soared. What a delicious, sweet, coconut flavor and creamy texture. And the crust was perfect.

"I've talked to Hoffman," Tom said. "I can be a hothead. I told him it's his business, and he should do what he wants." He paused. "He says your cheese is good. Better than good."

Brynn chastised herself for not bringing cheese. "You can come over anytime and try some cheese. Both of you."

"Thank you," he said.

"I have a very old recipe for cheese pie," Elsie said, as if she'd just remembered it.

"Good to know," Brynn said. As she sat there with the older couple, she tried to see why Willow had thought he was creepy. Complicated old curmudgeon, yes. Creepy, no. Also, hadn't Tillie mentioned something about him? She hated his history class.

But from where Brynn sat, it looked like he was trying to navigate change as best he could. At least he was trying.

"How has the investigation been going? Do you know?" Elsie asked.

"No, I'm sorry. I haven't a clue."

"We saw the sheriff over at your place earlier, and

we saw you taking a bit of a walk with him, so we wondered."

"Unfortunately, that led to nothing," Brynn said. Which wasn't quite true. It led to knowing Tillie was in trouble, anyway she studied it.

"We do get to see a lot from our front porch sometimes," Elsie said and grinned. "Mostly young people. Lover's trysts. Sometimes drinking beer and smoking cigarettes. That kind of thing. It all goes on in that old parking lot of the church."

"Or in the cemetery," Tom said.

Brynn stopped herself from saying anything about the box they'd found. It was best she kept it to herself, at least until she talked with Tillie. "I like walking over there," she said. "The tombstones are so interesting."

"There are unmarked graves over there, too," Elsie said.

"So they say," Brynn said, and shoved another bite into her mouth.

"Who do you think set the fire?" Elsie asked.

Brynn's stomach soured, even as her mouth enjoyed the texture of the creamy pie and flakey crust. "I truly have no idea."

But she felt an impulse to find out. Now, she could scratch Tom Andrews off her unofficial list of suspects. He was difficult, but he wasn't a murderer.

Chapter Forty-One

Brynn carried a White Christmas pie to her car and set it on the seat before waving at Elsie and Tom. He seemed much more pleasant when his wife was near. She made a mental note to remember that. Maybe she wouldn't have to deal with him much when Elsie wasn't around.

Tomorrow evening was the CSA Christmas party, and she looked forward to it. She understood Elsie would be there, so Tom would be on his best behavior. People were odd.

She pulled into her driveway and mentally checked over the things she wanted to get done with the rest of her afternoon.

She needed to clean her make. She planned on crafting a batch of cheese tomorrow, and she liked to clean the cheesemaking area at least twice, sometimes three times, before she actually made the cheese. Cleanliness was of the utmost importance in cheesemaking.

She also needed to check on the crème fraîche she would hand out as gifts tomorrow night. A calmness settled on her. Hoffman loved her cheese, and with Tom out of the way, they might move on with whatever his ideas were. She certainly had a head full of them.

But as she moved about her make, scrubbing, the quietness dinged at her. She was all alone and was trying not to feel vulnerable. She'd just crossed Tom off her list of suspects. Who else could it be?

She wiped off her counter and leaned against it, drawing in the scent of the clean make. She may have to wait to theorize until she spoke with Tillie.

None of it made sense to her. If Nancy had stumbled on something—like scads of money in the woods—she'd have told Brynn. And probably the police and the whole community.

Brynn walked out toward the barn area. Freckles was suddenly at her side, her tail wagging, and grinning up at Brynn. She reached down and rubbed her head.

Petunia wasn't far behind the dog, though she was busy chomping on a clump of grass. The two of them made quite a pair. And Brynn was happy that Freckles was more than a pretty face—she was quite a good guard dog, informing Brynn any time someone was around.

Brynn took her leave of the animals and dashed inside her house to the warmth. She was beginning to despise the cold. She'd heard someone say these were some of the coldest temperatures on record for the Shenandoah Valley. It didn't bother her girls at all. And she'd have been more concerned about Freckles, but she had that heated barn to retreat to—and she was one smart dog.

Brynn poured herself a glass of wine, turned on

some holiday music in the living room, and decorated her jars of crème fraîche, tying festive red and green ribbons around them and attaching handmade tags. On the one side, MERRY CHRISTMAS FROM BRYNN AT BUTTERMILK CREEK FARM, and on the other side, a list of ingredients: FRESH CREAM, LOCAL HONEY, AND SLICES OF ALMONDS. That list was important because food allergies seemed to be getting more and more prevalent. She didn't want anybody to get sick from her food.

She sipped her wine—red and spicy—and examined her jars. She ambled back into the kitchen and placed them on the counter, just as her cell phone rang. She heard it ringing but wasn't certain where it was. Once she found it, she picked up.

"Hey, Brynn, it's Schuyler. I'm just calling to check on everything."

"Thanks. We're all okay. I just came in from the make and the field. We're all well and accounted for."

"Good to know." She paused. "Have you learned anything yet from my brother or the sheriff?"

"Not really. Did Willow tell you about the money?"

"Yes, she did. I'm betting Tillie will clear things up, whether or not she wants to."

"What do you mean?"

"I mean, I'm certain she doesn't want to get in trouble. Her parents are very strict with her."

"When it comes to trouble, if she knows anything at all about what's been going on, her parents are the least of her worries," Brynn said. "But she seems so together. So smart. I can't imagine she'd be involved in anything."

"Kids make mistakes. Even smart ones," Schuyler said. "Even lovable ones with beautiful singing voices."

Brynn sat with the truth of that. Had she been blinded by Tillie's sweetness? Was it all a put-on?

"I spoke with the Sollittos. Talk about kids and mistakes."

"Who?"

"The folks who used to own this place. They ran it as a B&B, but it didn't last long because their son got involved with drugs."

"Funny, I don't remember that name at all."

"You were probably too young. It was about fifteen years ago."

Schuyler laughed. "I was in vet school then."

So she was a vet. Brynn had wondered if she was a vet, or just a person gifted with animals.

"Or should I say I was flunking out of vet school then?"

Oh, questioned answered.

"Flunking?"

Schuyler laughed. "Yeah, it wasn't for me. I was smart, graduated from high school top of my class, but, I couldn't wrap my mind around vet school for a lot of reasons." She paused. "I wasn't here then. But I bet Willow would remember."

"Well," Brynn said. "They said their son had gotten involved with a Flannery. But not Flannery's son. His nephew."

"Nephew? That'd be Jacob. Yeah, he's still around. I didn't realize about that trouble. I assumed it was only his son. But now that I think about it, it makes sense. That family has had it rough. Good people, but they can't seem to catch a break."

That sentence could describe a lot of families. Especially these days.

Brynn often wondered what the ingredient was for someone to become an addict. She'd seen many families torn apart because of it. She'd read about kids ripping off their parents, and vice versa, and worse. The impulse for the drug was so deep and fierce that it was the only thing that mattered. She set aside her wine—she was feeling buzzy, as she was a lightweight with alcohol. Which probably was a good thing.

Freckles's barking interrupted her thoughts, and she arose from the couch to see what all the fuss was about. When she opened her door, Reverend Higard was just about ready to knock.

"Sorry to disturb," he said.

"No problem. Please come in," Brynn said. "I've just been getting ready for the CSA's party tomorrow night."

He followed her into the living room. "I'd thought I'd peek in on you and Petunia. It seems she's quieted down."

"Please have a seat," Brynn said, so pleased with herself that even after two glasses of wine, she remembered her manners.

He sat down on the overstuffed chair.

"Yes, Petunia has a friend. A dog friend. They adore one another. The relationship is so cute."

His face soured. "Animals don't really have relationships. But in any case, I'm glad to learn she's better. Will you be using her for the living nativity scene or the one you've been bringing to rehearsal?"

This was the second time Brynn noted his attitude toward animals. She's didn't like it, and she wasn't sure she liked him—even if he was a minister.

"We'll stick with Buttercup," Brynn said. "So, what can I help you with?"

"Nothing really. I came to check in on you. As I said, I'm aware things haven't been easy, with all the stuff going on. The church. The fire. I just wanted to see that you're okay." He lifted his double chin in her direction.

"That's so kind of you. But things seem to have calmed down. Perhaps because Christmas is in a few days, and people are busy. Or maybe whoever was trying to scare me has given up."

His weight shifted in the chair, which squeaked beneath him. He folded his hands, almost as if in prayer. "Is that what you suspect has been going on?"

"That's what it looks like. Someone killed Nancy and nearly destroyed the church because they didn't like her plans."

His eyebrows gathered. "I know nobody who didn't deem her plans fabulous. Your theory makes no sense."

"Tom Andrews didn't like her plans. The historical society wasn't thrilled with them. Also, I understood she had a hard time finding a local contractor. She had to go with one from Lexington."

He sat back. "Lexington? That's not far away. Perhaps the others were just busy. Perhaps you're reading too much into all of that?"

Was he right? Had her imagination been working overtime? Was there another reason for the fire?

"I was contemplating trying to get the funds together to rebuild the church."

Brynn's heart skipped a beat. "Do you mean to keep a farm shop going?"

"No. I'd like to see it become a church again."

That was the oddest thing she'd heard in a while. "Why? There are plenty of churches around."

He shrugged. "It's just an idea I had. I've no idea if it's even possible. They have changed the zoning, I imagine. I've just always had this idea of a non-denominational country church. It's always appealed."

Brynn had to admit that it sounded good—it sounded better than a half-burned church sitting on the other side of her field. "I'd rather see a farm store, of course, something truer to Nancy's vision. But I wouldn't fight having a church there, if that's what you're asking."

He waved his hand around. "It's probably not possible, but I'll research it. It's good to know you'd not be against it. I had you pegged as a nonbeliever."

Brynn couldn't believe what he'd just said. Her mouth dried as she searched for the right words. She'd kept her mouth shut about his ideas and opinions on animals. But this was too much. Her spiritual life was none of his business. "Come again?"

"I said I had you pegged as a nonbeliever."

Brynn's face heated. "That's none of your concern, surely."

"Oh, I'm sorry. I didn't mean to offend. You're friendly with Willow and Schuyler. They've both been vocal about their views."

Both women were the kindest people she'd met since she'd been here. Okay, so Schuyler was prickly, but deep down her heart was gold.

"I'm not aware of their views," Brynn said. "They've just been extremely welcoming."

The two of them sat in silence for a few beats. Brynn wanted him to leave but couldn't figure out how to get rid of him.

"Well, that's nice, dear," he said, and stood.

Thank God he's leaving.

"I best be on my way. So glad to see things are looking up for you."

Chapter Forty-Two

When Brynn opened the door to let out Ed, it startled her to find Mike Rafferty there, looking official and grim. He and Ed exchanged how-dos.

"Do you mind if I come in?" He said it as a question, but Brynn felt she had no choice.

"Sure." She opened the door farther and led him to the living room. "Can I get you a drink? Water? Coffee?"

He sat down on the couch. "Nah."

Brynn sat next to him. "What's up?"

"I have a few more questions for you, if you don't mind."

"About the fire? I think I've told you everything I know."

"It's been my experience that sometimes people know more than they think. So humor me, will you?" He smiled a soft smile as if trying to reassure her. There, in that smile, she caught the resemblance between him and Schuyler.

"Of course." He didn't grasp how she'd wracked her brain about that night repeatedly, and was just about certain there was nothing left to explore. But she'd help if she could.

"You ran over to the fire when it was going on and you spoke to a few of the officers over there, correct?"

Brynn nodded.

"That's a nice tree, by the way."

"Thank you."

"But, as I was saying, you were there. Did you overhear the order to send Nancy to Augusta?"

Brynn pondered it and remembered nothing like that. She recalled the officer telling her people could survive fires. She remembered getting sick and waking up in the back of the ambulance. "No, I remember nothing like that. I'm sorry. I do recall the paramedic telling me that Nancy was sent to Augusta Medical, and that she thought it was odd."

His head tilted. "So people on site realized she was being sent there?"

She nodded. "Do you mind if I ask what the big deal is about it? I mean, I've heard over and over again that she should've been sent to the University of Virginia Medical Center. So why wasn't she?"

He lifted his chin. "Good question. I'm trying to get to the bottom of it. But I need to corroborate several stories before I can even raise the issue." He leveled a look of gravity. "If a firefighter sent Nancy to Augusta, he or she had bad intent. It's not protocol. You could ask anybody in this area where burn victims should go, and they'll tell you. So why was she sent to Augusta?"

"Could it have been a rookie mistake? Like a younger person who was nervous and stressed and made the wrong decision?"

He nodded, then sighed. "I figure. Trouble is, people are covering for this person."

The burn of anger rose in Brynn's throat. She was so

tired, and her "polite" filters had just about vanished. "Well, how about that? He makes a decision that played into someone's death, and people are covering for him. This place just keeps getting better."

"He's young and belongs to a huge, respected family." Rafferty sat back on the couch. "But here's something nobody knows. I figure he also set the fire."

Brynn sat in silence with her mind reeling. A young man who was a firefighter had made the call to send Nancy to Augusta—and was the same person who probably set the fire. She didn't know what to say. It was too much to ponder. It was horrifying.

"So, you see, I've got to be very careful here. I don't want to destroy a family." His voice cracked. His square jaw tensed.

"Sometimes families are stronger than you assume. I mean, what can you do, Mike? You can't leave this alone. Nancy Scors matters, too."

His eyes met Brynn's. "Oh, I'll do the right thing. But I just need to be certain."

She respected him for his methodical nature and work ethic. He'd been working on this case diligently day and night. They sat in silence for a few beats.

"You know, the young men who were staying here talked with me about pyromania. Is this a case of that? Because it sounds like it. A firefighter who set the fire? I gotta say, that worries me."

"Absolutely. It's interesting. We've seen it before, of course. More than we want. Believe me when I tell you most firefighters are salt of the earth and want to serve their communities. But once in a while, we see this. It's troubling."

"Don't fire recruits get psych evaluations?"

"Yes, they do, which makes it all the more troubling."

"So, the person who set the fire and decided to send Nancy to Augusta is probably the person who's been harassing me, as well."

"I didn't say that."

"You didn't have to. It makes sense. Even though I don't understand why I'm on his list. But it worries me, of course. I can't wait until Wes gets here."

"Wes?" His head skewed, and he crossed his arms.

"Nancy's grandson is moving in to help me out around here, and I'm going to teach him how to make cheese."

He looked relieved. Odd.

"Sounds like a good arrangement."

"I hope so," Brynn said, yawning. She couldn't help it. She knew it was rude. But it was late.

"Thanks so much for answering my questions again. I better get going." He stood, and she followed him to the door. He turned and looked at her. "Good night, Brynn."

There was something unsettling about the way he looked at her. She couldn't quite figure out if he liked her or not. After he left, Brynn thought to call Schuyler and Willow, but time was pressing on her. She needed to get the cows inside and milk Petunia.

The next day flew by, yet Brynn didn't hear from Tillie. She didn't want to alarm Tillie's parents by calling too frequently, so she didn't call her back. And she was certain she'd run into her sooner rather than later. But if she didn't hear from Tillie by to-morrow, she'd go over to the house with a cheese ball in hand.

As she readied for the CSA party, the doorbell rang. She threw her sweater on and ran to get the door.

"The fur babysitter is here," Schuyler said as Brynn opened the door.

"And thank goodness for that." Brynn smiled at her. "I wonder how much longer we'll have to worry about this."

"Until we find the culprit." Schuyler walked past Brynn, into the kitchen. "You look great. Love the sweater."

"Thanks. My parents brought it over from Ireland. Dad's from Ireland."

"Really? Didn't know that." She plopped herself down on a chair. "Has Tillie checked in?"

"Not yet. If I don't hear from her by tomorrow, I'll make a visit."

"They're nice people, but strict. But it's odd that Tillie's not called you back."

Just then, the door to Brynn's house flew open. It was Willow, with her long brown hair flying behind her, not dressed for a party.

Schuyler stood. "What's going on?"

"It's Tillie! She's missing! Her parents just called the sheriff, and Mike and the other guys are all out looking for her!" Her face was a red mess, half-covered in makeup.

Brynn's pulse quickened. "What's going on here? Where could she be?"

"She's involved in whatever scheme brought the church down," Schuyler said. "She's gotten herself in way over her head."

"What can we do?"

"We can join the search crew!" Willow said.

Tears pricked at Brynn's eyes. Poor Tillie.

"Wait. Are you sure she's not just a runaway? The kid was pretty unhappy," Schuyler said, walking back toward the door, reaching for her coat.

"She didn't come home last night. Her parents have called her. Texted her. No reply. The kids she went skiing with are all home, and none of them know anything about her whereabouts."

Schuyler snorted. "I need a list of their names. I don't believe that for a second. Nobody knows anything?"

"The sheriff has already been to talk to every one of them. They all have the same story. She left when they all left. She had driven her own car and didn't ride with any of them."

Brynn's mind raced. If she were Tillie, where would she hide? The valley was full of dips and sways, cracks and crevices in the ground, caves, and caverns. There were places cell phones could not get signals. It was a matter of course. "Tillie's smart. If she was in trouble, where would she go for safety?"

"If she was smart, she'd have gone to the sheriff," Willow said, crossing her arms.

"Maybe this isn't Tillie running off to avoid trouble. Someone might have her. Then it won't matter how smart she is." Schuyler reached for her bag. "I'm off to join the search crews. How about you two?"

It tore at Brynn—she didn't want to leave her place or the animals, especially now. But she wanted to help the search crews.

"I promised Mike I'd stay here," Willow said, tuning to Brynn. "I hope you don't mind. But she likes you. She might reach out to you. So we both need to stay here."

Which made Brynn let loose with her tears. She nodded.

"I'll keep in touch," Schuyler said, and flew out the door.

Brynn and Willow ambled back into the kitchen. Brynn reached for a tissue, then washed her hands. "I'll make a pot of coffee," she said, sniffing.

Willow nodded. "We'll need it."

As Brynn was making the coffee, Willow paced around the kitchen. It was a big farmhouse kitchen, but her pacing was setting Brynn's nerves on edge. As the coffee scent filled the room, Brynn took a deep breath to calm her nerves. "Please sit down, Willow. You're driving me mad."

"Oh, I'm sorry," she said and sat down, rubbing her hands on her jeans. "I can't stop imagining all the possibilities. Everything that could happen to her. For all her smarts, she's really quite naïve. Like most sixteen-year-olds—but especially from this valley. They are all a little overprotected."

"That's kind of nice." Brynn reached into the cupboard and pulled a couple of mugs down. Large mugs. They would need as much caffeine as possible. "Teenagers these days just grow up too fast."

"Sometimes they have to," Willow said.

Brynn poured the steaming brew into the mugs and brought them to the table. The two of them sat in the quiet, like vigils in wait, with one lone light shining on the table. They didn't know what they were waiting for, but they were both hoping for the best.

"You make the best coffee," Willow said. "And your hot cocoa is superb."

"Ah, thanks," Brynn said. But conversation felt hollow. Where was Tillie?

"We should watch some TV or something to get our minds off of Tillie," Willow said, her eyebrows raising.

"Good idea. We need something light and funny."

The two of them plopped onto the couch and found reruns of *Friends*. But both of them kept their cell phones in their hands.

At 2:31 AM, Brynn's phone rang. She was half asleep, but pressed the button to answer. "Yes?"

"Brynn, it's Schuyler. We haven't found her, but we found out she purchased a plane ticket to Boston. Do you know anybody in Boston?"

"Boston?"

Willow sat up as if she'd just awakened.

"Yes, she's probably there already. We found out she left in the middle of the ski party."

Brynn's brain clicked into gear. Who did she know in Boston? Nobody. But she did know someone in Massachusetts. "Wes."

Chapter Forty-Three

Within about an hour, the police confirmed that Tillie was safe with the Scors family in Massachusetts. Brynn stayed awake for another few hours so that she could milk Petunia, feed Freckles, then let the girls out. Once she was done, she climbed into bed.

She felt wired and exhausted all at once. Part of it was the caffeine and staying awake all night, the other part was trying to wrap her mind around Tillie running off to Wes and his family. When had they even gotten that close?

Brynn needed answers. She'd get them—or die trying.

She awakened at noon, realizing she'd left out her gifts for the CSA members. The crème fraîche wouldn't be good now. She'd have to pitch them all. She should make them something, though, perhaps cheese balls. They were safer than crème fraîche.

After pitching the cream and washing out the jars, Brynn sat down at the table with a bowl of cereal and a pot of coffee. Tomorrow was the day before Christmas Eve. She'd be spending her late afternoon and evening at the church with Buttercup. She needed to make certain someone would be here with her crew. A shot of resentment tore through her. Why did she have to have babysitters for her animals? What was the problem here?

She picked up her phone, hesitated, then dialed Wes.

"Yes, Brynn," he said. It always briefly shook her when someone recognized it was her calling. She'd never get used to the whole caller ID thing.

"You know why I'm calling."

"Yes. I suppose I do. Believe me. I was as surprised about this as you probably are."

"So, you two didn't plan this?"

"No. My parents weren't happy about it, either, but then . . ." He breathed into the phone.

"Then what?" Brynn's heart raced.

"She's afraid. She won't tell anybody why."

"Good God. She doesn't seem like she'd scare easily."

"No." He paused. "This is serious. Which is why my parents were chill about it."

"Is she there? Can I talk with her?"

"Nah. She's at the police station. My parents are with her."

"Why not you, Wes?"

"My parents took over. That's all. I'm sure Tillie would have preferred me."

Brynn poured herself another cup of coffee, figuring she shouldn't have another one, but feeling like she needed it.

"We've been texting since I left."

Brynn's heart ached. Didn't Tillie have any other trustworthy friends close by? Why did she have to run all the way to Wes? Was she that frightened? "Is she okay?"

"She's upset. Nervous. Not herself. So I don't consider 'okay' as a good term for what she is."

"Did she say why?"

"No. But I surmise it has something to do with my grandmother's death. She witnessed something, or someone."

Brynn figured that, but she kept her opinion to herself. "What makes you think that?"

He let out a long sigh. "They were close. Tillie was around her place a lot. I imagine she was there more than we knew. But she said something that made me sense she knew Gram well. Like how her favorite tea is Earl Grey. Was, I mean. Like how she loved Keats. She's also talked about her cinnamon scones. So I know Gram fed her at least once."

Brynn considered Tillie's reaction in the barn when she told her about Nancy. It made sense now. "But she didn't tell you what she witnessed?"

"No. I asked. And she smiled that crooked little smile of hers and shrugged. She said something about not wanting to involve me." He snorted. "But I am involved now, aren't I? The police have been here. My parents are with her at the station. And, hey, I'm moving into the guest cottage in a few days."

Brynn wanted him there as soon as possible. A couple of days seemed very far off right now.

"My parents are not thrilled with me right now."

Brynn smiled. "But they love you. It's going to be okay. When you're a famous chef, they'll be very proud."

After they hung up from their conversation, Brynn's mind focused on Tillie and what she could possibly have witnessed that made her run off like that. Perhaps she'd glimpsed who started the fire. But she certainly would have stepped forward by now. Or, maybe she observed who took the money out of the box in the woods. She's so bright. She may have spotted all of it and then put together the pieces, leading her to run off.

But what other pieces could there be? What could she have seen?

Brynn stood from the table and walked toward the door. She slipped on her coat and boots, wrapped a scarf around her neck, opened the door, and headed for the half-burned church.

The cold was numbing. Her breath puffed out in billowy streams. She walked up the hill and across the field. A car sat in what used to be the parking lot of the church. But she observed nobody sitting inside. Nor did she glimpse anybody lurking around. Perhaps it was a hiker who'd left his car there. Or someone visiting the cemetery.

She focused on finding the box, not that she would even peer inside if she found it. She wanted to take in the view from where it was while it was still light outside. She made her way through the little cemetery, leaves swooshing beneath her feet.

She found the place. She turned to make out what would have been in Tillie's view if she'd seen something from here. Her breath caught as she scanned the scene. Of course, the church was in view, and beyond that was Buttermilk Creek Farm. Perched on the next hill was Tom Andrews's house. She looked in the other direction, through the bare trees and observed nothing but woods. She turned around and viewed nothing but woods. But hadn't someone said the Old Glebe Woods was the boundary between the

church and the apple orchard? Brynn hadn't planned
on exploring the woods amid such a cold winter. But
she was here now, and so she marched forward.

Brynn walked through the wooded area and noted
how rocky it was. She'd had no idea. The land dipped
down into a small valley where Buttermilk Creek trick-
led, and then back up again. Once she climbed to the
other side, she turned around and peered back at the
church. Nothing unusual. But even from this spot,
Tillie would have had a good view of someone lurking
around the church. Brynn shivered.

She walked up the slope to the top, sweating by this
point, and took in the view of the apple orchard. A
man walked along the tree line. Nothing unusual
about that, Brynn surmised, even though it was cold.
She squinted her eyes to see who it was, but he was too
far away and heading into the distance. Neatly aligned
trees spread out for what seemed like miles. Smoke
puffed from the chimney of what must be Tillie's
family's home. Only the roof was visible from here.

She turned around to head back through the woods
to her house.

As she made her way down, back toward the frozen
creek, she glimpsed an oddly shaped rock ledge poking
out from the side of the hill. She traipsed along until
she could get a better view.

Beneath the ledge was a deep, dark space. As she
investigated closer, she observed that it was a small
cave. Interesting. She had no idea there was a cave
here. She stopped walking and had a conversation
with herself. Curiosity plucked at her. Common sense
did, too. She wanted to explore the little cave, but she
figured bears and other animals might hibernate

inside. Besides, she hadn't brought a flashlight. Cave exploration could wait for another day.

But as she got even closer, she spotted a piece of red fabric along the edge of the space. Well, it wouldn't harm anything just to check out what the fabric was. She'd not go any farther inside. No—not without a flashlight.

She crouched next to the cave, almost losing her balance on the rocky earth. A blanket was spread out, along with two ratty pillows and a wooden box brimming with supplies, like water, canned food, kindling, and a lantern. Her breath caught. Was someone living here? Was she intruding on someone's property or home?

Brynn climbed away from the cave and started back toward the church, taking the path Tillie must have taken to visit Nancy. She continued searching around for anything suspicious. Nothing. Which led Brynn to conclude that what Tillie had witnessed was not there—that it had come and gone. It was not what Brynn had been hoping for, because now Brynn surmised that what Tillie observed must have been the person who set the fire. The question was why wouldn't she step forward and tell Mike Rafferty, or the police, or her parents? As Brynn walked past the church, noting that the car was still there, she tried to make sense of it all, and figured the question to ask was why was Tillie so afraid to come forward? So afraid that she ran off to the Scorss' home in Massachusetts?

As she walked by the car, she spotted the top of a hat in the passenger's seat. Her heart almost stopped. Was there someone in the car? She ran over to it. She peeked in through the window. Sure enough, someone was inside sleeping in an awkward position. Sort of twisted up. Why would someone be sleeping in a car in the church parking lot? Were they okay? A runaway?

She tapped on the window. "Hello?"

The person inside didn't move. At all.

She knocked harder on the window. No movement.

Was this young man drunk? Sick? Dead? What should she do? Open the car? She reached for the handle and pulled. It was locked. In fact, all of the doors were locked. Whoever this young man was, he'd locked himself in the car.

"Hello?" she said again, to no avail.

She reached in her coat pocket and pulled out her phone, dialed 9-1-1, and waited for the police to arrive.

"And what were you doing here, again?" the sheriff said.

"I was just taking a walk through the woods."

He placed his hands on his hips. His leather belt and holder squeaked. "On a cold day like this?"

Brynn nodded. There was no way she could tell him she was out looking for clues as to what Tillie may have seen to scare her off. Obviously, Tillie didn't trust the local police, or she would have gone to them instead of running away. "I needed air."

The paramedics were pulling the young man out of the car. Brynn choked back tears. She didn't know him—but he was young, in his early twenties. Why would he lock himself in a car? What was he doing here?

"Who is he?" Brynn asked. "Do you recognize him?"

"Yes, but we've got to inform his family first."

"So, he's local." Brynn was thinking out loud.

"That's right. Chances are, this is a drug overdose. Maybe suicide." His voice cracked. Brynn watched his Adam's apple move as if he were swallowing—or holding back. "I doubt any foul play."

"Speaking of foul play, how is the other investigation going?"

The ambulance door shut after the paramedics slid in the body of the young man.

"We've got some leads we're following."

"So you're getting close?"

He smiled at her. "You never give up, do you?"

"It's just that I've been harassed. Someone killed Nancy. I don't feel safe in my home. So I'm concerned. I want resolution."

"Well, we all want that, believe me, and we're working on it. Now, do you mind telling me what you were really doing over here?"

Brynn grimaced. "I told you. But I found something strange in the woods."

"More secret stashes?" He grinned, and Brynn wanted to slap him.

"No, I found this cave, and it looked like someone's been staying there." She told him what she saw in detail.

"Sounds like someone's hunting cabin," he said and shook his head. "But there's no hunting allowed on this property. These woods are too close to the population. If I find someone hunting over here, I'll arrest them on the spot." He looked around as if he was looking for the hunter right now.

Hunting? That was all she needed. She was always reading about hunting accidents and didn't want her cows being shot.

"I've not heard any gunshots. But if I do, you'll be the first to know."

The two of them quieted, as did the other rescue officer on site, as the ambulance carried off the body of the young man.

Chapter Forty-Four

Death and doom hung in the air.

Brynn's usual optimism was wearing thin. Happening on a dead body like that had sealed it. Even though it was locked from the inside, Brynn still thought it suspicious. She was certain that a killer could have figured out how to lock the door and make it look like it was from the inside.

Her heart sank as she considered the young man, dying right before Christmas. The holiday would never be the same for his family.

Would the holiday ever be the same for her?

She didn't like to dwell on her years with Dan, but the Christmases they spent together had made the holiday even more special. She was bound and determined to get herself into the spirit of things. But it seemed as though the universe conspired against her.

Nancy's death was the beginning of a downward spiral she had to figure out how to dig out of.

She lay in bed that night, replaying the events that had happened. Nancy died. Someone tried to set Brynn's yard on fire. Someone placed a stuffed crow on her door. And she was certain someone had taken Freckles, though she had no proof of that.

Then, she and Willow stumbled upon money in
the woods, which had vanished by the next day. Tillie
ran away—which was the weird icing on the even
weirder cake.

She would feel so much better when Wes moved
in—and she hated that. She wanted to be independ-
ent. But she had to admit that having another person
around—male or female—would not only give her
more of a sense of security, but maybe some time to
get some other things done—a website for Buttermilk
Creek Farm, a farm shop for the CSA, and heck,
maybe even a haircut. Yes, that would be nice.

Her cell phone awakened her. It was 5 AM, just a
half hour before she usually arose to get Petunia
milked. "Hello?"

"Hey Brynn, it's Willow. Are you up?"

"I am now." Brynn's mind was struggling to keep
up with her mouth. "What's up?"

"Hey, I heard about yesterday. I'm just calling to
check on you. Must have been a bit disturbing."

"Yeah." Brynn sat up, still wrapped in her quilt.

"I heard this morning on the news that it was a
drug overdose."

"Do you ever sleep?" Brynn asked.

Willow laughed. "Yes, but I'm such an early bird. I
figured you were, too, because of the cows."

"I am. What kind of drugs?"

"Heroine," Willow answered. "It's a huge problem.
These kids try it for fun and find it addictive. I'm certain Carsen was addicted."

"Carsen?"

"Yeah, he was the guy you found," Willow said. "He
graduated from James Madison University last year.

He was a prelaw major and was taking a year off before law school. He was working for Flannery."

Brynn shot up out of bed. "Flannery?"

"Yes, why?"

"The name keeps coming up in connection with drugs."

"Unfortunately, there're reasons for it. You know the story."

"Yeah, but I knew nothing about the nephew until I talked with the Sollittos. Did you?"

"That family has cleaned up its act. But I've got to admit, I'm wary of them. I can't quite put my finger on it. But I really do like Zach, the father. He's been through the ringer."

Brynn slipped on her jeans and considered his kind blue eyes. "So I gather." Brynn didn't have the same local concern for the family. If they were involved in Nancy's death, or the death of this boy, they needed justice served. While she pondered justice, she thought about the sheriff and Mike Rafferty. Perhaps she'd call them both today to check on how the investigation was going. She had every right to be concerned.

"Have you heard from Tillie?" Willow said.

"No. But I talked with Wes. He doesn't understand what's going on with her. But as far as I'm aware, she's still in Massachusetts."

"She is very frightened."

"But why?" Brynn walked downstairs. "What does she know? What did she see? I tried to figure that out yesterday. I walked in Glebe Woods."

"What? What for?"

"I just wanted to check out what she may have seen. There's a perfect view of my place and a view of Tom's place. In any case, I concluded that it must have been a person she noticed. Perhaps she observed the person who set the fire."

"Surely she'd have come forward?"

"I'd like to think so. But for all her smarts and maturity, she's still only sixteen."

"If she did spot someone, I'm sure it scared her. But it makes little sense she'd not come forward. I know her. I know her people. They are honest sorts."

Brynn's thoughts circled around. "It must be more complex than we realize. What if she recognized the person?"

"The killer? The person who set the fire?" Willow's voice raised.

"Yes. What if you were sixteen and witnessed someone you knew, maybe someone you trusted, or liked, setting a fire that killed someone?" Brynn slipped on her boots. That must be it. Poor Tillie had viewed someone she recognized doing this terrible thing. It must be tearing her up.

"If that's the case, then I'm glad she's not here," Willow said in a hoarse whisper.

Brynn chilled. She put her coat and hat on, along with a warm scarf. But her garments did no good against the deep-down bone cold she felt. But when she opened the door, a foul stench greeted her, along with a huge bag of garbage on her front porch. Someone was here last night and dropped off a bag of trash. Where was Freckles?

"Willow, I've got to go. Someone dropped a bag of trash off on my porch, and it stinks to high heaven."

"What?"

"Someone is not giving up. They really want me gone." Prickles moved up and down her spine.

"Why didn't Freckles bark?"

Brynn rushed to the barn to open the door and was greeted with happy, excited cows—and a dog who was still curled in the corner, fast asleep.

"I don't know," Brynn said. "She's here, but she's sleeping. Freckles!"

The dog stood and shook herself.

Brynn ran her hands through the dog's warm coat. "Some watchdog you are."

Chapter Forty-Five

"Well, it looks like you're right. It's trash," the sheriff said. "It's illegal to dump your trash on someone's front doorstep. We'll go through it to see if there're any clues as to who it belongs to."

"Clues?" Brynn said.

"Mail, magazines." He walked away from her and headed to his car.

She followed him. "What's really going on, Sheriff? It's one thing after the other."

"Now, you don't worry about anything. We'll figure it out." His tone was so condescending, it turned Brynn's stomach.

"I need to worry. I'm being harassed. Who knows what they will do next time?"

"Maybe you should get an alarm system."

Just then, Freckles, who she'd assumed was her alarm system, walked over and licked the sheriff's hand. "My alarm system likes you."

He cracked a smile. "It's odd she didn't bark."

"Maybe she did, and I slept through it. Looks like the person may have just driven up and dropped off the trash. Probably not here long."

"Well. We can cross Tillie O'Reilly off the suspect list. She's not due home until tomorrow."

"Why was she even on the list? She's a good kid."

He nodded. "I agree. But she's young, and sometimes young people make huge mistakes. See it all the time." He paused and looked around. "Love what you're doing with this place." He looked back at her, directly. He wasn't lying. Or if he was, he was a very good one—there were no tells. "She lives just beyond those woods on the other side of the orchard. So, she has easy access to your place, and, unfortunately to the old church."

Brynn's heart fluttered wildly in her chest. "What are you saying? That she set the fire?"

His face lost all expression. "No. I'm not saying that at all."

A police truck drove up the driveway, and a crew of two exited the vehicle, scooped up the trash, and placed it in the back of the truck.

"Search it thoroughly," the sheriff said to the two officers. "We need to find out who did this."

The young police officers slipped surgical gloves on their hands and dug through the trash in a methodical manner. Brynn felt a little sorry for them on this cold day, digging around in the stinky trash. Though she supposed it might be worse if it was a warm day.

After a few minutes, one of the officers came up to her and the sheriff. "We've found nothing with an address or name on it."

The sheriff nodded. "Let's bag it up and take it to the station. I want prints done on each piece of trash that we have. Understood?"

"Yes, sir."

He turned back to Brynn.

She recognized the concern in his eyes. "Would you like to come in for some coffee and Danish? Or something? I also have some Christmas cookies if you'd like."

He looked at his watch. "I can take time. I'd love that. Thank you."

The police truck pulled away, and Brynn and Sheriff Edge drifted into the house. Brynn was grateful for the warmth.

"So, tell me about the Flannery family," Brynn said, after they'd sat down, and the sheriff was up to his elbows in cookies.

"What do you want to know?" He drank his coffee.

"I've heard they had trouble with drugs." Brynn sipped her coffee. Nonchalantly, pleased with her cool exterior. Someone had dumped trash on her beautiful front porch. She felt violated. Angry. Frightened. And nothing seemed to happen—nobody was taking this seriously enough to prevent whatever might happen next. She needed to investigate further on her own.

He nodded. "Yep. That was years ago, though."

"Are drugs bad here?"

"Just like they are everywhere." He sounded a little indignant. "Rural kids get into trouble just like big city kids. And you know it's not just kids. I arrested a teacher a few years back for possession and selling."

"As a newcomer, I have to say, I'm more than a little surprised."

He set his cup down. "I'm sorry to hear that. Folks from the outside look at us as if we're some bucolic community that time forgot." He bit his cookie, chewed, and swallowed. "It's true to some extent. But we deal with modern problems, modern crime, every day."

"How is the fire investigation going?" Brynn's fingers circled the rim of her cup.

"You'd have to ask Rafferty about that. It's his territory."

"What are the chances they'll find the person who set the fire?" she said, and lifted the cup to her mouth.

His eyes met hers. "Maybe they already have."

"What's that supposed to mean?"

"Sometimes it just takes time to gather strong enough evidence to make the case. Careful police work takes time."

Brynn mulled over everything she learned. She'd warmed up to the sheriff. He did seem concerned, and he couldn't possibly be watching her place all the time to catch the perp. She supposed he was right. That it took time for them. The trouble was, in the meantime, she appeared to be a sitting duck. She was getting increasingly nervous. A big part of her wanted to leave and go home to Richmond until they found out who'd set the fire and who was harassing her. But she couldn't leave the farm. Even if she could hire someone, she wasn't sure she could live with herself for giving up that easily.

"Are you in possession of any weapons?" The sheriff interrupted her thoughts.

"What? You mean like a gun?"

"Yes. If you don't have one, you might get one. When you live in the country, it comes in handy."

Brynn chilled. She never wanted to have a gun in her home. She knew the statistics about guns in homes.

She didn't want to be another statistic. "I don't think guns are for me." She tried to smile.

He sat back in his seat, which squeaked beneath his weight. "Get one of those toy guns then. The ones that look real. You could at least scare someone with it."

Brynn laughed. "Well, now that I might do."

Chapter Forty-Six

Brynn hated to need someone. But she really needed someone now. She was in a bind. Every time she turned around, another incident happened. Another person here would be helpful. But it was the day before Christmas Eve. More than hating the vulnerability in her gut, she hated the embarrassed feeling of not wanting to impose, especially at this time of year.

So she kept herself as busy as possible, to keep her mind off of all the incidents that had gone on around her. She flipped on the stereo and rolled up her sleeves. It was Christmas, dammit. What it needed was Christmas baking.

She marched into her kitchen and took stock. She had nut filling, poppy seeds, Rice Krispies, peanut butter, flour, sugar, chocolate chips—and plenty of eggs and milk.

Dolly's rendition of "Jingle Bells" blared over her speakers. She reached for the mixing bowl and started to make a poppy seed cake. It was her grandmother's recipe. Her family had a deep history in Richmond, but her mother's family had come from Poland. She was a healthy mix of Polish and Irish, seeped in southern life. One way her Polish roots came through was from the recipes handed down. This poppy seed cake was an old recipe. And it wouldn't be Christmas without it.

She measured the flour, cracked the eggs, and plopped the poppy seed filling into the bowl. The scent of the nutty mix brought memories flooding back to her. Memories of Christmas mornings filled with magic, Christmas Eves sitting in church impatiently waiting for the service to be over, and visits with family and good friends to exchange baked goods.

She slid the cake into the oven and focused on making the rest of her goodies—sugar cookies, nut cups, and cherry squares.

Brynn's mind kept circling back to the fire that killed Nancy, the trash on her front porch, the bird, the attempted fire in her front yard, and poor Freckles. Then it wandered to Tillie. Did she really know something about all of this? Poor kid.

Brynn filled the last of her nut cups and slid them into the oven. She stood and glanced at her counter, where the poppy seed cake cooled, along with a couple of batches of snowball cookies. Her kitchen smelled of sugar, cinnamon, and nuts. She couldn't imagine a scent she liked better—except for cheese.

Which reminded her she had cheese balls to make.

But instead, she walked into the living room, sat down, and looked out her window, allowing the Christmas music to lift her worries, if only momentarily. Her cows were hanging out with Freckles. The grass was brown and scraggly—but they still ate it.

Her eyes gazed along the horizon to the hill and the clouds dotting the sky. Would things ever really work out for her here? Should she cut her losses and move on? How much longer could she put up with this?

Brynn needed to stay focused on her business, or it just would not work out. But it was difficult to stay focused when someone was dropping trash on your front porch.

She didn't understand how to backtrack on a decision and wanted to make this work. Brynn had used all of her grandmother's money to pay for the farm. Should she sell it and take her girls somewhere else?

Where else could she go?

This place seemed perfect with the revitalization of the community and an active CSA, one dedicated to healthy, organic practices. And the price was right. She figured she couldn't afford to move on. She absolutely had to make this work.

Dan's words came to her then, through his laughter. "You think you can take care of cows, the farm, and make good cheese?"

Anger jabbed at her. "Yes, I do. Or I will die trying."

She blinked back a tear. Damn. Not only had they planned to live the rest of their lives with one another, but they had also planned the rest of their professional lives together. For all his problems, he was a fine cheesemaker. He worked hard and made incredible cheese.

His cheating on her had shaken her to her core. She'd had herself a good cry, then kept moving on with her life. But at moments like this, where she was alone, mulling over her life and what had happened with Dan, she realized she had barely given herself time to reflect on it.

It wasn't her fault that he cheated on her, so why did she sometimes have this huge sense of guilt? Why did she sometimes feel like she could have done more?

That's just crazy talk. She could hear Becky's voice loud and clear in her mind.

"Well, Brynn, stop feeling sorry for yourself and get to work."

She stood and marched into the kitchen to check on the cream cheese she had left out to soften. She poked it with a fork: perfect. Homemade cream cheese was so easy to make—and fresh was ten times better than store bought—just like anything else.

Freckles interrupted her thoughts with her loud barking. Brynn dropped the cheese and for a minute wished for that toy gun that the sheriff had suggested. Then she willed away the thought. *Don't be ridiculous.*

She made her way to the front door, opened it, and spotted nothing that should have made Freckles bark. She slipped on her boots and set off to her backyard field where Freckles still barked.

She rounded the corner and blinked. Freckles's behind was sticking up, her nose was pointed down, and her tail was wagging furiously. Did she have something cornered? Brynn ran over to her. "Freckles!" The dog backed off reluctantly.

What looked like a dead possum was tucked in the grass. But Brynn was certain it was alive—it was playing possum. But what to do with the creature so Freckles wouldn't bother it? "Freckles, come with me," Brynn said, and headed for the barn.

Petunia stood nearby, overseeing the scene.

Brynn breathed hard, and her breath came out in smoky puffs into the cold air. In the back of the barn, she rummaged around for boxes. She searched until she found them and chose one that she could place the creature in, to get it out of harm's way.

She headed back outside for the possum, shovel in one hand and box in the other. But the possum was gone. Well, that was a relief. She set the shovel and box aside.

And headed back into the house.

"Would you like to come in the house with me?"

Freckles looked up at her with a quizzical expression.

"C'mon."

Up until this point, the dog had preferred to be outside, but this time she followed Brynn toward the house. Brynn glanced at Petunia, who watched as the dog followed her. The cow blinked but didn't seem to mind.

Freckles followed Brynn into the warm house.

Brynn's phone rang—it was Becky.

"How's it going?" Becky said.

"Fine, just made cookies and poppy seed cake," Brynn said, heading into the kitchen, where she spent the next hour fashioning cheese balls and chatting with her sister.

Chapter Forty-Seven

After Brynn hung up from talking with her sister, she wrapped her cheese balls in craft paper, tied them with raffia, and attached her homemade Buttermilk Creek Farm tags. She readied to leave to deliver her gifts to the CSA members, but when she opened the door, a jolt of fear zoomed through her. She couldn't step out of the house.

If she left, who knew what she'd come home to? If she stayed, slept, and woke up, who knew what she'd wake up to? It was a dilemma.

She was afraid for her animals. She absolutely couldn't leave until they figured out who'd been harassing her, and if it had any connection to the fire that killed Nancy.

She hated to call Willow as it was the day before Christmas Eve, and she was certain Willow had better things to do. But Brynn needed to get the cheese balls delivered.

"I'll be right over," Willow said.

There were only twelve active members of the CSA, but they were all spread apart, so it would take time to deliver her gifts. "Thank you," Brynn said as she left.

"Sure thing," Willow called after her.

Brynn set the box holding her gifts on the passenger side of her car. First stop, the Andrews, because they were the closest to her farm. One by one, she'd make her way out to the farthest farm, and then she'd have one more stop to make—the O'Reillys'. Her heart sped at the idea. Would Tillie be home? She hoped the girl was home safe and sound. She also hoped that whatever had troubled her was solved.

Brynn parked her car, not turning off the engine, and popped out to the Andrews' front door.

Elsie answered the door. "Why, hello, Brynn."

"Hi, Elsie. I didn't make it to the party the other night, so I'm delivering gifts to the members."

"Oh, how sweet. Can you come in for some tea or pie?" She opened the door wider. The alluring scent of sugar and cinnamon plucked at Brynn's nose.

"As tempting as that is, you're my first stop. I need to get going. I wanted to wish you a Merry Christmas." Temptation averted.

"Thank you. Same to you."

As Brynn drove through town and delivered her cheese balls, she again mulled over the events of the case. The Sollitto family had set her mind to wondering about all the drug problems here and in the country. But Nancy wasn't involved in drugs. Was Tillie? She seemed too smart for that. Even though she'd briefly suspected Tom Andrews, Brynn certainly didn't anymore.

She considered Flannery, the contractor, and his kind blue eyes. His family had had a rough time. But were any of his kin so messed up by drugs they'd gotten involved in murder? She also mulled over the conversation she'd recently had with Mike Rafferty. It sounded as if he had a very good idea of who the guilty party was. There were so many local boys she'd met—and most of them were in the volunteer fire department.

Then she recalled the deceased young man in the parking lot. What was his story? And did it fit into any of the other incidents?

She drove along the two-lane road and turned into the long drive of the Christmas tree farm. The smaller plantings dotted the hilly land. As she drove closer, the house and barns came into view, along with the larger trees. It looked as if Kevin only had a few left.

She knocked on the door, and Kevin answered. He cracked a smile. "Well, hello there, Brynn. We missed you the other night."

"Yes, sorry I couldn't make it, but I brought you some cheese to celebrate the holiday. Merry Christmas." She handed him the wrapped cheese ball. It dwarfed in the large man's hand.

"Thank you," he said. "Is everything okay?"

"Oh sure. The night of the party was the night Tillie went missing, and I was a mess."

He stood holding the cheese ball. "I didn't know you two were close."

"I wouldn't say we're close. But I like her. She's spent time at my place. I was just upset to hear she was missing."

"Oh, I see. We love her," he said. "She's a special girl. Is she home?"

Brynn shrugged. "I have no idea."

"Would you like to come in?" he asked after a few seconds.

"I'm sorry. I'd love to, but not this afternoon. I've got to deliver the last of these cheese balls."

"Merry Christmas," he said.

"Same to you!"

As she drove off, she remembered being here the night Tillie was singing. The Ryder family must have taken her under their wing. Good to know.

Brynn made several stops. Few people were home, which was to be expected. She had two more stops to make—the honey farm and the O'Reilly Orchards.

She hadn't expected the honey farm to be so cute. Fancy bee houses that looked like miniature houses, painted beautifully, even artistically, lined the driveway.

"Love your bee houses," she said to Josh.

"Oh yes, thanks. There's a woman down the road who makes them. Samantha Hildebrand is her name."

"Really? How fascinating!"

"They are little pieces of art. We're all proud of her. She, um, is a veteran, and has PTSD. Stays at home on the mountain most of the time." He gazed off as if he were remembering something from long ago.

Brynn felt awkward. "Enjoy the cheese! Merry Christmas!"

"Hey, thanks, same to you!"

Brynn ambled off to her car. Before she started it, she texted Willow to see how she was doing.

Watching Frosty was her response.

Brynn smiled and drove on.

The sun hung low in the sky as Brynn drove along toward Tillie's family's farm. She needed to make this quick.

She pulled into the drive and was surprised to find the sheriff there. She should just turn around and go home, but curiosity picked at her. And, besides, she needed to give the family their cheese ball. If everybody else got one, and they didn't, it would not be a good thing.

So, she parked her car and exited.

She walked up the sidewalk to the front porch, admiring the Christmas decorations. A wreath and one glowing white candle hung in every window, so understated and beautiful. She rang the doorbell.

Mr. O'Reilly answered. "Hi Brynn. Can I help you?" He only cracked open the door enough to stick his head out.

"Just dropping off a gift, since I didn't make it to the party the other day."

He smiled. "Thank you." He took the cheese ball and started to close the door. "Merry Christmas."

"Same to you," Brynn said. "Mr. O'Reilly?"

"Yes?"

"Have you heard from Tillie?"

"Yes. She's fine. No worries."

He shut the door. As Brynn turned to go, she caught movement in a window. Tillie and the sheriff were sitting in the living room.

Just what was going on?

Chapter Forty-Eight

Brynn knew something was wrong the minute she entered her house. It was too quiet. Willow had said she was watching TV. A strange prickle traveled along Brynn's spine.

"Willow?" Silence answered her.

Calm down, she told herself. She may have had to leave.

But her car was still in the driveway.

Maybe she was in the bathroom. Yes. That must be it.

Brynn walked into the kitchen and placed her purse on the counter, hoping that Willow would exit the bathroom at any minute. She walked from the kitchen to the living room and spotted Willow's purse, an empty wineglass, and a plate with crumbs on it. She shivered.

She'd not have gone far without her purse. Willow must still be in the house.

Brynn sat down on the sofa, crossed her legs. Uncrossed her legs. Stood back up. Surely, Willow would be out of the bathroom by now, if that's where she was.

Could she be in the barn? Brynn paced between

the couch and the Christmas tree. It was the day before Christmas Eve, and she was certain Willow had a million things to do. Where had she gone off to?

Brynn couldn't shake the cold creeping over her. She reached for a throw she had hanging over the arm of the couch and wrapped herself in it. She then checked the thermostat. Sixty-eight. That's where she usually liked the temperature. Why was she so cold? She nudged the control needle up to seventy, just to take the chill off.

She was hoping Willow would come bounding into the room at any moment. But there was nothing but silence. No opening and closing of doors. No creaking of floorboards.

Maybe she'd gone up to take a nap in a bedroom.

Brynn ascended her stairs, alert to any noises, any breath, anything.

She poked her head in the first guest room. No Willow. She poked her head in the next room. Empty. She poked her head into her own bedroom. Unmade bed, a book on the foot of the bed, but no Willow.

Maybe she'd gone for a walk. Yes, that must be it.

Willow loved to walk. It wasn't like her to sit in the house—or anywhere—for hours.

She must have gone for a walk. Brynn yelled her name out loud one more time, as if to assure herself that Willow was not in the house.

Brynn texted her. **Where R U?**

No reply.

The sun was hanging low through the windows, and Brynn hightailed it to the field to bring the cows in. On an evening like this, she'd be happy to use the milkers. It was cold, and she was freaked out by the absence of Willow. Heck, perhaps she'd run into Willow outside.

She put her coat and boots on and headed for the girls and Freckles, who all greeted her. Freckles's tail wagged a mile a minute, and the girls followed her to the barn.

"Hello, ladies," she said to them as they walked. "I've made all my deliveries to the CSA members, who now have lovely cheese balls, thanks to your sweet cream."

She settled Buttercup and Marigold into the barn and Petunia into the milking stall, flipped the music on the stereo, and attached the milkers. While she was waiting on the milking to be finished, Brynn swept the floors, trying not to think about Willow.

Okay, yes, she liked to walk, but wouldn't she have left a note? Or have gotten back to her on the text? Some of these areas, between the hills and winding roads, didn't have much reception. But still.

She continued to sweep the floor until the milking was finished. She busied herself with taking care of milk and cow, and then made her way back to the house, watching for Willow to walk over the hill or to come around the other side of the house. But neither happened.

Was Willow okay?

What was going on?

She stepped inside the house, slipped off her coat and boots, and headed for the kitchen. Perhaps Willow had left a note on the fridge. But there was no note—just Brynn's collection of cow magnets.

Okay. She'd had enough wondering about Willow. It was time to call the police. She reached into her pocket and pulled out her phone. She slid her cold fingers on the screen, but a sharp pain in her head interrupted her. A voice hissed, "You couldn't leave it alone!"

Her phone flew out of her hands. The sound of it hitting the kitchen floor was the last thing she remembered before everything went black.

Chapter Forty-Nine

One dim light shone in the cellar among the rows of cheese. Brynn blinked, trying to focus her eyes. Slowly, she honed in on Willow, who appeared to be sleeping. Brynn hoped and prayed she *was* sleeping.

Willow was bound and gagged the same way she was. Arms tied together at the wrists and pulled behind her back, legs crossed and tied at the ankles, and mouth taped.

Brynn glanced around the room, searching for whoever it was that had done this to them. There didn't seem to be anybody but her and Willow. The quiet was unnerving. Nothing was stirring. Not even Freckles was barking. There was no sound coming from the direction of the barn. Her stomach gathered into a ball of nerves.

"You couldn't leave it alone." The words echoed in her pounding head.

She pressed against the rope that was holding her hands together behind her back and tried to move her fingers along the edges to investigate if she could, and perhaps, figure out how the rope knotted. But it was hard to twist her fingers around. She wanted to scream—and she tried, but because of the way the tape was over her mouth, it came out sounding like an angry, muzzled pig.

But it was enough to startle Willow into waking up.

Her huge eyes looked bright and frightened in the dim light. She grunted something as if she was trying to talk. Then she gave up and slumped back onto the wall.

Brynn wasn't quite ready to give up. *Think, think, think. There must be away out of this.*

The trouble was, what would happen if they got out of the cellar? Was the person who placed them there still in the house? In the barn? Were her girls okay?

Hot tears streamed down her face. She heard herself sob. Shocked that such sounds could come out of her, it was as if another person had taken over her throat. She dizzied and gave way to an utter and complete sleepiness.

Brynn awoke with a gentle nudging. Someone was kicking her.

She sat up quickly, wondering why she was being kicked. But then she spotted Willow pushing her ropes against Brynn's with her foot hooked in between the knots in Brynn's ropes. She worked at the ropes with her feet. Then she seemed to give up. Then she worked again.

Brynn nodded, noticing the ropes on her feet give way.

While Willow was working, Brynn was mentally sorting the cheese tools in the cellar. Was there anything she could use to cut them free once she was out of her leg ropes?

Her mind circled around and wondered if she couldn't find something in the cellar, could she find something upstairs in the kitchen? But first, they had to continue to work to free her legs.

Willow rested, breathing heavily, sweat pouring down her face.

Who did this? Had Willow observed the person? Or had he snuck up behind her like he did Brynn?

Brynn's head still pounded and fuzzed, like it hurt to think. But she couldn't remember seeing a person. Only the shocking and harsh shove, and hearing her cell phone fall on the floor.

"You couldn't leave it alone."

Yes! If she could get free, she'd get her cell, and they could call the police. If her phone was still on the kitchen floor.

Waves of weariness came over her. She wondered if she'd been drugged. What time was it? She was supposed to have met with the others tonight one more time before the living nativity tomorrow. They'd judge her a shirker. How she hated that.

But she had a good excuse. She would probably die right here in this cellar among her cheese and with Willow. A pang of guilt shot through her then. Poor Willow wouldn't be in this situation if it wasn't for her.

Please let Willow live, she prayed.

Willow was back at twisting her feet around Brynn's ropes. Suddenly she let loose, kicking her feet furiously. Brynn yelled because she was getting kicked hard. But soon, her legs were free.

Now, all she had to do was stand. She pressed her back up against the wall and tried to lift herself to her feet. But her legs felt like rubber. She took another deep breath and pushed herself again. Off balance, she almost fell to one side, then angled to pull herself up.

She stood. If she could have managed, she'd be grinning. Her mouth was as dry as sandpaper, and her shoulders and arm sockets ached from being pulled in an awkward position.

Willow looked up at her and tilted her head toward the stairs.

But what if the person was still there?

What then?

Brynn stood for a moment, looking around the cellar for a tool. But there was nothing sharp enough to cut the ropes from around her hands—or around Willow's.

Willow tilted her head again toward the stairs. Brynn took one step and then another, with her shaking legs protesting all the way.

She stood for a moment. It sure sounded like there was nobody upstairs.

She lifted her foot and placed it on the first rickety stair. If she got out of this thing alive, she would fix these darn stairs. If she could free her hands, it would be so much easier!

She took one stair at a time and kicked open the door, left slightly ajar. The air and light from the rest of her house filled her with the lightness of hope.

She slowly made her way to the kitchen where she figured her cell phone might be. But she couldn't find it.

It had to be here! Her eyes searched the counter and the floor, but it didn't seem to be around.

Waves of panic tore through her. *Now what?*

She breathed hard. Thoughts circled. What to do?

Okay, people survived worse than this without cell phones, the voice of logic came to her. You're in the kitchen, get something sharp. But since her hands were tied behind her back, it wouldn't be easy.

She turned her back to the kitchen drawer and slipped her fingers along the edge of the handle; she pulled. The drawer came open.

Brynn reached for a knife, grabbed it, then it slipped right through her fingers. Darn. She hadn't realized how much she was shaking until she tried to lift that knife.

She tried to will away the shakes. But it wasn't happening. She tried to get the knife again. This time she succeeded. Now, all she had to do was clutch it long enough to get it down the stairs to Willow.

Her eyes glanced at the faucet and the fridge. She was so thirsty, she ached. But first, get down the stairs with the knife, and then worry about being so parched.

She could do this. She hung on to the knife as if it was a treasure. And it was. She took it slowly, even though she wanted to run. She couldn't take any chances on losing that knife.

If she got out of this, she was selling the place and leaving the area. She didn't need this. The police weren't taking her seriously. Brynn figured poor Tillie had run off because she'd glimpsed something so disturbing that she surmised she had no other choice. Brynn had found a dead body in the parking lot of the church. If she didn't watch her step, she or Willow would be next. Maybe she'd take her girls elsewhere and start again.

She didn't even care about finding out who attacked her—she just wanted out.

As she walked toward the cellar door, the doorbell rang. Her heart almost stopped. Whoever did this to them wouldn't be ringing the doorbell. It must be someone else.

"Hello?" came Schuyler's voice. "Anybody home?"

Brynn ran to the front door, dropping the knife on the floor with a loud clang.

Chapter Fifty

After Brynn and Willow were free of all their constraints, they sat in the kitchen drinking water, trying to calm themselves down and figure out what to do next.

"We need to call the police," Willow said.

"They've known about all the other things that have happened here and haven't done a thing. Maybe we should just take care of this ourselves," Brynn said.

Schuyler held Willow's wrists, which were red and raw from where the ropes burned into her. "You probably should both be checked out by a doctor. You're not thinking right. You're in shock. We need to call the police. Someone was in your house and tied you up in the cheese cellar."

"Did you see who it was?" Brynn looked at Willow, still pale and shivering, even though she was wrapped up in a blanket.

"No. He came up behind me. He was large. Very strong."

Brynn would agree. But that described half the men in these parts. At least half.

Schuyler called the authorities, and while they

waited for them to arrive, the women tried to figure out who their assailant was.

"Where were you this afternoon?" Schuyler asked. "Willow was here watching the place. Where were you?"

"I was delivering cheese balls to the CSA members."

"So, they all knew you were gone. Anybody else?" Schuyler stood from her chair and paced.

Brynn mulled it over before answering. "No."

"Did you tell anybody you were going to be here?" Schuyler turned to Willow.

Willow sat and drank from her water. "Sure. I didn't know we were keeping it a secret."

"Who did you tell?"

"I ran into Tom Andrews at the store, and we chatted." Willow took another drink of water.

"He wasn't home when I dropped off the cheese ball."

"But he's not a very tall man," Schuyler said. "You both said he was tall and strong."

"Besides, he's prickly, but I don't suspect he'd do such a thing," Brynn said.

The three of them sat quietly.

"His hands smelled of something familiar." Brynn's mind grabbed and clutched, trying to remember where she'd smelled that scent before.

"Yeah." Willow lifted her head up. "Now that you mention it. I recall that, too. A certain spicy scent. Cinnamon?"

"Cinnamon and apples . . ." Brynn said. "Come to think of it . . . I smelled it the night of the fire. Standing next to the man who helped me. It was . . ."

"O'Reilly!"

"Tillie's father?" Willow stood.

"Or her brother?" Schuyler said.

"Tillie's in more trouble than we imagined. I saw her earlier. She's home."

"Probably the very place she shouldn't be," Willow said.

"Let's go," Schuyler said, just as the police and ambulance sirens were getting close. "Damn."

"I told you not to call them." Brynn crossed her arms. Once they told the police their theory, they would probably lock all three of them up. And poor Tillie, who knew what she was dealing with in her house, right this moment? A man in her family—either her father or her brother—was at the root of all of this.

As Brynn considered it, it made sense. Their property bordered on the woods that bordered on the church property. She was missing a huge piece of the puzzle, but the other pieces fell into place. An O'Reilly would have easy access to Nancy, the church, and Brynn's place. Nobody would have imagined it odd at all if they were seen in the area. Brynn's heart ached as she realized that what Tillie had witnessed, what had upset her so much, involved her father or brother.

But it didn't answer the question why. What did O'Reilly hope to accomplish?

The sheriff entered Brynn's home, looked around, and placed his hands on his hips. "Okay ladies, what's going on?"

Schuyler relayed the information—what had happened here tonight. But she mentioned nothing about the apple-cinnamon scent.

"Did you notice anything about the man other than he was tall and strong?"

"He smelled of apples," Willow said. "He smelled like an O'Reilly."

The sheriff's face dropped. "What the—"

"Look," Willow said, standing. "I know she's your sister, but you need to get her out of there."

Brynn was learning many things today.

Schuyler cleared her throat. "She may be in trouble. We think that Tillie is. If she saw him or Frank . . . up to no good . . . I don't know what they are capable of."

"You're talking about my in-laws," he said. "I'll have to get someone else to take over this case. Conflict of interest. I'll call Charlie."

Brynn wasn't acquainted with Charlie. Had they met? Her head swam knowing that Mrs. O'Reilly and the sheriff were brother and sister. She found herself impressed, probably for the first time since meeting the sheriff. He definitely needed to step away from this case, and he realized it.

The knot in her stomach hardened. Poor Tillie. If only the police hadn't shown up, they would have run to her home. Brynn shivered as she connected their assailant, Nancy's killer, to sweet Tillie. Living in the same house with her. Brynn prayed it wasn't her father.

Chapter Fifty-One

Brynn and Willow both wanted to head over to the O'Reilly place. Curiosity was killing them. But they both stayed put out of respect for the family. Brynn fought her compulsion to run to Tillie and hug her.

After the paramedics checked them over thoroughly and left, Schuyler gave them a homemade herbal concoction to relax them.

"I suppose it was her brother, Frank," Willow said, stretching out on Brynn's couch.

Brynn recalled the lone figure walking through the orchard when she'd gone exploring in the woods. He must have seen her, which is why he came after her later that day. Willow just happened to be in her house. She also recalled his icy blue eyes during the CSA meeting, and now that she focused, she remembered him the night of the fire more vividly. "I really hate it, but I agree with you. Her dad isn't quite that big." Brynn pondered a moment. "Is he?"

"He's tall, but thin. The guy that grabbed me was solid, like a brick wall." Her chin quivered. "I assumed he would kill you. I was just lying there in the cold cheese cellar, dreading your coming home."

Brynn's heart fluttered. "Thank you for worrying about me."

"Of course," she said and yawned.

"Hey, I have extra rooms upstairs."

"Don't think I can make it. I'm fine here."

Brynn took her leave and made her way to her bedroom, feeling more at ease than she had in weeks. She was certain the police had nabbed their guy by now. Probably Tillie's brother. Poor Tillie. No wonder she had been acting so strangely. She must have known the whole time. Brynn certainly understood now why she'd hadn't come forward, though she should have.

But why? Why had he done it? Brynn slipped beneath her covers. What was the reason? Would they ever understand? Did he also kill the young man in the church parking lot?

Frank's parents must be heartbroken.

Before heading to bed, Brynn downed more of the herbal remedy, hoping for a good night's sleep.

The next morning, someone knocking at her bedroom door awakened her. "Brynn, are you all right?"

Brynn pulled the covers over her head. She was okay, but just needed to sleep.

"Brynn?" Her door popped open. "You need to get Buttercup ready to go. She's on tonight, remember?"

The covers came off in a most cruel way.

Schuyler looked down at her. "Are you sick?"

Was she? She felt so completely and utterly tired. Drained. "I don't think so."

"Willow milked Petunia this morning, and let the girls out, but she's gone. She had to go home because it's Christmas Eve. And you need to get up. I've got Willow's trailer."

"Have I slept all day?"

Schuyler nodded.

"Well, that's one way to get through the holiday alone," Brynn blurted.

"Besides, you've just been through quite an ordeal."

Brynn sat up. She could still use another good eight hours.

Even though she'd never been bound and gagged before, she'd also never reacted to any kind of traumatic event by sleeping. Perhaps it was the herbal medicine she took. Medicine that was wearing off. They bandaged her wrists and ankles, and they burned. Every part of her body ached.

She placed her feet on the floor.

"I'll leave you to it," Schuyler said. "But you know Higard. I wouldn't be late if I were you." Schuyler grinned.

Brynn moaned as she placed her weight on her legs. "I'm so sore!"

Schuyler turned around. "There's more medicine for you on your kitchen table. But I'd wait until tonight to take it. I think you've had too much. Are you going to go tonight?"

Brynn nodded. "Give me a few minutes. I'll be downstairs."

"Get a shower, and I'll make some coffee."

As the hot water rained down on her, Brynn's brain slowly awakened. She still couldn't grasp she'd slept all day. As her mind played over the events of the past twenty-four hours, she found it hard to fathom any of it. She and Willow had been tied up and left for dead. She shivered in her steamy shower stall.

After she dressed and drifted downstairs, coffee scent leading her, she looked around for her phone. "I still can't find my phone."

Schuyler shoved a mug of coffee into her hands. "I'll call you. Do you think it's still here? Or maybe the cops took it?"

Brynn sat down at the table in her kitchen nook and breathed in the steamy coffee. "I have no idea. It's a blur."

Schuyler pulled out her phone and slid her fingers around on the screen. No sound came from anywhere.

"Does *he* have my phone?" Brynn said. "I need my phone. It's Christmas Eve. I have calls to make. If my sister calls and doesn't hear back, she'll alert the FBI and the army."

"The cops might have it." Schuyler slid her fingers around again on the phone.

Brynn drank her coffee and looked out over her backyard field where her cows and Freckles ran in the winter sun. The sky was so blue, it almost hurt her eyes.

Schuyler focused on her phone, but Brynn wasn't paying attention. She enjoyed the view and drank her coffee. If only Dan could see her now. Not only was she making a go of the farm and the cheese-making business, but she'd survived an attack in her own home. And she was getting through this holiday, wasn't she?

"They have your phone," Schuyler said. "They'll bring it tonight."

"Thank you, Schuyler," Brynn said, with tears suddenly pricking her eyes. She swallowed. *Don't cry in front of this strong, kick-ass woman.* But a tear escaped.

"Are you okay?" Schuyler crouched and slipped her arm around her. "You've been through a lot the past few weeks, but especially last night. It will take some time."

Brynn nodded. "I'll be fine." She swallowed another gulp of coffee. She would be fine. But she wouldn't quite be at ease until she spoke with Tillie. She whispered a little prayer that she was okay.

Chapter Fifty-Two

The O'Reilly family would not visit the living nativity tonight. Of that Brynn was certain. Whether it was Tillie's father or her brother—and she'd not heard yet—theirs was a family in crisis.

"Have you heard how Tillie's doing?" Brynn asked Schuyler as they drove to the church grounds.

"She's in shock."

"Have you seen her?" Brynn looked out the window at the passing scene. Snow floated through the air, but so far hadn't clung to the grass.

"I didn't, but Mike did. He's been watching Frank for years." Schuyler stopped at the stop sign and then continued driving. "The boy has been a problem. Quite a little pyromaniac, when he was little. We all thought he grew out of it. But, he was on Mike's radar. In fact, I guess, he was Mike's first suspect all along."

Brynn mulled that over. It would have been nice to be aware of that. There she was, phoning the Sollittos, interviewing contractors, and digging into the history of the church. Plus, she and Willow had gone traipsing into the graveyard, and stumbled on money there.

"What did the money and the books and everything have to do with any of it?"

"That's a good question. I have no idea. We'll find out soon."

"Did he also kill the young man in the parking lot?"

"I don't know. I'm not privy to everything. Mike is pretty tight-lipped. But that makes little sense. Perhaps someone else killed him. Unless he witnessed Frank starting the fire, and Frank had to get rid of him."

It was Christmas Eve, and they were in the truck conjecturing about who were fire starters and who were killers. Brynn hated that. Of course, as she kept telling herself, Christmas was just another day. All the fuss meant nothing and usually didn't have anything to do with the meaning of the day, anyway. Yes, that's right, just another day.

"What exactly did Tillie see?" Brynn asked, more to herself than to Schuyler.

"That's pretty obvious, isn't it? She saw her brother set the fire that killed Nancy Scors."

"Yes, but why did she run off like that? Was he threatening her? Her own brother?"

"That's another thing I don't know. I'm sure it will all come out, eventually."

Brynn hoped so. In fact, she hoped she'd get the lowdown from Tillie herself.

Schuyler pulled the truck up to the living nativity area in front of the church. Joseph, Mary, and the Baby Jesus were there, and Reverend Higard was barking orders. The sheep were in place and so was the donkey and camel. Brynn and Schuyler worked at getting Buttercup out of the trailer, and Brynn led her to her spot.

"I'll park and be right back," Schuyler said.

Brynn nodded.

The church was softly lit, sitting up on a hill, through a little patch of lightly wooded fields, and the nativity scene was set in a sort of enclave, between the church and the parking lot. Right outside the church, women were setting up tables with drinks and snacks. The smell of hot apple cider hung in the air. Brynn choked back a wave of sick. Would she ever be able to smell that scent and not flash on what had happened to her? If Willow hadn't been able to untie her ropes with her feet, they might still be lying there on the cheese cellar floor.

She ran her hands along Buttercup's coat. She was nice and warm. "How are you, sweetie?"

The cow looked up at her, her ears flicked, and she blinked. Those big brown eyes exuded even more warmth. Brynn rubbed her under her chin—a gesture the cows all appreciate, but Buttercup loved it. If a cow could coo or purr, this cow would.

"Good to see you, Brynn." Reverend Higard came up alongside of her. "Sorry to hear about what happened."

"Oh?" She turned to him. "Word's gotten around already?"

He smiled. "Small town and all that. Plus, people tend to bring their problems to me."

"Tillie?"

"No, unfortunately. But her dad has been quite torn up through the years about Frank. I've known his family for years. Good people."

"Except for Frank?" Brynn ran her hands behind

Buttercup's ears, prompting the cow to squint her eyes in pleasure.

"Look at that, would ya? She really likes your attention." He paused a little. "One thing I've learned is there's no truly bad or truly good people. We are all shades of everything in between. Frank is troubled."

He's also a killer, Brynn thought, but kept it to herself. She didn't know the young man, but she knew Nancy, and the woman didn't deserve to die like that. Nobody did. "So, you're the keeper of everybody's secrets? Next time I'm harassed, I should come to you for answers?"

He laughed. "Let's hope you won't be harassed again."

He turned to the others in the scene. "Okay people, we have about ten minutes before the official opening. Can we get some photos?"

A photographer stepped forward. Brynn stepped out of the manger and took in the scene. Joseph and Mary took their places, and the animals stood in place, behaving themselves nicely. Someone took a few shots before the baby let out a huge wail. Baby Jesus was tired and cranky. This was going to be a long night.

Every time the baby cried, the sheep bleated. And eventually Buttercup got in on the noisy action and mooed her annoyance. Halfway through the night, Mary sent Jesus home with his grandmother, and a lifelike doll took his place.

"How are you holding up?" Schuyler asked, coming up alongside of her. "Can I get you something? Water? Apple cider?"

"No, I'm good. Just a little cold. We've only got another thirty minutes. I'll be fine."

The scene was lovely, now that the fussy baby was gone. The church's lawn had tufts of snow all over it. Not like Bethlehem at all, mused Brynn. She hoped the church was making a lot of money here to support the Blue Ridge Food Shelter.

"Why don't you go into the church and get warm?"

Brynn laughed. "Because I'm afraid lightning would strike."

Chapter Fifty-Three

Brynn wished she could dream of sugar plums instead of apple cider and huge men and cheese cellars. She gave up on half sleeping about 4:30 AM and climbed downstairs to watch the TV. She flipped on the Christmas tree lights and then the TV, deciding to watch something light, instead of her usual murder mysteries. Funny, they didn't hold the same appeal when a couple of murders had happened in your backyard.

She flipped on the *Downton Abbey* Christmas special, snuggled up on her couch, and watched it for an hour, and then got up and saw about her girls. Just like she did every day.

And then she came back inside, grateful for the routine for there was comfort in it.

Being alone wasn't the worst thing that could happen; there were other things surely. She had a roof over her head, her girls and Freckles, plenty of food in the fridge, and cheese in the cellar. But her thoughts turned to Dan, wondering how he was doing. Blast it, who cared? She shoved those thoughts out of her mind and turned back to watching *Downton Abbey*, wrapped up in a quilt on the couch. Soon enough, she fell asleep, only to be rudely interrupted by a knocking on her front door.

Who could that be? On Christmas day?

"Yoo-hoo!" A familiar voice echoed as they opened the door. "Anybody home?"

Brynn stood. "Becky?"

"Aunt Brynn!" Her 5-year-old niece, Lily, came running to her.

Brynn's heart nearly exploded, and she crouched down for the hug. "What a nice surprise!"

"We brought you some gifts," Lily said.

"You did? How wonderful!" She led her niece and sister into the living room. "But you must tell me what Santa brought you."

Becky stood and folded her arms as she took in the living room, TV blaring *Downton Abbey*, pillow and blanket scattered haphazardly. "Looks like we came just in the nick of time."

After the place was straightened up, and gifts exchanged, Lily wanted to give the girls gifts. She loved the cows with her whole little heart.

The cows were always gentle with her. Freckles, on the other hand, nearly knocked her over.

Lily giggled as Freckles stood on her hind legs and placed her front paws on Lily's shoulders. "I brought you a treat." She reached into her pocket and pulled out a dog treat, which the dog gladly took in her teeth and darted off to see about chewing on it. Wrapped around Lily's shoulder were three thick, red ribbons with beautiful old cow bells dangling from them.

She slipped one on each of the cows, who were compliant, as Lily always charmed them. In fact, they were charmed by almost any child—except a crying baby. At least Buttercup couldn't abide a crying baby.

As the cows moved around, the bells rang, which for today, anyway, sounded Christmassy. Brynn blinked back a tear.

"I thought you said you couldn't afford a visit this year," Brynn said.

Becky shot her sister a grin. "Christmas bonus, which was a complete surprise. We can stay a few days. If that's okay."

Warmth spread through Brynn as she stood there, with snow all around, and her breath puffing out in the cold air. "You know it is."

After the cows were duly decorated with their new bells, the three of them went back inside. As Brynn and Becky made pimento-cheese sandwiches for the three of them in the kitchen, Becky asked about the shenanigans.

"Have they caught who's been creeping around here?"

Brynn spread the cheese on a piece of bread. She hadn't told Becky all of what had happened to her. "You'll need to sit down for this."

She told her sister the story of how she and Willow were held in the basement, and Becky's eyes lit with anger. "Why didn't you tell me?"

"It just happened two nights ago. I slept most of the day yesterday, and today is Christmas. I was going to tell you, but I wanted to wait until the holiday was over."

"So the man who did it is behind bars?"

"I assume so. I haven't heard a word, it being Christmas. I'm sure it will all come out soon. There are a lot of questions about how this all fits together. Frank set the fire that killed Nancy. But it's a mystery whether he killed the young man I found, and, if so, why. I also don't know exactly what Tillie has to do with any of this."

"Tillie?"

"The neighbor girl I told you about. I assume she saw her brother set the fire, and that's what had her so edgy. But she took off at one point, which I don't understand."

"Maybe she felt the sudden need to get some distance. She was trying to figure out what to do."

Brynn contemplated that. "It could be." She paused. "That sounds like something you'd do."

Becky cracked a smile as she placed a sandwich on a plate for Lily. "Yeah, I would."

Brynn's sister was more complicated than she was. Brynn was a simple sort, who faced things head on. Not so with Becky. She mulled and took space and time to make important decisions. She took two years to decide to marry Lily's father, who was a police officer in Richmond. Three years later, the worst had happened, and now she was a single mom.

The two of them brought their plates of cheese sandwiches, along with a tray of Christmas cookies, into the living room, where Lily was reading an old Trixie Belden book of Brynn's.

She didn't even look up from it.

"Are you hungry?" Becky said.

She set the book down. "I am." She reached for a cookie, and her mom playfully slapped her hand away. "A sandwich first, then you can have some cookies."

"That's harsh, Mom," Lily said.

"You think that's harsh? Let me tell you about your grandmother . . ." Brynn said and laughed.

Later, the three of them called Lily's grandparents,

who seemed to be in good spirits, even though their family was not with them this Christmas.

"How are the girls?" Becky and Brynn's father asked.

"They're good. Looking spiffy with their new bells."

He laughed. "God, I love cows."

"He loves cheese even more," their mother chimed in from the other line.

It was true that Brynn had come by her love for cheese quite naturally. Her grandmother's family came from a long line of dairy farmers and cheese-makers. In fact, sometimes she felt like it was in her blood. She didn't know if there was any truth to the theory of genetic memory and disposition, but if there was, she was living proof.

After they hung up from chatting with their parents, Brynn and Becky played cards with Lily and listened to Christmas music.

"It's almost time to bring the girls in," Brynn said, which prompted a smile from Lily.

But just then, the doorbell rang.

"I wonder who that could be," Brynn said as she rose to answer the door.

When she opened it, a grinning Wes stood there with open arms. "Surprise, and Merry Christmas!"

Brynn squealed. "Wes!"

"Okay, Wes, give me the scoop," Brynn said, after the girls were back in the barn for the night, and Lily was fast asleep. "I've been trying to keep my nose out of the O'Reillys' business, but I'm dying to learn what happened. Do you know?"

He sat back into the couch as the MacAlister sisters sat forward. "What do you want to know?"

"Did Tillie see her brother set the fire?"

"Yeah, and she saw some other things, too," he said, grimacing.

"Other things?" Brynn felt her pulse quicken.

"The police suspect he was a part of a local drug network."

"What? Here in Shenandoah Springs?" Becky gasped.

Wes nodded. "Yeah. I guess the story's ready to break in the news tomorrow or the next day. But they were running a drug-trafficking ring up eighty-one, and the church was a meeting place. And a place where money was exchanged. Big money."

So, finally, an answer that made sense. It didn't really make Brynn feel any better. "Yes, I saw the money one night. But the next day, it was gone."

"What?" Becky said. "You didn't tell me that."

"Tillie found it, too," Wes explained. "But she took it."

Brynn's heart nearly jumped into her throat. They had suspected she took it.

"But she gave it to the police with a note attached, and then hopped on a plane to get some distance."

"She came to you?" Brynn asked. "Interesting."

"We'd been texting and talking. We bonded over the parent thing."

"What do you mean?"

"Her passion is music, and her parents don't like it." He paused. "Sound familiar? My parents didn't want me to be a chef."

"So, let me get this straight. Tillie saw her brother set the fire, and she also took the money and gave it to the police? Why didn't she come forward about the fire?" Becky said.

"He's her brother. She was torn and upset. He'd been in trouble before, and she didn't really want to send him to jail. Also, I figure she was a little scared of him. She was afraid he'd set the family home on fire. She really didn't know who to turn to. But, ultimately, she did the right thing."

Silence hung in the air as each of them considered the complexity of the situation.

Brynn remembered another question she had about the situation. "Why were there books left in the box in the woods? Do you know?"

He shrugged. "I don't know anything about that. Maybe it had something to do with the way she and Gram exchanged books in secret."

"That kind of makes sense." Brynn would never understand why Tillie's parents objected to her reading certain books. She was intellectually curious and wasn't that a good thing?

"So, is this young man in jail?" Becky asked.

"You bet. He'll be gone for years. He's twenty years old. A year older than me."

"He killed Nancy. I hope they throw away the key," Brynn said.

"I doubt he meant to kill her. He meant to scare her off. It was an accident. But he is still responsible for it."

"Arson is a serious crime, whether or not anybody is killed," Becky said, and sipped her eggnog.

"Dang, this is good eggnog," he said.

"Old family recipe," Brynn said.

"Go easy. There's at least three kinds of booze in it," Becky said.

"Then I guess I shouldn't be drinking it," he said, smiling, setting the glass aside.

Brynn drank the thick brew. Sadness moved through her. She felt awful for the O'Reilly family—and for Nancy's family.

Brynn didn't really want to ask, but she really had to know. "Why was he trying to get rid of me?"

"You're the closest neighbor. He was afraid you'd interfere with the drug business. And you kind of did."

Becky giggled. "My sister. The sleuth. The drug-lord slayer."

"You're getting a bit tipsy," Brynn said, and smiled.

She was uncertain if it was from the whisky in the eggnog, or the fact that she was surrounded by some of her favorite people, but a wash of contentment came over her. She'd prepared herself to be alone today. But she had to admit, this was so much better.

There was her sister, who she couldn't imagine her life without—even if she couldn't stop drinking the boozy eggnog and giggling. And there was Nancy's grandson Wes, her new friend and partner, who may just be the closest she could get to having her old friend close by.

Something was in the air that evening—a kind of sweet, warm magic. Niece, Freckles, and the cows tucked safely away. Sisters giggling. Christmas music playing. And mystery solved.

Chapter Fifty-Four

One Month Later

Brynn stood behind Wes as he revealed her new website.

She gasped as tears formed in her eyes. "It's stunning! Thank you!"

"This is going to grow the business, and we're ready for it."

It had been a month since Wes moved in, and, as Brynn had suspected, he was a fast learner. They were creating inspired, brilliant cheeses, and experimenting with cheese sidelines—like cheesecakes made with homemade ricotta cheese, and cheese balls.

Wes beamed. "I'm glad you like it. Before you know it, we'll be getting our first order."

The doorbell interrupted the revelry, and Brynn ran to answer it. When she opened the door, she was stunned, relieved, and happy to see Tillie. She reached out and hugged her.

"Come in," she said after the hug. She hadn't seen her since the incident with her brother.

"Really? You're okay with me being here?" Tillie asked timidly.

Brynn's heart sank. "Of course, I am."

Wes barreled around the corner. "Tillie! Good to see you."

The three of them walked into the living room.

"Can I get you anything? Hot cocoa?"

Her eyes momentarily lit up, but then she said, "I'm sorry. I can't stay, but I wanted to see you and apologize."

A light fluttery feeling erupted in Brynn's chest. "You've got nothing to apologize for. I know you were in a bind. The worst kind of bind."

"Well, you see, I wasn't sure if I saw what I thought I saw. It was dark. And I witnessed everything from the woods, and I didn't really want to believe it. I kept coming back and looking at the scene and trying to figure it out. But there was no denying that Frank set that fire."

"It must have been difficult for you, and I'm so sorry you've had to go through this."

"Thank you. Frank is my big brother. I hate that this has all happened, but at the same time, he's finally getting help." She turned to Wes, who was sitting in a chair on the other side of her. "I'm sorry about your grandmother. If I could go back in time and do anything . . ." Her chin quivered. Brynn's arm slid around her.

"You don't have to apologize for your brother," Wes said.

She nodded. "Well, I feel like I do. What he did was . . . so bad and so wrong. I just can't . . ."

"Hey," Brynn said. "You are not your brother. Everybody is responsible for their own actions."

They sat in silence for a few moments before Wes said, "Hey, do you want to see the new website?"

"Website? For the farm?"

"Just finished it this morning."

As the two of them left the living room, Brynn yelled out, "I'm making cocoa!"

Tillie turned around, grinning. "Okay."

Brynn moved into the kitchen and gathered ingredients for hot cocoa, which was the perfect drink for a cold winter's day. A soft and warm critter rubbed against her legs—Romeo had decided to move in with her, too. Brynn theorized the cat had a bit of a crush on Wes—for even though Nancy had named the cat Romeo, Brynn discovered the cat was a girl. Wes was her guy, but when Brynn was in the kitchen, the cat was at her feet.

As Brynn made the cocoa, her cell phone rang. It was Mike Rafferty.

"Hello."

"Hi Brynn, I'm just calling to thank you for all the help on the church fire."

"What? I didn't help much at all."

"You helped more than you think. We just left our meeting, and after we all debriefed the whole case, we decided that your investigating was what led the team in the right direction. And you made Frank nervous, so he kept doing things that really helped to build a case against him."

Things like attempting to set a fire in her yard, nailing a bird to her front door, taking her dog, and dumping trash on her front stoop. She'd felt like a sitting duck—or cow, as the case may be.

"What we can't figure out is why you were calling all of the contractors."

"It was Nancy. The last thing she said to me was 'call the contractor' or 'Paul the contractor.' So I thought the contractors had something to do with her death. But it turns out that they had nothing to do with it."

There was silence on the other end of the phone.

"But I guess it was enough to stir things up a bit," Brynn said.

"I'd say so. The man you found in the car was known as 'The Contractor.'"

Brynn's breath rushed out of her. "What?"

"Nancy must have seen some drug deals going down. She must have been trying to tell you about it."

Brynn felt like a fool having circled the community, trying to find out information on the contractors in the area.

"And the O'Reilly boy was heavily involved in it," he went on. "So you stepped into a bit of a hornet's nest."

"So much for my sleuthing skills."

He laughed.

After they finished their conversation, she turned back to her steaming hot cocoa. She stirred and stirred, reached for the cayenne pepper, and flicked them into the mix.

Tillie's laughter filled the house.

If Tillie could laugh, it was a good sign that she'd be okay. Her burden would never completely vanish, but she would be able to manage it. Knowing your brother killed someone, and witnessing it, was heavy business.

Brynn poured the cocoa into three mugs, set them on a tray, and delivered them to the living room.

She wandered into her makeshift office, where Tillie and Wes were oohing and ahhing over the website.

"Cocoa is ready," Brynn said.

The three of them sat in the living room, drinking hot cocoa, and watching the snow fall. The girls were unfazed by the snow at this point. It was way beyond the first snowfall, and Brynn thought they were no longer amused by it. She looked out her window at the fields, hills, and valleys of Buttermilk Creek Farm, with Petunia, Buttercup, and Marigold hanging out in the snowy fields, Freckles along with them, and felt content.

The past few months hadn't been easy. But there had been good things, too. She glanced over at Wes and Tillie, enjoying their cocoa, becoming good friends. She now had a website, had signed a contract with Hoff's Bakery, and already had several return clients.

There was so much work ahead of her, on the farm and with her cheese, but she never minded hard work. In fact, she loved it.

For the first time since moving here on her own, she thought about the future, and she was hopeful. She was growing friendships, had someone to help her with the business, and plenty of cheese to make. Of course, there would be challenges, but nothing on the same level as murder. Not anymore.

Shenandoah Springs was a safe place. And it was getting safer by the minute. Arrests had been made, and it felt like the place was getting a clean slate.

Life was good—and it promised to get better.

RECIPES

Pimento Cheese

Pimento cheese is quintessentially southern. And like most old southern mainstays, each family has its own variation of the delicious cheese spread.

- 8 ounces sharp cheddar cheese, shredded
- 8 ounces mild cheddar cheese, shredded
- 8-ounce package cream cheese, softened
- ¼ cup diced pimentos
- ½ teaspoon salt
- ¼ teaspoon freshly ground black pepper
- 2–3 tablespoons mayonnaise or Greek yogurt (optional)
- Optional Ingredients: Add garlic powder, onion powder, cayenne pepper, or hot sauce to your preference.

Cream together cheddar cheeses with the softened cream cheese.

Stir in pimentos, salt, and pepper.

For thinner, spreadable cheese, add in optional mayonnaise, Greek yogurt, or liquid from the diced pimentos to achieve desired consistency.

Store in an airtight container in the refrigerator for up to a week.

Not Your Mama's Cheese Balls

1 package (8 ounces) cream cheese, softened
1 cup crumbled blue cheese
¼ cup butter, softened
1 can (4¼ ounces) chopped ripe olives
1 tablespoon minced chives
¼ cup chopped walnuts
Assorted crackers

In a large bowl, beat the cream cheese, blue cheese, and butter until smooth. Stir in olives and chives. Cover and refrigerate for at least 1 hour.

Shape cheese mixture into a ball and roll in walnuts until coated. Wrap in plastic and refrigerate for at least 1 hour. Serve with crackers.

Yield: 2 cups.

The cheese ball can be made a day in advance. Cover and refrigerate until 20 minutes before serving.

Quick and Easy Cream Cheese Danish

1 sheet puff pastry dough, thawed
8 ounces cream cheese, softened
1 teaspoon vanilla extract
4 tablespoons sugar
1½ cups canned cherry pie filling
1 egg
2 tablespoons water
powdered sugar
shaved chocolate, optional

Preheat oven to 400 degrees F. Line a baking sheet with parchment paper or use a silicone baking sheet.

On a lightly floured surface, roll out thawed puff pastry into a 12×9 inch rectangle. Cut in half lengthwise, yielding two 4½ inch strips. Cut those two strips crosswise into thirds, to yield six 4×4½ inch pieces.

With a knife, score a ½ inch border around the edge of each piece of puff pastry. Use a fork to make five or six pricks into the dough within the border of each piece. This will help keep the middle of each piece from rising.

In a bowl, stir together softened cream cheese, vanilla, and sugar. Spoon 2 to 3 tablespoons of the mixture into the middle of each piece of dough and spread around evenly, ensuring the mix stays within the borders.

In the middle of the cream cheese, add about 6 cherries.

Whisk egg and water for brushing the edges of the pastry.

Bake for 20 minutes on the middle rack and rotate the baking sheet halfway through baking. Remove from baking sheet and cool on a wire rack. Serve warm or at room temperature. Sprinkle with powdered sugar before serving. Shave chocolate over the top as well, if desired.

Christmas Pie

10-inch Pie Crust
   6 tablespoons unsalted butter
   1½ cups all-purpose flour

½ teaspoon kosher salt
1½ teaspoons granulated sugar
2½ tablespoons cold vegetable shortening
¼ cup ice cold water, plus more as needed

Filling

1 envelope unflavored gelatin
¼ cup water
⅔ cup granulated sugar, divided
¼ cup all-purpose flour
½ teaspoon salt
1½ cups whole milk
¼ teaspoon almond extract
¼ teaspoon vanilla extract
½ cup heavy cream
3 egg whites
¼ teaspoon cream of tarter
¾ cup shredded coconut plus more for sprinkling
    over top

Topping

2 cups heavy cream
2 cups fresh diced strawberries
½ cup confectioners' sugar

To make the crust, cut the butter into pats and place flat on a plate. Place the plate in the freezer while you work on the remaining ingredients.

In the bowl of a food processor, place flour, salt, and sugar, and pulse to combine. Add cold shortening and pulse a few times. Add frozen butter and pulse until the butter is pea size.

Continue to pulse while adding cold water, stopping and checking frequently by pinching some dough.

If it is crumbly, add a tablespoon of water at a time until the dough comes together.

Pour onto a floured counter and press together into a disc. Wrap tightly with plastic wrap and refrigerate 30 minutes.

Remove dough, and on a floured surface, roll the dough until it is two inches larger than your standard 10-inch pie plate. A 9-inch pie plate can be used, though the filling will be right up to the top. Place the dough over the pie plate and gently press in and up and over the edges. With a knife or scissors, cut off the extra dough. Pinch the overhanging dough into a high ridge all around, and then go back over and make a decorative edge, again, keeping it high. Place the completed pie dough in the freezer for 30 minutes to set up, so that the sides don't collapse while baking.

Preheat oven to 375 degrees, and once the pie plate with the dough has been in the freezer for 30 minutes, remove, add parchment paper, and either pie weights or dry beans. (To make the parchment fit, cut parchment into a circle larger than the pie plate and make four slits a few inches long around the edge halfway to center so when you place it in the shell, the slits overlap and fit up the sides.) Place in the oven for 20 minutes. Remove pie weights or beans, and with a fork, puncture the bottom in a few places to release the steam, and then return to oven without the weights and parchment and bake for 15 more minutes. Cool to room temperature. The shell is now ready to be filled.

While crust is baking, make the filling by first blooming the gelatin. Place gelatin in the water in a small bowl to dissolve, and set aside.

In a medium saucepan, mix ⅓ cup of the granulated sugar, flour and salt. Add milk and whisk to combine. Over medium heat, bring to a boil and cook one minute.

Add gelatin mixture and whisk to combine over medium heat then remove from heat. Whisk in the almond and vanilla extracts then place saucepan in a bowl with ice to quickly cool.

Beat the ½ cup of heavy cream until thick and set aside.

Beat egg whites with cream of tartar and the remaining ⅓ cup of granulated sugar until stiff peaks form and set aside.

Place the filling into the mixer and whip just long enough to make the mixture creamy.

Into a large bowl, add the cooled whipped filling and gently fold in whipped cream, beaten egg whites, and shredded coconut. With a rubber spatula, scrape mixture evenly into baked, cooled pie shell.

For the topping, whip the two cups of heavy cream to stiff peaks, and, using a large pastry bag with a large star tip, make a decorative top over the filling and then sprinkle some coconut over the top.

Dice the strawberries and mix in a bowl with the confectioners' sugar. The strawberries will eventually give up enough liquid to mix with the confectioners' sugar and create a sauce.

Cut and serve pieces of the pie with the strawberry sauce spooned over the top.

Brynn's Spicy Hot Cocoa

Serving: 2 large mugs

4 cups milk
1 cup dark chocolate chips
¼ cup sugar
1 teaspoon ground cinnamon
¼ teaspoon ground cayenne pepper
Pinch of salt

In a heavy-bottomed saucepan, heat 2 cups of milk until scalding. Remove from heat. Add chocolate chips, sugar, cinnamon, cayenne, and salt, and whisk until combined. Add remaining milk, heat, stirring until hot.

Wes and Max's Baked French Toast

1 loaf sourdough bread cut into one-inch pieces
6 large eggs
1½ cups whole milk
½ cup half and half
½ cup sugar
1 tablespoon vanilla extract
1 teaspoon ground cinnamon
pinch of salt

Streusel Topping
¼ cup all-purpose flour
¼ cup brown sugar

1 teaspoon ground cinnamon
¼ cup butter diced
confectioners' sugar for dusting, optional

Liberally spray a 13×9 inch baking dish with nonstick cooking spray (or coat with butter). Add bread cubes to baking dish and distribute evenly.

In a large bowl, whisk together eggs, milk, half and half, sugar, vanilla, cinnamon, and pinch of salt. Pour over bread cubes. Press bread cubes into the baking dish to make sure they absorb the custard. Cover baking dish tightly with plastic wrap and refrigerate overnight.

In a small bowl, mix together flour, sugar, cinnamon, and butter for the streusel topping, being sure to break up butter into small pieces. Cover tightly with plastic wrap and refrigerate overnight.

When ready to bake, preheat oven to 350 degrees. Remove baking dish and streusel topping from the refrigerator. Sprinkle streusel topping liberally over the top of the French toast. Bake 45 minutes. Remove from the oven and allow to rest for about 3 minutes before serving. Dust with confectioners' sugar, if using, and serve with maple syrup.

If you enjoyed *Christmas Cow Bells*,
be sure not to miss
Mollie Cox Bryan's
Cora Crafts Mystery series,
including

ASSAULT AND BEADERY

All of Cora Chevalier's dreams are coming true.
Since moving to Indigo Gap, North Carolina,
the busy crafting maven has been blessed with
a great boyfriend, a lovely home, and a
booming craft-retreat business. But on the eve
of her first Crafty Mom's Escape Weekend,
tragedy strikes again in Indigo Gap.
This time, it's curtains for Stan Herald, the
disagreeable director of the local theater
group, who's murdered on the opening night
of their new production. Worse, Cora's friend
Zee is accused of the crime.

Cora is determined to prove her friend's
innocence, but Zee's mysterious past is making
that difficult. And with a list of suspects longer
than a double spool of satin cording, getting a
bead on the real culprit won't be easy.
With her friends Jane and Ruby at her side,
Cora must string together the clues and solve
Stan's murder before the killer
gives an encore performance.

Keep reading for a special excerpt.

*A Kensington mass-market paperback
and eBook on sale now!*

Chapter One

"How did we let ourselves get involved with this?" Cora Chevalier whispered to best friend and business partner, Jane Starr.

"It's not too bad, is it?" Jane whispered back.

The voice of one of the cast members performed the vocal gymnastics otherwise known as warm-ups. Cora grimaced.

"What do *you* think?" Cora said, hands over her ears.

Jane was in her element. She loved designing and painting the sets for the local theater group, IndigoArts. Cora would rather be at home with her cat, Luna. Besides, their next craft retreat, with a back-to-school theme for moms, beckoned with countless tasks requiring their attention.

Fiddler on the Roof opened tonight and along with excitement in the air, frayed nerves ran rampant. Cora and Jane's work essentially was done a week ago, but the sets needed a few touch-ups. They planned to be on their merry way as soon as possible.

Jane stood back and examined her work. "It will do. Good thing the audience won't be close enough to see the details," she said as she looked over the log house façade. It consisted of painted brown logs in be-

tween soft blue lines representing mud or clay Jane
drew. She had also painted two windows and a door,
along with the roof. No curtains hung in the windows,
which was a subject of about a week's debate between
Jane and the director, Stan. Should there be curtains?
Or not?

Earlier, Jane and Cora finished painting a purple
night sky with mountains fading in the distance,
which took most of the day. Since they were already at
the theater, they checked out a few of the other set
pieces and façades to see if any touch-ups were needed.

"It looks beautiful," Cora said, picking up and then
dropping her paintbrush into a bucket. She grew
dizzy from the scent of paint and turpentine. "Let's
get this cleaned up and go home before we're com-
mandeered into doing something else."

She spoke too soon.

"There you are!" Zee said as she walked onto the
stage as if she owned it. Others milled about, cleaning
and making quick repairs and changes. "I wondered
if you two are going to make the show tonight?"

It was their burgeoning friendship with Zee, otherwise known as Zora, that brought them here. Soon
after Jane and Cora met her, she told them to please
call her Zee, as she hated the name Zora, which had
belonged to an evil old aunt. She was the musical
director for the theater group. When she learned of
Jane's artistic ability, she approached her.

"No," Jane replied. "We figured we'd attend next
Sunday's matinee. We've got a retreat starting."

"Oh, that's right," Zee said, and wrote something
on a paper attached to her clipboard. "Thank you
both for all the work you've done." She lowered her
voice. "I know it wasn't easy at times. So I owe you."

"We'll remind you of that," Cora said with a joking tone.

But Cora meant what she said. The politics of the local theater group was like an intricate game of chess. Cora found herself with her foot in her mouth on more than one occasion. She loved theater and had been in plays in college and briefly thought she might get involved with IndigoArts. Until this experience. She adored Zee, but they'd need a long chat about all this someday.

Besides, Cora needed to focus on the upcoming retreat. Her guest teacher was scheduled to arrive bright and early in the morning. Lena Ross was a beading artist. Just thinking about learning how to work with beads lifted Cora's spirits. It was a craft that was easy to make for non-crafters. No special talent was necessary, but beading could become an art in the right hands.

Lena Ross crafted across the spectrum of what made up the beading scene. She made everything from French bead floral arrangements to gorgeous lampwork necklaces. Cora was fascinated.

"You've done such a great job," Zee said. "Do you have a full house for this retreat?"

"Not yet," Cora said. "We've got some room. Do you want to come and craft with us?"

"Heavens no," she said, waving her plump hand. "I just thought if you needed room you could send them my way."

Zee owned and operated the Blue Note, one of the bed-and-breakfasts in quaint Indigo Gap. "I'm all thumbs with anything but music and flowers," she said. "Believe me. I've tried."

"Well, if you ever change your mind and want to

give something a try, we're here for you," Cora said, grinning. "And if we're ever in need of rooms, we'll send our retreaters to you."

"What are you going to be doing? Crochet? Quilting? I've no interest whatsoever in making that stuff. I do love to buy it, though," Zee said with a Cheshire cat grin.

Jane and Cora had tried to guess Zee's age to no avail. And she wasn't one to tell. She'd had a whole other life before "retiring" to Indigo Gap. She was a musician, and her B&B featured a shiny baby grand in the sitting room. She had silver-blond hair and wore black kohl eyeliner over blue eye shadow, every day.

"Zora! There you are! Can I have a word?" It was the musical's director, Stan Herald, who took himself a bit too seriously for Cora's taste. He also refused to call Zora by Zee, even though she'd asked him to several times.

"Catch you two later," Zee said, and followed Stan into the wings. "I'll bring the flowers by then."

After they had finished cleaning up, Cora whispered, "Let's get out of here . . . while we still can."

Chapter Two

Cora and Jane made their great escape from the theater to the streets of Indigo Gap. They walked briskly, passing several local businesses: the florist, the paper shop, and the Blue Dawg Diner.

"Do you have everything you need for your class?" Cora asked. "I know you were expecting more materials."

Jane nodded. "Everything is set."

Jane planned a mini-class on making raku beads. As a potter, she understood all about clay and already possessed the tools and materials for the class. Embellishments and instruments were ordered for the crafters. Cora had peeked at the beads Jane fashioned while practicing for the class. Jane thought of them as whimsical projects, but Cora was amazed by them. Because of the firing techniques and the materials used, the clay resembled glass. Jane's beads shimmered with colorful translucency, reminding Cora of swirly carnival glass.

"I'm so looking forward to this retreat," Jane said. "What a great idea to hold a retreat for moms after the summer. Maybe we can make this an annual event."

"Let's see how the first one goes," Cora said. "For now, I'm all for it."

"I like the idea of a single craft, but with each teacher adding their own unique element," Jane said.

This crafty moms retreat was the first. Up until this point, at each retreat Cora and Jane had offered two or three different crafts.

"Well, beading lends itself to it," Cora said. "I'm looking forward to Ruby's herbal beading class."

"She's a bit more prickly than usual," Jane said. "I hope everything is okay with her."

Now the third partner in their craft retreat business, Ruby lived in the gardener's cottage on the property and came with the purchase of Cora's house-turned-retreat center. She was a local and a gifted herbalist, both of which benefited the business.

"I wouldn't worry about it. I think she's just a moody person," Cora said.

"It's almost time for me to pick up London from school," Jane said, as they approached Kildare House. "I'll catch you later."

"You should come by later and check out Zee's floral arrangements," Cora said.

"I'll try," Jane replied as she walked around the side of Kildare House and back to her carriage house abode. She and London lived in a second-floor apartment, over Jane's pottery studio and shop.

Tomorrow, along with their guest teacher's arrival, a few of the crafters would be arriving as well, so Cora took this time to once again make certain everything was prepared for them. She walked through each room and each bathroom, inspecting things. Did everybody have enough towels? Soap? Sheets? Extra blankets? Satisfied that everything seemed to be in order, she moved along at a brisk pace until she arrived at Mémé's Boudoir, where she always paused because the room was filled with her grandmother's things. Worn French linen covered the bed, lacy antique linen hung on the walls in French-inspired, gilded frames, and old family photos sat on the dresser on top of a long frilly doily. Perhaps it was just the memory of the woman who saved all these treasures for Cora, or maybe the items themselves held a comforting vibe. She smoothed over the bed, and the feel of the soft linen on her skin calmed her.

When she thought of calm and comfort, Cora's thoughts moved to Adrian, her boyfriend, who was working late tonight at the public elementary school. As the school librarian, he was readying for parent night, tidying up his library. She'd not gotten to see him much over the past few weeks because school was in session and she'd been recruited into helping out with the IndigoArts play. Never again, she told herself.

Just then her cell phone rang. "Cora Chevalier," she answered.

"Hi, Cora, this is Roni Davis."

"Hi, Roni, how can I help you?" Cora asked.

"I'm one of your retreaters and I completely miscalculated how many days it would take me to drive to Indigo Gap from Virginia, so I'm almost there. Should I get a hotel room, or is it okay for me to just come to Kildare House?"

So much for having the night to herself.

"You're welcome to come here. No worries," Cora said. She wondered what Jane would say. She'd been telling Cora she ought to work on her "need to please" and set more boundaries.

"Thanks so much," Roni said. "I'll pay you for the extra night."

"Thank you," Cora said, thinking that would make Jane happy. "We'll see you in a bit."

Cora sat on the edge of the bed, surrounded by her grandmother's worn but beautiful objects. Sometimes she felt like pinching herself. Could it be that her dreams were all actually coming true? The Crafty Mom's Escape Weekend was her third retreat—and the arrangements were all in place. She expected blips, such as a guest arriving earlier than intended. Cora could manage. She *was* managing. She hadn't had a panic attack in months.

Not only was her professional life coming together, but she and Adrian were moving along in their relationship. She had a great boyfriend, a lovely home, and a booming craft retreat business. Dare she hope for even more success and happiness?

After giving everything a final check, Cora called Zee. She was late with the flowers, which was totally unlike her. She didn't answer her phone, which was also unlike her.

Oh well, Cora thought, maybe she'd gotten busy at the theater. After all, it was opening night.

Cora set off to check over the gift baskets, which had become a signature of their retreats. Each crafter received a basketful of tools and crafting goodies on arrival. Almost everything they needed was in the baskets—beads, wire, felt. Gifts from a few local crafters were also included, such as a paper pack from the new paper shop and tiny felted birds from an art teacher at the high school who had a craft business on the side.

Her phone rang, interrupting her thoughts and her checking over the baskets. "Cora Chevalier."

"Hello?" Cora said when no one spoke at first.

"It's Zee."

Cora's heart raced. "What's wrong?"

"I can't bring your flowers. I'm at the . . . I'm at the police station."

"Whatever for?"

"It's Stan. He's dead."

"What? What happened?"

Zee inhaled and exhaled into the phone before answering. "It was no accident. Someone killed him, and they think it was me."

Connect with

Us

Visit us online at
KensingtonBooks.com
to read more from your favorite authors, see books
by series, view reading group guides, and more.

Join us on social media

for sneak peeks, chances to win books and prize packs,
and to share your thoughts with other readers.

**facebook.com/kensingtonpublishing
twitter.com/kensingtonbooks**

Tell us what you think!

To share your thoughts, submit a review,
or sign up for our eNewsletters, please visit:
KensingtonBooks.com/TellUs.